To: Is it after ... yet?

A DUSK WITHOUT DAWN

SABRINA ALBIS

Best wishes
xoxo
Sabrina

To Joseph

Is it after midnight yet?

For Jeff.
Thank you for all your love and support.

Best wishes

xoxo

Sabrina

PROLOGUE

The man sat, tapping his foot impatiently.

He looked at his watch; the same watch he had glanced at a handful of times in the last hour.

It was agony, the waiting.

He was late.

Still, tardiness aside, this was the least of his concerns.

The thoughts rattling around his head without refrain? *Those* were concerning.

Why was this meeting called? Why was he summoned by him in such haste?

He said it was urgent.

Considering his delay, how urgent could the matter really be?

Alas, when someone of such knowledge, such as a Perceiver, said something was *urgent* it was *rarely* good news. This much he had deciphered.

The anticipation made him restless, made him uneasy. He tapped his finely crafted Italian leather shoe into the thick muddy dirt. He stood up, pacing back and forth like a caged animal. He needed to think about something, *anything* that made him happy, something pleasantly distracting.

His cause, the one he had fought for so many years now. He thought of that.

His group of friends, how they would all, live or die for him, and vice versa.

The world becoming a better place, a place where he and those like him, might be accepted, perhaps even revered.

The thoughts stopped abruptly at the sound of crunching leaves and cracking branches.

Moments later, a man stepped forth through the forest bramble.

The Perceiver hadn't changed much since the last time they had met, though it seemed like eons ago.

His silver hair was long and silken, framing a rosy-cheeked face adorned by crisp blue eyes. A ceremonial red robe with gilded decals dragged along behind him through the mud and debris of the forest floor.

"Blaze," he said, hand outstretched from his robe. "Thank you for coming."

"Edmond," Blaze replied, the ghost of a smile on his ruggedly handsome face. "I was starting to worry you weren't going to make it."

Edmond swept his hand through the air, gesturing for Blaze to follow him.

"Sorry to keep you waiting," he said as they began trekking through the sea of trees and bushes. Their limbs protruded every which way, providing an obstacle course for them to move past.

"I had a vision on my way here," he went on. "It's unfortunate, you know, not being able to control it." He smiled at Blaze meaningfully. "Unlike you with your *gift*."

This statement made Blaze let out a genuine chuckle.

"A gift is it?" He retorted, amused. "Perhaps most days but let me tell you Edmond, some days it can be a curse. As for control? It took me the better part of my life to master."

Blaze remembered those days distinctly. When his *gift* caused him so much anguish. He didn't like to remember the early days, because that led to thoughts of her, of Annalise. He was never forgiven for what happened to Anna, not by anyone that knew the truth.

It didn't matter.

He would never forgive himself it, either. No matter how many times he told himself it wasn't his fault. His past haunted him like a tireless ghost.

He shrugged the thoughts away and took in his surroundings. Edmond had guided him to a place buried deep in the trees. They were in the heart of the forest. The heady scent of pine overcame Blaze's nostrils. In front of him was a stone carved table, with two large flat boulders for chairs.

"My hideaway," Edmond said, grinning, almost childlike. "I come here for solitude."

Blaze heard the soft rustling of branches as wild life scampered along, and the gentle hoots of an owl perched nearby.

"It is quite peaceful," Blaze said, taking in the scenery around him.

"Please sit," Edmond said, as he took a seat himself. Blaze nodded and sat across from him.

"I was rather pleased to hear you took my last vision to heart," Edmond said, adjusting one of many large bangles on his wrist. "You managed to save them I reckon?"

Blaze frowned. "Of course I took it to heart. Have I *ever* disregarded your visions Ed?" He paused. "And yes, we saved them."

"I'm sorry it was such short notice," Edmond said. "The vision came quite abruptly. I haven't had one like that since my early days."

Blaze felt his heart clench as he remembered. He was terrified he would lose them to the cave beasts that night.

The picture Edmond painted him when he reached him, panicked about his visions of impending death. His dire warnings still resonated in Blaze's mind.

"If you don't go tonight and aid them, they will all die," Edmond had said. "There is no other outcome unless you intervene. The path they are on now, is the one to their graves."

Time wasn't on his side but Blaze managed it. He gathered the troops and together they saved them. If there were miracles to be had, that was one of them.

Edmond looked at Blaze with watchful eyes. There were times Blaze felt he could see inside his soul and considering the secrets Edmond knew, he would bet his life he was right.

"Do you still believe the chosen one is among them?" he asked.

Blaze nodded his head.

"I've kept a close eye on them and all the signs are there. Everything is coming together nicely."

Edmond tapped his hand lazily against the stone table.

"They haven't realized you are watching them?"

"They are all very astute," Blaze paused, looking uncertain. "But I don't think they have caught on to any of us *yet.*"

Edmond smirked, impressed.

"I shouldn't have doubted you. You are quite the covert agent when you need to be."

There was a lapse of silence before Blaze leaned across the table towards Edmond.

"So let's get down to it," he said quietly. "You said the matter was urgent."

Edmond was silent for a long moment. He appeared to be choosing his words carefully.

"The chosen ones mate," he began slowly.

Blaze felt his pulse quicken at the mention of her.

Was Edmond's warning pertaining to her? Was she in peril?

"Is she in danger?"

"No danger Blaze," he said reassuringly. "I called on you because I had visions of an obstacle involving her. It directly hinders the fulfilment of the prophecy."

Blaze's entire body tensed.

Absolutely *nothing* could stand in the way of the prophecy.

It *had* to come to fruition. If it didn't, Whitan would suffer and inevitably, the rest of the world.

"Did you see the obstacle?" Blaze asked hopefully. "We can stop it right?"

Edmond looked down, his face bearing a frown.

"I can't see the obstacle, just the terrible outcome. The vision is still rather hazy. I hope with my prayers to the goddess, I can gain clarity." He looked at Blaze. "I will let you know as soon as I see something."

Blaze felt oddly reassured by Edmond's words. With Edmond's Perceiver powers and the guidance of the goddess of the moon, the answers would surface in no time.

"I appreciate you letting me know about this Edmond," Blaze said, as he observed a lone fowl landing on a tree branch. "You always go above and beyond your duties when it comes to our cause."

Edmond stood up, grinning from ear to ear. Edmond was a humble man, but he did love praise. His *gift* wasn't an easy burden to bear. Receiving accolades made it a little bit easier.

"I am always glad to help Blaze."

He reached out his hand. "Please send the others my regards."

"I will do that," Blaze stood up, shaking his hand.

As always, Edmond's handshake firm.

Blaze's father always told him, a firm handshake equals unwavering loyalty. A weak handshake shows weak character. Since then, he found himself judging people based solely on their grip. The advice hardly ever led him astray.

After goodbyes were exchanged, Blaze headed through the maze of trees and bushes and back to his car. As he walked, Edmond's words nagged at him.

The prophecy *needed* to be fulfilled. *Nothing* could stop the inevitable. They were all pawns in the game of kismet now.

A chilling thought entered his mind and he knew he couldn't deny it.

Whatever the cause required, he would gladly abide.

Even if it meant sacrificing himself.

1

"Am I in trouble Mr. Steel?"

Autumn knew she might come to regret the question, but she needed to know.

As she sat in the principal's large office, she racked her brain relentlessly and couldn't figure out why. All she knew was one minute she was in homeroom with Rick, listening to Mr. Brown discuss final exam schedules when suddenly she was called to the principal's office.

It didn't forebode well.

She stared blankly out the square window across from her, as a bird landed on the grass outside. It looked around cautiously before bopping along, hunting for some semblance of nourishment.

Free as a bird, Autumn thought as the bird dipped its beak into the ground. It wasn't long after another bird joined the feast that Mr. Steel cleared his throat.

"Trouble? Hardly," he chuckled, amused. "It's quite the opposite actually."

Mr. Steel had a rotund face, rosy cheeks and a white impeccably groomed beard. His jovial features, in conjunction with his round belly, made Autumn think fondly of Santa Claus.

"I am absolutely honored to be the one to tell you that you've been chosen as this year's valedictorian," he smiled, his eyes wrinkling.

At first, Autumn thought she had misheard.

Of course her grades were above average, and her attendance was perfect, but she had just matriculated to Whitan High recently. She was certain that counted as a strike against her.

Mr. Steel was staring at her expectantly.

What did he want her to do, she wondered. Should she squeal with excitement, act modest and demure or go all out and start jumping up and down on his desk? The image of the latter made her smile but she knew exactly how to react in a situation such as this.

"I am truly thankful for this opportunity to represent Whitan High," she began cautiously. "But-"

"Why is there *always* a 'but'?" Mr. Steel said, rubbing his temples.

Autumn smiled weakly. "I am relatively new here. Don't you think some of the other students might be bitter about this?"

Mr. Steel leaned back in his chair and put a hand through his beard, his brow furrowed in thought. It took him a moment to respond and when he did, his jovial smile had returned.

"I understand your concern Ms. Kingston but if I am being truthful, the other students don't get to choose the valedictorian here. I do. And I think you are best suited for the job. If you would be so kind as to accept."

Autumn couldn't deny it. Being the valedictorian *was* something she had always dreamed about. Her parents, Aunt Katherine and Uncle James would be so proud. Audrina, her older sister, would be so jealous.

"I accept," she said finally and Mr. Steel let out a long drawn out sigh of relief.

"Thank goodness! You had me worried for a second there."

※ ※ ※

The cafeteria was eerily quiet. Autumn noticed the absence of overlapping conversations and raucous laughter as she sat awaiting Rick to return with food.

A pin drop could be heard as students studied their massive textbooks, prepping for exams that were only two weeks away.

Autumn had left Mr. Steel's office an hour ago but she was still reeling from the good news.

She needed to hear something good.

With high schools anticlimactic end just around the corner, she had found herself dwelling on the future.

Would she go to college? University? Would she abandon education in lieu of a job?

While many people had their aspirations etched in stone, she had never been one to think too far ahead. Even her parents, who in their youth were considered strict pragmatists, hadn't bothered to ask her what she wanted to do after high school ended.

The anticipation of graduation coupled with the anxiety of aimlessness made her sick to her stomach.

So any good news was a welcome distraction right now.

The other thing that kept her going was her blooming relationship with Rick. Her friendships with Mandy, Nathaniel and Eric. And of course, her training.

The days and nights spent in the backyard of Eric's mansion, her hands clenching her machete, her limbs moving fluently and effectively.

Once, Rick lent her the rapier from his sword collection.

She remembered the first time she held it in her hands. The sunlight glinted off the blade, shimmering like it was heaven sent, like the Gods themselves were smiling down on her saying:

This is your destiny.

It moved like lightning, with ease and grace.

It felt so light in her grasp, she nicknamed it.

Blink.

It could kill you, just like that.

A kiss grazed her cheek, startling her from her reverie. Rick, with his adorable face-framing curls and ice blue eyes, looked upon her.

"I got you pizza. One slice, double cheese, mushrooms and olives no pepperoni," he placed the food in front of her, complete with a can of soda.

"You know me so well," Autumn kissed him on the mouth as he sat beside her. "Thanks."

"You are more than welcome," he replied.

As usual, Rick's tray was loaded to the nines. Three huge slices of pizza, a water bottle, chips and veggies and dip.

Rick began digging in, pizza first.

"So what did Steel want?"

"Apparently I am this year's valedictorian," Autumn said casually.

Rick stopped mid-bite, his blue eyes flashing with excitement. Autumn couldn't hide her astonishment. Nothing, short of a fire, would cause Rick to stop eating.

"That is amazing!" he exclaimed, reaching over to hug her tightly. "I know I tease you for being a go hard but all the homework and studying was *actually* worth it!"

"Imagine that!" she said sarcastically. "Hard work and achievements are somehow connected!"

Rick patted her shoulder and went back to his pizza, a huge goofy grin on his face.

"Sure. You become the valedictorian and suddenly it's cool to mock us ordinary schmucks."

"Trust me Ricky," Autumn said, starting on her pizza. "There is nothing ordinary about you."

The two continued to eat and chat when Autumn spotted Mandy and Nathaniel sauntering through the cafeteria.

Mandy, dressed in a white tank top and jeans had her pixie cut held back with barrettes. Her brown Bambi-like eyes were lined perfectly with black eyeliner and framed by black mascara.

Since dating Nathaniel, Mandy had begun wearing makeup daily. Though still a tomboy at her core, Autumn noticed she had started wearing skirts to school a few days a week.

Nathaniel, on the other hand, still dressed like a hobo.

Today he wore his favorite, worn-out, ripped jeans paired with a tattered blue t-shirt. His ginger hair looked like it hadn't met a brush in days.

"Hey dude," Nathaniel said sliding in the seat across from Rick. He lifted his arm to give Rick a high-five but Mandy was holding his hand.

Mandy looked at him, bemused. "You want your hand back sweetie?"

Nathaniel smiled at her, exposing perfect, white teeth.

"You can have it back when I am done with it."

Mandy rolled her eyes, relinquishing her grip.

"I suppose it wouldn't be a *normal* day if you guys didn't high-five like two igits."

Nathaniel sat down, a mischievous expression forming on his freckled face.

"So Autumn, I heard about your big meeting with Steel," he said, pulling out a brown paper lunch bag.

Mandy nudged him sharply in the side, nearly knocking the bag from his grasp.

"Ouch! What was that for?" he asked, rubbing his arm.

"We discussed this remember? No teasing Autumn about her meeting!" she snapped as she started on her lunch.

"No teasing? You are no fun!" Nathaniel sulked as he bit into a sandwich.

Mandy looked at Autumn apologetically.

"I didn't tell him *anything* Aut. He heard from some big mouth in his homeroom."

"Good news travels fast huh?" Autumn said apathetically.

"It's high school. Good or bad news, everyone knows about it by lunch," Mandy said.

"Is everything okay?"

Autumn took a bite of her pizza.

"Everything is fine. I was chosen for valedictorian."

Mandy reached across the table and grabbed Autumn's hand, squeezing it tightly.

"That is better than fine Aut! I am so proud of you!" she was grinning ear to ear. "My bestie, beautiful and smart. Rick, you realize how lucky you are right?"

Rick nodded, his mouth full of pizza. "Like a duck."

"Eric! Wait up! Please!"

Autumn spotted Eric King coming towards their table, a look of mild exasperation on his handsome face.

"Hey Eric," Autumn said.

Eric placed a finger over his lips to indicate silence and ducked down beside Mandy.

Nathaniel chuckled. "King, she's *short*. She can't hide you."

Mandy responded with a sharp jab to his side.

"Ouch!"

Eric sat up reluctantly, looking unimpressed. "Will you keep it down Abrams?"

"Eric?"

The lilting voice spoke again as a pretty girl appeared behind Eric.

She was tall and slender with long corkscrew curls framing her round face. She wore a yellow sundress and a smile just as bright.

She placed both hands over Eric's eyes and giggled.

"Guess who?" she asked, a wicked smile on her face.

Eric pursed his lips in disapproval.

"Brittany?"

Disappointment flashed across her face as she removed her hands from his eyes.

"How did you know?"

"You were just chasing me down the hall."

Autumn met Eric's gaze, grinning at him impishly.

Ever since the caves had been sealed and Eric had found peace, it was like he was a different person. He had always been arrogant but his days of constant brooding were over.

Eric's new carefree attitude had made him the schools most eligible bachelor.

Now all the great qualities Autumn saw in Eric, other girls saw as well.

He had gone from high school outcast to mysterious guy with a Camaro and mansion.

Brittany wedged herself between Mandy and Eric.

"We should go out this weekend," she said, flipping her long hair in Mandy's face.

Autumn watched in horror as Mandy attempted to yank the curls, only to have Nathaniel restrain her.

Eric looked at the girl, his face deadpan. "I told you before. I don't go out."

Disappointment flickered across her face. "Even on dates?"

"*Especially* on dates."

Brittany looked at the table sheepishly.

"You do like *girls* don't you Eric?"

Nathaniel's thundering laughter ripped through the air, causing Autumn to jump out of her skin.

"Sometimes I wonder!" Nathaniel said amid cackles.

Eric's jaw clenched. Autumn could tell he was about to blow. Eric only had so much patience and this girl was wearing his thin.

"I happen to *love* women," Eric replied sharply. "I'm just not interested."

Brittany nodded her head, clearly deflated.

"If you change your mind," she handed him a piece of paper. "Call me."

When she was finally gone, Rick frowned at Eric disapprovingly.

"Man that was harsh and painful to watch."

"She never bothered with me when I was the *prince of darkness*," he made air quotations with his fingers.

"No one did buddy," Rick pointed out.

"Aut?" Eric looked at Autumn, clearly seeking validation.

"You were a little vexing back then," she admitted. "Still, I tend to agree with you. Brittany isn't really girlfriend material."

"I concur," Eric said. "I want someone intellectual and witty," he glanced at the paper Brittany had given him and frowned. "Not someone who dots their *I*'s with hearts."

* * *

As the final bell chimed, Autumn and Rick were stationed by their lockers discussing their plans for the evening.

"Are we studying tonight?" Rick asked, looking up at Autumn from his cell phone.

"We probably should," she replied, grabbing a textbook from her lockers top shelf.

Rick leaned into her, kissing her neck gently. Autumn giggled.

It tickled.

"Are you talking studying with our books or our *lips?*" he murmured into her ear.

She felt her face heating up. "Rick, come on. Exams are coming up."

"Yes, but its *Friday* night. Even the most disciplined of minds need a break Aut and Nate just texted me..." he trailed off.

"Let me guess. He wants to go skateboarding?" Autumn finished his thought, a huge grin on her face.

"Bingo," Rick said, putting his arm around her shoulders. "You are free to come along."

After her bag was sufficiently stuffed with books and binders, Autumn shut her locker and looked to Rick. He had a valid point. They had been studying nonstop the past couple weeks.

They had earned a Friday off.

"I appreciate the exclusive invite but Mandy and I are going shopping," Autumn said finally.

"You guys go ahead and enjoy the skate park."

Rick beamed as he pulled out his cell to text Nathaniel.

"You are an amazing girlfriend," Rick said, kissing her gently on the cheek.

"How did I get so lucky?"

Autumn shrugged her shoulders, as they began walking towards the exit doors.

"Just remember how lucky you are when we are studying *next* Friday night."

When they arrived at home, Autumn rushed upstairs to get ready while Rick snagged a snack from the fridge.

She slipped out of her school clothes, and pulled on a pair of comfortable black leggings and a turquoise tunic. She was just touching up her makeup when she heard Rick and Nathaniel chattering in the foyer.

"The video is ridiculous! This dude caught some serious air on that ramp!" Nathaniel said animatedly.

"Dude that is sick!" Rick said, as Autumn strolled down the stairs.

Mandy's eyes lit up at the sight of her.

"Autumn! You're here," she said, relieved. "All this skateboarding talk. Save me! Please!"

"Consider yourself rescued," Autumn said as she began lacing up her shoes.

Nathaniel put his arm around Mandy. "Sorry babe. I didn't mean to ignore you."

Mandy smiled mischievously. "You've already made it up to me sweetheart."

Nathaniel stared at her blankly. "I did?"

"Yep," she said. "Dinner is on you. I borrowed some money."

Nathaniel's brow furrowed in confusion. "When did you go into my wallet?"

"At lunch."

"How did I *not* notice that?"

"I am a skilled pickpocket baby," Mandy said proudly. "And you were distracted at the time."

Realization flashed across his face. "Oh! At *lunch!* When I was looking at Autumn's boobs!"

Mandy glared at him and pinched his forearm tightly. "You sicko!"

"Ow!" Nathaniel grumbled. "That hurt you fierce imp!"

"You deserved that one Nate," Autumn said smugly.

Mandy nodded. "Now that that's all settled, Autumn and I have some shopping to do."

Right on cue, Rick gave Autumn a quick kiss on the lips.

"Have a good time honey," he said. "Call me if you need anything."

Autumn nodded in acknowledgment before going in for another peck.

"You guys have fun too. Don't break anything."

Mandy waved then linked her arm in with Autumn's and they headed out the door.

2

The mall was virtually deserted when Autumn and Mandy arrived. It was strange for a Friday night to see the mall corridors mostly empty and shops with very few shoppers inhabiting them.

By seven o'clock Autumn had splurged on two bags of books and Mandy had run up her dads American Express. Both girls had worked up a sufficient appetite and headed towards the food court for dinner.

"So how are things going with you and Nate?" Autumn inquired as the escalator transported them to the upper floor.

Autumn noticed Mandy was glowing, her pixie-like features lighting up at the mere mention of his name.

The ghost of a smile appeared on her face.

"He makes me happy Aut. I haven't felt this way about any other guy I dated. Well, not for long anyway."

From what Autumn knew about Mandy's past relationships, they were definitely not healthy.

The guys she dated stole, did drugs, and got arrested regularly.

Her interest in guys was based on a scale: how much would they drive her well-to-do, snooty parents crazy?

"With other guys, their tricks got old fast," Mandy said. "You can only steal from the local variety store or sneak into the movies so many times before it becomes dull."

"Did you try just paying for things for a change?" Autumn joked.

Mandy smiled. "Nathaniel is decent. He may say *everything* that pops into his head without remorse, but he has a good heart."

The girls had finally made it to the top floor of the mall when Mandy mentioned Rick.

"You guys are perfect together," she said. "What's it like living with Rick? Because if I had to live with Nathaniel *and* go to school with him, I actually might consider homicide."

Autumn grinned impishly. "Well there are the *obvious* benefits."

Mandy's brown eyes lit up. "Like late night make out sessions in bed when his mom and dad are sound asleep?"

Autumn chuckled lightly. "That and I never feel alone. When I need Rick, he is just down the hall."

"Much to your father's discontentment, I am certain."

"I think he avoids that train of thought altogether," Autumn admitted.

She looked around the food court, taking in the sea of mostly empty seats and restaurants devoid of customers.

"So Chinese?" Autumn offered.

"Sounds good."

* * *

Carrying their red trays of chicken fried rice, sweet and sour pork and steamed vegetables the two girls claimed a much sought after booth to slide into. Though tonight, competition for the best seating was non-existent.

It wasn't until they arrived at the booth, that Autumn saw him sitting at the round table a few tables over.

Mandy had noticed him too.

She began approaching the handsome guidance counselor who sat, oblivious to his surroundings, reading the local newspaper.

Balancing her tray with one hand, Mandy used her other to grasp Autumn's forearm.

"What are you doing?" Autumn asked under her breath. She felt her cheeks blazing.

She already knew.

"We are going to sit with him of course!" Mandy said, grinning from ear to ear.

"Oh no. We are *not*," Autumn protested.

"And why is that?" Mandy asked, a frown replacing her giant smile.

"Because he's my guidance counselors and it's *weird*," Autumn began. "And Rick doesn't like him."

Mandy made a point of scanning the food court.

"Well, lucky for us, Rick isn't here," she said sardonically. "And we aren't at school. So he isn't your guidance counselor. Just some guy sitting at the food court reading the paper."

Autumn opened her mouth to protest but she knew it was a losing battle.

She was being dragged along, whether she liked it or not.

"Fine," Autumn grumbled, as she ran a hand through her dark waves.

Mandy glanced at her. "You look hot. No worries."

Autumn rolled her eyes. "I'm not worried."

Mandy smirked. "Yes you are."

As they got closer, Autumn took in the guidance counselor.

It didn't take a genius to realize he was handsome.

His chocolate eyes, dark hair checkered with light flecks of grey, and sharp jawline made the girls at school stare with admiration.

"Mr. Garrison!" Mandy exclaimed, as they stood in front of him. "Fancy meeting you here this fine evening!"

Autumn narrowed her eyes at Mandy, who relinquished the death grip on her arm.

Mr. Garrison looked up from his newspaper and smiled.

"Why hello there," he said pleasantly. "Ms. Jensen and Ms. Kingston, how nice to see you both."

"Likewise!" Mandy said. "What a darn coincidence huh?"

She looked at the round table and the vacant seats surrounding it.

"We just grabbed dinner and were looking for a place to sit," Mandy said pointedly.

Autumn frowned. Mandy was fishing for an invite to join him and she silently prayed she wouldn't get it.

She couldn't think of anything more awkward than having dinner with Mr. Garrison.

Mr. Garrison looked around the empty food court.

"Picky are we?" he teased. "Or did you guys want company? If so, by all means, take a seat. I would love some dinner companionship."

"Oh we would *love* that!" Mandy said, a huge grin on her face.

She nudged Autumn in the side. "Right Aut?"

Mr. Garrison glanced at Autumn, who nodded her head. "The more the merrier I always say."

The girls sat down and started in on their Chinese food.

"So Mr. Garrison," Mandy began.

Mr. Garrison looked up from his garden salad. "I know it might not be commonplace but please, if we aren't in school, call me Ryan. I feel like mister is too formal."

"Does it make you feel old?" Mandy asked searchingly. "Like older than whatever age you are currently. Which is?"

Autumn glared at Mandy. She was so transparent she was ghostly.

"Twenty four," he replied. "A little young to be a guidance counselor, I've been told. I had to pull some strings with people to get the job. I really love the idea of helping others. I enjoy touching people's lives."

"And I am sure they love being touched by you Ryan," Mandy said, putting a forkful of rice into her mouth.

Ryan politely ignored Mandy's innuendo and took another bite of his salad.

"So Autumn, how's the tutoring coming along?" he asked.

"Rick's grades are up," Autumn replied. "It really is a miracle considering his attention span."

Ryan chuckled. "Miracle? Hardly. After all, he has the schools *valedictorian* helping him out."

Mandy stared at her food, but Autumn could see the smirk on her face.

"You heard about that?" she asked, surprised.

Ryan took a drink from his water bottle.

"Guidance counselors hear everything. I must say Autumn, being chosen is quite an accomplishment."

Autumn's cheeks turned scarlet. "Thanks but it's not a big deal."

Ryan's eyes met hers and he smiled, his trademark crooked grin.

"Don't be modest. You worked hard and persevered, at a new school, nonetheless. That is admirable."

"That's Autumn," Mandy piped in, beaming. "Exceptionally gifted and yet, so humble."

The rest of dinner, Mandy questioned Ryan. Autumn imagined him, sweating profusely under hot lights, as Mandy interrogated him.

Despite her loutish methods, she *did* manage to get information out of him, much of it personal.

Ryan wasn't married or divorced. He lived alone, and just moved to Whitan within the last year or so, which explained why Rick didn't know him.

His hobbies included reading, going to the gym and playing darts and pool at the local pub with his buddies on weekends.

As Autumn listened intently to Ryan's backstory, she noticed something she hadn't seen before. She blinked her eyes, thinking she might be imagining things.

She wasn't.

His dress shirt was open a bit on his left side. The button must have come undone. It was just enough to reveal an image on his upper chest.

Autumn squinted, forcing her eyes to look closer.

It was a tattoo.

A black tribal design, with intricate swirls and lines. It was rather extensive and noticeable.

Autumn wasn't sure why, but something about it intrigued her.

This tattoo is important, her instincts told her.

It is something you don't want to forget.

3

"So you had dinner with Garrison?"

Rick was fuming. He paced back and forth, his fists clenched into tight balls.

If Autumn didn't know better, she might assume he was a rambling lunatic.

She had made the dire mistake of telling Rick that she had run into Mr. Garrison at the mall. Then she followed the first mistake with yet another: admitting she had dinner with him.

Now, Rick was on a rampage.

"We weren't alone Rick. Mandy was there," Autumn began feebly.
"Mandy? The same Mandy that thinks Mr. Garrison is, direct quote, *gorgeous*? Not helping."

The volume of Rick's shouting mounted and Autumn was thankful that Aunt Katherine and Uncle James were out at a charity gala for the night.
Mandy had warned her to keep their dinner with Ryan a secret, but Autumn knew she couldn't.
She didn't like harboring secrets, especially from Rick.
Secrets were dangerous.
When shared with another, they bonded people. When kept from someone, they tore people apart.

"You know what I think? He probably *followed* you to the mall!" Rick went out, arms flailing about manically.
"He was biding his time until he *accidently* ran into you. I bet having dinner with you just made his whole night!"

Autumn, who sat on Rick's bed picking absently at a stray string on his comforter, looked up at him.

"You sound absolutely insane."

Rick stared back at her, wild eyed. "I'm insane? Your guidance counselor is stalking you Autumn! Seriously! You should be worried!"

"I *am* worried about someone!" she snapped. "And it isn't Ryan!"

"*Ryan?*" Rick shouted. "Ryan! Did he tell you to call him that? Oh please, call me *Ryan!* Trust me, confide in me, so I can steal you away from your immature high school boyfriend!"

Rick's shoulders shook violently as he headed towards his shelf and began propelling books off it at random.

Autumn headed towards the door, afraid she might get caught in the crosshairs.

She had never seen Rick so irate. She hated to admit it, but it frightened her.

"You need to calm down Rick," she said cautiously. "Take a deep breath. You are overreacting."

Rick, holding a school textbook above his head, looked at her, incredulously.

"What I *need* is to punch *Ryan* in the face!"

He chucked the tome across the room and it landed with a thud on the wooden floor.

He reached for another but Autumn grabbed his arm.

"STOP!" she shouted. "You are making a mess and acting ridiculous."

"Me? Ridiculous?" Rick shot back. "I'm not the grown man chasing a teenager!"

Autumn couldn't believe how preposterous Rick sounded.

She wasn't blind. She could see the signs when someone had feelings for her and Mr. Garrison wasn't showing any.

Rick was being paranoid and jealous.

She was relieved that he seemed to be calming down. His trembling had subsided and his coloring returned to normal.

"I have a gut feeling. The guy is hiding something," Rick said, his voice even now.

The image of the huge tattoo flashed through Autumn's mind.

She wasn't telling Rick about it, not now.

"That may be so," she said. "But it has nothing to do with me. He is friendly with all the students Rick."

Rick blew a raspberry. "I bet he doesn't have *dinner* with all his students."

He placed the books back on the shelf and flopped onto his bed.

Autumn sat beside him.

"He is a guidance counselor Rick. It is his job to be friendly. Otherwise, no one would tell them their deepest, darkest secrets." She grinned, nudging him playfully in the side.

Rick grimaced. "I'm sorry Aut. I just lost it. I don't know what came over me."

Autumn looked up at the ceiling, the ghost of a smile on her face.

"Well, you never did like books."

The next morning, Autumn awoke to the heady scent of fresh baking. There were numerous things to love about Aunt Katherine, her homemade baking being one of them.

Autumn inhaled deeply, taking in the delectable aromas. Banana, chocolate, strawberry and vanilla scents invaded her nostrils as she got dressed to head downstairs.

As she pulled on a tank top and yoga pants, memories from her fight with Rick came rushing back.

Rick promised he was going to curb his jealous tendencies and though Autumn believed him, something still nagged at her.

Rick's moods had been like a rollercoaster of late. His behaviour was erratic and his fuse short.

Autumn knew Rick had a jealous streak, and that Ryan was the proverbial thorn in his side but his reaction last night was unsettling.

Autumn pulled her hair into a topknot, took a quick glance in the mirror and shrugged her worries off.

This was a puzzle she would have to figure out later.

She would add it to the list.

* * *

Autumn entered the kitchen to see her aunt mixing batter at the counter with her hair pulled into a ponytail. She wore her trademark red lipstick and her blue checkered apron.

She was humming a song Autumn didn't recognize.

"Autumn, you are awake," her aunt said, looking up from her baking.
"Rick just left with James."

Autumn had almost forgotten. Rick and his dad were taking advantage of his rare Saturday off from work at Cesus Corp. to engage in a father and son golfing day hosted by his employer.

"Rick ate six of the dozen muffins I made," her aunt sighed wistfully. "So here I am, baking more."
She gestured to an array of baked goods tucked behind her blueberry and banana muffins.
There were tarts, lemon and date squares, brownies and gingerbread and chocolate chunk cookies.
"Help yourself to whatever you like dear."

Autumn looked at the clock. It was nearly lunch and she hadn't even had breakfast yet.
"Thanks!" Autumn said as she snagged a blueberry muffin and a brownie.
She took her food to the table, along with a glass of milk.

"So I hear congratulations are in order?" Aunt Katherine said. She glanced at Autumn, a twinkle in her brown eyes.
"Rick told you did he?" Autumn asked, her cheeks turning pink.
"He did. This morning actually. Me and James are so proud of you Autumn," she said. "You had so much to contend with this year, between helping Rick and your own studies."
And slaying monsters in dark dank caves, Autumn thought grimly.
"Did you call your parents and tell them?" She asked, pouring batter into a large muffin tray.
Autumn shook her head as she bit into her muffin. "Not yet, but I will."
Aunt Katherine beamed. "They are going to be thrilled. Your father was valedictorian at his graduation as well. "
Autumn was about to respond, but the cover of the *Whitan Weekly* newspaper on the table caught her eye instead.
She read the headline and grabbed the paper frantically.

SIXTEEN YEAR OLD BOY PRESUMED MISSING.

Sixteen year old Andy Carson of Jamestown High School has been reported missing by his father. Last seen a week ago yesterday, he was said to be heading to Glendale Forest in Whitan to meet with friends.

"He told me he was going to camp out with friends for the weekend," his dad, 40 year old, Neil Carson said in a statement. "He was with a couple other guys. Next thing I know, they are calling me, panicked and saying they can't find Andy."

The two other boys, whose names have not been released to the public, said they went to sleep with Carson in their tent and awoke to find he'd vanished.
When asked if they heard anything throughout the night, one of the boys said Carson had gotten up to have a cigarette at around 2 in the morning then promptly returned to the tent.

The police have stated that neither of Carson's friends are currently suspects in the investigation but they won't rule anything out. If anyone has any information, police ask that you please contact -

Autumn stopped reading, as the nausea overcame her.
She looked at her hands. She was gripping the paper so tightly, her knuckles were white.

Glendale Forest was the woods near the cave.
The cave *they* had sealed with Eric and the elusive wolf men so many months ago.
The spell had banished the creatures and the evil lurking inside the cave.
They hadn't gone back to confirm, but the reports of missing people and mysterious accidents in the area had come to an abrupt halt afterwards.
The spell had been successful.
Autumn wanted to ignore it, but the thought nagged at her, begging to be acknowledged.
Did they screw something up that night?
Eric's spell would protect the caves from *anything* else taking them over.
Plus, the wolves knew what they were doing right?
Unable to focus on anything but the dreadful news, Autumn thanked her aunt for breakfast, politely excused herself, and promptly texted the person she could trust most on this subject.
By the time she had showered and brushed her teeth, she had gotten a message back from Eric. *See you in fifteen minutes.*

4

Fifteen minutes on the dot, Autumn heard the doorbell chiming.

Dressed in a simple white V-neck shirt and grey cords, her long hair pulled into a ponytail, she grabbed her tan knit sweater and threw it on as she headed downstairs.

"Eric! So nice to see you honey. Please come in!" She heard her aunt's jovial greeting.
"Autumn will be with you in a moment."
"Mrs. Jacobs how are you?" Eric asked pleasantly as Autumn hit the bottom of the stairs.
"I am well Eric. How about you? I haven't seen you around in a few weeks. What have you been up to?"
"Studying for exams," Eric said, a crooked smile on his face as he glanced at Autumn, who was putting on her brown suede boots.
"Not all of us are effortlessly shrewd like Autumn."
Autumn looked up from her boots and grimaced at him.
"Or as effortlessly beautiful," he added slyly.
Aunt Katherine looked from Eric to Autumn, grinning impishly.
"She is very beautiful inside and out. Rick is lucky to have her."
"He is," Eric agreed.
"So what are you two up to?" Aunt Katherine asked, as she fiddled absently with her apron.

"Coffee downtown," Eric said, placing a hand on the small of Autumn's back. "Autumn is going to help me with quadratic equations."
Autumn saw this as her chance for revenge after the *effortlessly smart and beautiful* comments.
"Poor Eric," she smiled sweetly. "He can't even do simple addition without his trusty calculator."
Eric smiled tightly, unable to deny it. "Yeah. I really can't."

Aunt Katherine looked at Eric pityingly.

"Oh Eric, don't be ashamed," she said, putting a hand on his shoulder reassuringly.

"Math was my worst subject too. The only thing that helps is practice *and* a good teacher of course."

Then she looked at Autumn.

"You're a good friend helping Eric, but don't spread yourself thin. You have your speech and your own studying to do. It's Saturday. Go see a movie when you're done."

"We just might. I'll text Rick and let him know where I am," Autumn said, hugging her aunt. "I'll be home for dinner."

Aunt Katherine hugged her back. "Alright sweetheart. Have fun. It was nice seeing you again Eric."

"Likewise Mrs. Jacobs. Enjoy the day."

When they were finally out of earshot, Eric looked at Autumn a scowl on his handsome face.

"A *calculator?* Really?"

Autumn shrugged her shoulders. She saw Eric's gold Camaro parked by the curb. Polished to perfection, it glimmered in the sunlight.

"*Effortlessly smart and beautiful?* I am dating her son Eric!"

Eric said nothing and just grinned, as they walked towards the car.

He opened Autumn's door for her but it wasn't until they were both in the car that he spoke.

"I didn't mean to make you uncomfortable but it isn't news to your aunt that you are pretty. She isn't blind."

Autumn's cheeks were on fire.

"That is ridiculous."

Eric glanced at her. "Hardly. You are beautiful. Just accept it."

Autumn sighed. "Aunt Katherine doesn't know the truth."

Eric's brow furrowed. "The truth?"

"About us dating. As far as she's concerned, Rick was my first choice."

The car engine roared to life and Eric shrugged his shoulders.

"Wasn't he?" he asked apathetically.

Autumn frowned. "No. He wasn't but she doesn't need to know that."

"Fair enough," Eric said as he headed down the winding street.

The car was thick with silence for a moment. Eric stopped at a red light and looked at Autumn.

"I read the newspaper. After I got your message," he said.

"Not before?" Autumn asked as she adjusted her seat.

"I'm surprised you have no interest in the local news."

The light turned green and Eric hit the gas.

"I spent years looking at that paper. Reading about the travesties caused by those demons," he said bitterly. "I thought it was finally over. I gave up my morning routine of scouring pages for strange occurrences masked under the guise of news."

Autumn knew what Eric meant. Reading about the missing boy was like a kick in the teeth.

"Do you think I jumped the gun?" she asked.

Eric's expression was unreadable.

"I think anytime someone goes *missing* in these parts, it is never a coincidence," he replied.

"But we may be looking in the wrong place."

Autumn looked out her window. She saw a couple walking in the street. They were young, maybe in their 20's. They were laughing, grins wide, teeth exposed, looking like they hadn't a care in the world.

For a moment, she envied them.

Their naiveté, their blindness to the truth she knew all too well.

The true darkness of the world was hidden to most.

"The wrong place?" Autumn repeated Eric.

He turned onto a main road. It was packed with weekend traffic.

He stopped the car, claiming his rightful place in the gridlock.

"I'm saying that between the spell being cast and the big bad wolves, we are covered. Which leads me to believe something else is responsible for this abduction."

They were stuck in traffic for fifteen minutes before cars finally began moving. Eric slipped off the main road onto a side street. He took backroads all the way to their local haunt, a cozy coffee shop that was tucked neatly between a launder mat and a drug store.

As the Camaro pulled into the lot, Eric glanced at Autumn.

"I assume we are getting our order to go," he said, his trademark half-smirk returning.

"Unless you prefer discussing elaborate monster theories in public?"

"You're sharp," Autumn said, teasing.

"Remind me to pick you as my trivia partner next time Aunt Katherine hosts game night."

* * *

Walking into the coffee shop, the first thing Autumn saw was the crimson brick gas fireplace. Gathered around it were groups of plush oversized arm chairs. Beyond that, was a large rustic wooden counter, and in between were chairs and tables, all ornately rustic to match the rest of the décor.

The design seemed to be very cabin in the woods.

Autumn thought it looked rather cozy.

As they approached the counter, a young girl with a choppy blonde bob and large blue eyes greeted them warmly.

"Hi there! What can I get you?"

The girl looked quickly past Autumn to the handsome Eric. She batted her lashes at him, reminiscent of a cartoon character with hearts floating around its head.

Autumn wasn't dense. She saw how Eric entered rooms and made heads turn. Gone were the days of Eric's black wardrobe and constant brooding.

Today, dressed in a blue polo shirt and khakis, his brown eyes alight, he was irresistible.

The female population *loved* the new Eric.

The girl stared at Eric, cheeks flushed, awaiting a reply.

"A large coffee black for me and a large green tea, for my gorgeous girlfriend here," Eric said lightly as he nodded in Autumn's direction.

Autumn looked at Eric inquisitively, wondering if she had misheard him, when he lunged towards her, kissing her gently on the lips.

Autumn was frozen in place as memories of Eric and her came rushing back.

Eric pulled back, winked at Autumn and turned back to the girl.

"That'll be 3.50," the girl said, deflated.

Eric reached into his pocket to fish out money. "No problem."

"Thanks," The girl smiled weakly before heading off to make the drinks.

When she was out of earshot, Autumn shot Eric a deadly glare.

"What the hell Eric," she snapped.

"If looks could kill," Eric muttered, an arrogant smirk on his face.

"What were you *thinking?*" Autumn whispered.

"If someone we knew saw us, Rick would find out and..."
"And Rick would tighten your leash?" Eric offered.
"He does *not* have me on a leash!" Autumn barked.
Eric shrugged his shoulders nonchalantly.
"Relax. I was just deflecting that girl. I don't need another lovesick girl on my heels. Brittany is hard enough to evade."
"Wow, arrogant much?" Autumn asked, narrowing her eyes.
"Look who's talking," Eric shot back.
"Excuse me?"
"This wasn't about *you* Aut. If Mandy had been here, her lips would've sufficed."
Autumn clenched her fists, barely resisting the urge to sock Eric. She had zero interest in Eric's *kiss* and him assuming cared, made fury bubble over inside her.

Finally the blonde barista returned with their drinks, her expression composed. She handed Eric his coffee first.
"Here you are. Enjoy."
Eric smiled his best one hundred watt grin. "Thank you. Enjoy your day."

He gave Autumn another coy wink that made her want to slap him, and went to find seats.
Sighing loudly, the girl handed Autumn her tea, looking forlorn.
"You are a lucky girl. He is so adorable."
Autumn gritted her teeth and nodded.
"He is just wonderful," she managed.

Eric managed to secure them seats by the fireplace. This spot was by far the most coveted and also Autumn's favorite.
She hadn't decided whether or not this act warranted forgiveness, when she sat down across from Eric.
He looked up at her innocently.
"Are you still mad sweetie pie?" he grinned.
Sweetie pie? Oh, forgiveness is on the backburner now, Autumn thought.

"You just better hope Rick doesn't get wind of your..." she paused, feeling like she might explode. "*Shenanigans!*"
"Shenanigans? I was more concerned about my tomfoolery," Eric jested.
He leaned back in his arm chair, looking untroubled as he stretched out his long legs.
"Seriously. You worry too much. No one here knows us."

"Autumn! Is that you?" a familiar voice rang out from an unseen corner of the coffee shop.

Autumn turned to see the Stuart, the homeless man she and Rick saw around town, coming towards her.

She couldn't believe her eyes.

Stuart looked rather presentable and unsoiled, in tan khakis, a grey shirt and a navy bomber jacket.

"Hey Stu," Autumn said, smiling. "How are you doing?"

He shrugged. "I just ate a half a dozen doughnuts, so I can't really complain."

He looked at Eric, inquiringly. "I didn't realize you and Rick split. Is this your new beau?"

Eric looked up from stirring his coffee. "So much for our secret affair Aut."

Autumn rolled her eyes. "No Stuart. Rick and I are still together..."

"*Oh* I get it. It's one of those open relationships," Stuart said surely. "Or as we called it in my day, polygamy."

"It isn't like that," Autumn interjected. "Eric was just trying to deter the barista."

Stuart put a hand on his stubbly chin. "Why?"

Eric shrugged his shoulders. "She is not really my type," he said, noncommittally.

Stuart nodded his head. "I understand. Oh, I'm Stuart by the way."

He studied Eric, sizing him up. "You must be Eric."

Eric raised his eyebrows. "How did you know?"

It dawned on Autumn that Eric and Stuart had never *actually* met, though she often spoke of one to the other.

"Fancy clothes, arrogant demeanour, the classic Camaro parked outside," Stuart said, sipping his coffee. "I can only assume you are the friend Rick referred to as, *the rich jackass.*"

Eric grimaced but didn't argue. "That's me. In the flesh."

Stuart joined Autumn and Eric at their table. She remembered something Stuart had said to her during one of their many aimless conversations. He had told her that being homeless meant being the eyes and ears of Whitan, and *beyond.*

"Stuart, I need to ask you something," Autumn began, her fingers tracing the rim of her cup absently.

"Uh-oh," Stuart said, looking mildly worried. "I hope you don't want advice on love kid because I am the *definition* of lone wolf."

"No nothing like that," Autumn said, raising her hand. She looked around at the people in the coffee shop. "We'll need to go somewhere more private to talk."

Stuart shrugged. "Alright. I know a place."

He looked at Eric, a grin appearing on his face.

"That is, if you don't mind letting a bum into your pristine automobile."

Eric sighed. "I let Nathaniel in it. So why not?"

Autumn stepped out of the coffee shop, looking up at the increasingly darkening sky. The sun was still glimmering, but the grey clouds were moving in, threatening to overshadow the light that bathed the streets.

"Alright, whose got shotgun?" Eric asked and Stuart face went stern.

"Guns are dangerous you know. Not things to be trifled with. Machines of death. I could go on."

Autumn let out a chuckle. "What Eric meant to say is, do you want to ride up front?"

Stuart ran a hand through his tousled brown hair. "Ladies always sit up front."

"I appreciate that Stuart but if you take the backseat you won't get to watch Eric play with the radio dials and tailgate other vehicles."

"I do not tailgate," Eric said in disbelief.

As they got into the Camaro, Autumn saw her phone flashing.
It was a text from Rick.
I miss you. What are you up to?
Autumn texted back.
On a road trip with Eric and Stuart.
Stuart the bum?
Yep. I'll fill you in later. Have fun. XOXO
You too. Talk soon.

"So where are we going anyway?" Eric asked as he slipped on a pair of aviator sunglasses.

"A forest out of town," Stuart said mildly. "Nice and quiet, no one around. People used to say it was haunted or something ridiculous. You know it?"

Eric nodded as he revved the engine. "Yup."

Autumn saw his eyes glance at her in the rear-view mirror. They exchanged perturbed looks.

"Listen to that kitten purr," Stuart said gleefully. "What a beaut."

Eric smiled with pride, gave the car another booming rev and began pulling out of the parking lot.

When they were finally on the road Autumn zoned out while Stuart and Eric discussed cars.

She stared out the window, taking in the endless sea of beautiful trees and blossoming flowers.

She tried to ignore the tight feeling in her stomach.

The caves were sealed. There was nothing to worry about right?

Still, the nagging dread persisted.

"How are you doing back there Aut?" Eric asked.

They had been driving fifteen minutes and she hadn't said more than two words.

"I'm great," she lied.

"Sorry. We got carried away with the automobile conversation," Stuart offered.

Autumn forced a smile. "No worries."

"She's good Stuart. Probably just speechless remembering that kiss I laid on her back at the coffee shop," Eric said haughtily.

Autumn met his eyes in the mirror and glared at him. "Not a chance King."

Stuart turned to face Autumn. "So how is Rick doing? I haven't seen him around lately."

"He's good. He's with his dad playing golf as we speak," Autumn replied.

"Is he close with his father?" Stuart asked and Autumn nodded.

"He's close with both his parents. They are tightknit."

The conversation lulled for a moment before Autumn spoke again.

"Where is your family Stuart? If that's not too personal."

He waved his hand dismissively.

"Nothing's too personal when you live on the streets kid. My parents live in New York. My mother owns a small coffee shop chain and my father is a lawyer."

Autumn arched an eyebrow. Perhaps she was being presumptuous but it sounded like Stuart's parents were well-off.

She wondered why he was living on the streets in another country, but she didn't want to ask.

Stuart seemed to read her mind. "I know what you are thinking. My parents are loaded and here I am, not asking them for a dime," he paused. "I love my parents. They raised me and took care of me but I could never *be* like them. Maids, chefs, gardeners and hoity-toity shindigs. That's not my bag. I don't condone servitude. I'd much rather live simply. With the clothes on my back, food in my stomach and a place to sleep at night." He looked to Eric. "No offense moneybags."

"None taken," Eric said coolly.

Autumn wasn't surprised by this. Since getting to know Stuart, she noticed he had an upstanding moral obligation. He was a person of high scruples.

"That is very noble of you," Autumn said.

"Or selfish, depending on who you ask," Stuart said. "I enjoy my independence. That's why my lifestyle suits me. Though it isn't for the faint of heart."

"Or stomach," Eric muttered.

"Do you miss them? Your parents I mean," Autumn asked.

"Every day," Stuart said wistfully.

"You must have friends though," Autumn said, feeling a sudden urge to probe him for more information.

Stuart laughed. "Oh sweetheart, when you live on the streets you make friends. *Good* friends though? People that stand by you through thick and thin? I can count those friends on one hand."

Autumn knew exactly what he meant. Some friendships came and went as quickly as seasons.

Real friends stood beside you forever. You might spend time apart, but when you come together again, it's like no time had passed. You share an unbreakable bond, a tether to one another that nothing, time nor life's trials, can destroy.

It didn't take long for them to arrive at their destination.

Being here again, with the caves so close, caused chills to dance along Autumn's spine.

Eric put the car into park in the familiar lot. They had always parked here before heading to the caves.

Stuart undid his seatbelt and got out, stretching his limbs towards the sky.

Eric turned to Autumn. "Are you going to be alright?" he asked softly.

Autumn nodded, forcing a smile. She was trying to convince herself as much as Eric.

"I'll be fine. Now's our chance to investigate, see if trouble is brewing again."

"Are we going to tell him?" Eric pointed to Stuart who was doing lunges across the mostly empty lot.

"I think we can trust him," Autumn replied. "Besides, it's no secret what goes on here, especially to someone like him. Stu is usually privy to local goings-on."

The two of them proceeded to get out of the Camaro and walk over to Stuart.

"Are you guys ready?" he asked as he finished stretching. "We can walk and talk."

"Sure," Autumn said but her limbs felt like lead when she tried to move them. The familiar sense of dread creeped down her spine as she recalled the many nights spent in this very spot.

Eric reached his hand out and touched her forearm discreetly. His eyes were fixed on hers.

He was wondering if she was alright. She took a deep breath.

The demons can't hurt you, she told herself. They are dead and gone.

You made sure of that. The wolves *definitely* made sure of that.

So they began walking.

Autumn fixed her mind on the scenery. The emerald grass, flowers blossoming, everything brimming with the possibility of summer. Birds cawed nearby, probably telling tales of their journeys through the sky. With wings, anything is possible, Autumn mused. Limits don't exist when you can soar away, wherever and whenever you want.

Autumn could see the cave in the distance. Even now, as benign as it was, it still towered menacingly. She shuddered involuntarily and Stuart caught it.

"The caves give you the heebie-jeebies do they?" he asked, as they walked through a patch of tall grass.

"They do," she admitted. She looked at Stuart. "Do you believe in the supernatural?"

Stuart, who didn't seem fazed by her question, looked at Autumn, his brow furrowed in confusion.

"Are you talking about ghosts? Or something else?"

Autumn shrugged her shoulders noncommittally.

"Anything out of the ordinary in or around Whitan I guess."

They trekked up the incline of grass and up towards the masses of overlapping trees and brush.

"I have seen things," Stuart said hesitantly. "But I don't really think I should be telling you guys all this."

Eric chuckled lightly. "Trust me Stu. We can handle it."

They came upon a camping area, a small clearing shrouded by clusters of Evergreens. There were remnants of a campfire and large boulders surrounding it. Stuart took the opportunity to take a seat on a rock and Eric and Autumn followed suit.

"I don't want you guys having nightmares on my account," Stuart said finally. "Why are you asking Autumn?"

Autumn suddenly felt uncertain. Should she really have brought the subject up?

She looked at Eric for guidance but his face was blank. She couldn't backtrack now. Only go full steam ahead.

She sighed deeply before beginning.

"Eric and I, we went into the caves. The stories, they are true."

Stuart raised an eyebrow. "They are haunted?"

"Worse. There were monsters. Demons actually," she paused, gauging his reaction.

He said nothing at first, his expression unreadable.

Autumn was aware of how she sounded. Like a lunatic. Like she belonged in a rubber room with the door padlocked and the key thrown away.

"That is a relief," Stuart said after a moment. "I thought I was losing my mind when I saw those things."

Autumn and Eric looked at each other, stunned.

She wasn't sure if Stuart was teasing her or not. She waited a few beats then she spoke.

"Are you joking?"

"Would I joke about something like that?" he deadpanned. "I saw them. Stuff of nightmares those things were. The bulging eyes, the veiny arms, the dead eyes."

"Throw in sharp teeth and lust for murder and we have a winner," Eric chimed in.

A memory rushed through Autumn's mind.

The beautiful and regal wolves fighting in the caves and saving their lives.

"There is more," Autumn said. "Rick, Mandy and Nathaniel were with us too. That night in the cave, we were in over our heads. We were fighting a losing battle. We would've died but these wolves showed up."

"Wolves?" Stuart repeated.

Autumn nodded. "Four of them. Well, it started out as three but another showed up."

"They were huge and towering. They were bipeds and seemed to have almost human intelligence too. They were just amazing."

She knew she sounded star struck but she couldn't help it. Those wolves were the reason she was still alive today.

"Werewolves," Eric added in for good measure. "That is my hypothesis."

"Werewolves?" Stuart reiterated, a hand on his chin. "I ain't surprised. These parts seem to attract many supernatural beings."

"Have you ever seen one?" Eric asked.

"A werewolf? Never had the pleasure," Stuart said outstretching his legs in front of him. "What were you doing that night at the caves?"

Autumn and Eric spent the next hour filling Stuart in on everything he needed to know. The caves, Eric's parents and his plan to finish what they started using his magics. How Autumn and the others trained to help him. Bianca the queen of demons. The mysterious and beautiful enchantress that aided Eric.
They left out nothing.

"So these mighty wolves saved you did they?" Stuart said. "Truth be told, I'm a little surprised you didn't get eaten alive."

"By the demons?" Autumn asked.

"By the wolves," Stuart said. "From what I've heard of werewolves they are temperamental buggers. You rub them the wrong way and they will turn on you."

"So much for loyal dogs," Eric jested.

"To be fair, that is just hearsay," Stuart said. "From what you told me they saved your asses. Which probably means they are the good guys."

Autumn remembered the intensity in the wolves' eyes as they fought. They weren't there by coincidence. It was evident they came to kill the demons that plagued the cave.

"Speaking of the caves, I usually keep abreast of all the comings and goings in the area," Stuart said. "Those caves have been dormant for months. Looks like your mission was a success."

"We thought so too," Eric said. "Until today's paper reported another teenager went missing in this very forest."

Autumn and Eric explained to Stuart what the article entailed. How Andy Carson had gone missing last weekend while camping out with friends and how this forest was the scene of the crime.

Stuart looked thoughtful before he finally reacted.

"I *can* see how it might seem like the caves are somehow to blame for that kid disappearing but I think it's just a coincidence. I hang around here frequently and I haven't seen *or* heard anything. Not since around the time you guys sealed those caves up."

Autumn let out a breath she hadn't realized she was holding in. Her muscles relaxed and her stomach unclenched.

If the monsters *were* back surely Stuart would know *something*.

That only left one problem that troubled Autumn again and caused her mind to race. If it *wasn't* the cave monsters, what happened to Andy Carson? What else was lurking out there?

5

He screamed.

A piercing shriek that no one would ever hear.

He figured it out early on, not long after he was introduced to his glass prison.

He wasn't alone completely. He could see the others in glass cubes adjacent to him.
A pretty blonde girl with huge terrified eyes. A tall lanky boy wearing a ratty band t-shirt.
Their outfits, ragged and worn, spoke volumes about the length of their captivity but it wasn't just that. It was their eyes. Their eyes were devoid of hope and that is when he deduced it.

He was going to be a prisoner for a long time.

When he first awoke he was groggy. He didn't recall how he got here or where here was. He realized he had been tranquilized.
A man was standing above him. Dressed in dark clothes, his face set in an unwavering scowl.
He set down a plate of food and water on the floor.
"Eat," he snapped, his dark eyes cold. "You will need your strength for what comes next."

He looked around for signs of where he was being held. He saw nothing. He did manage to read the embroidered letters on one of the guard's uniforms.
DSI.
Not like it mattered. He had no idea what DSI stood for.

Today would be like all the others since arriving in this hellhole.

He would cause a commotion and hope someone might give him answers. He demanded to know why he was taken. Were his friends here too? Were they grabbed and being held somewhere in this colossal room?

He continued screaming and banging.
They really didn't care if he screamed.
They let him. What harm did it cause?

They were probably underground. He had gathered that much from his surroundings. It smelt damp and earthy and he heard the consistent sound of dripping water.

Time passed so slowly he thought he might go insane. He waited, determined to get answers today.
Eventually a guard arrived. Wearing a black uniform with the letters *DSI* stitched on it, he was a guard he hadn't seen before.

The guard unlocked the door and walked into the glass cell, armed to the nines with weaponry. A gun, crowbar, Taser and a large hunting knife.
He knew better then to attempt escape. He had seen what happened to the last person who tried to run.
Days ago, a boy about his age in the cell across from him. Though he was built like a linebacker the guard took him down with ease. Then he was beaten with a baseball bat and dragged away.

He never came back.

The guard placed a bowl of oatmeal on the foldout steel table along with a bottle of water.
"Where am I?" he asked the guard his heart thudding in his chest like a drum.
The guard looked at him, a flash of bewilderment on his face that was quickly replaced with a sneer.
"You don't get to ask questions!" he growled.
"I have a right to know!" he snapped back, hands balled into tight fists. He was shaking now. From fear or anger he wasn't sure.
"Calm down!" the guard instructed as he pulled out his baton. It glinted menacingly in the light. "Or you will suffer the consequences!"
"Why me?" he was pleading now. "Why am I here?"

The guard looked at him, eyes narrowed.

"You got guts boy. For that, I will answer just this once. We needed more samples."

"Samples?" he echoed. He didn't understand.

The guard nodded, grinning wickedly. "And you boy, might be our finest most promising specimen yet."

* * *

Autumn's phone alarm sounded from her bedside table, reminding her it was Monday.

Back to school. After her visit with Eric and Stuart, she spent the night with Rick and the following day studying and writing her speech.

Her entire weekend had been jam-packed. So much so that the mere thought of getting out of bed now exhausted her.

Knowing her snooze would wake her up she began dozing off when she heard a gentle rapping on her door.

"Come in," she said groggily.

Rick appeared before her dressed in jeans and a t-shirt, his brown curls damp from showering. Usually it was Autumn waking *him* up first but not today. Rick seemed bright-eyed and bushytailed as he plopped down on her bed.

"Morning sweetheart," he murmured, kissing her on the forehead.

Autumn yawned loudly. "Morning."

Rick studied her, frowning. "I've *never* had to wake you up for school."

"And I've *never* seen you up before eight A.M.," she jested. "Is this one of the signs of the apocalypse?"

Rick chuckled lightly. "Nope. I am just excited. School is almost finished and freedom is merely days away."

Autumn smiled and leaned up towards Rick, kissing him.

"Didn't your mom say you needed to get a job this summer?"

"It's that or I can spend the summer mowing the lawn, taking out the garbage, washing the cars," he paused. "You get the idea."

"But enough of this depressing talk," Rick said. "Breakfast is ready. I can smell it."

"You go ahead. I am going to hop into the shower first," Autumn said kicking the covers off.

She stood up in her white tank top and yoga pants and stretched.

"Alright. I promise to save you some bacon," he said, wrapping his arms around her waist. He pulled her against him and kissed her. His fingers threaded into her hair and his lips lingered on hers.

Autumn pulled back and grinned. "Don't make promises you can't keep Jacobs."

6

"All students are to report to the gymnasium in an orderly fashion for the school's end of the year assembly."

The announcement came when Autumn was in homeroom. Mr. Brown had just let them start studying and she was practicing quadratic equations. She had completely forgotten the end of year assembly that Rick had warned her about. It would be boring, lengthy and made studying seem exciting.

Autumn turned to Mandy who sat in the desk behind her. She grimaced and mouthed to Autumn: *we should ditch*.

Autumn smirked and turned back around. Though the idea *was* tempting Autumn couldn't just skip. If she was caught, and with her luck she would be, she would never hear the end of it from Principal Steel. She could just imagine it. The upstanding student chosen as valedictorian ditching the end of the year assembly. It wouldn't be pretty.

"This blows," Rick, who was sitting in the desk next to hers, grumbled closing his math book. "I was just getting the hang of equations and now this? How can anyone get anything done around here?"

Rick was irritated that his *studying* was being interrupted? Autumn couldn't help but grin.

"We can study at home after dinner," Autumn offered.

Rick sighed, rolling his eyes. "That was what I was trying to avoid."

Autumn's cell vibrated in her jeans pocket. She pulled it out cautiously and read the text. It was from Mandy.

Let's ditch the assembly. We are seniors!

Autumn texted back:

I think Mr. B will notice our absence.

Autumn got a message back not long after.

Doubtful...The guy forgets to zip up his fly.

Autumn looked back at Mandy, who was grinning widely when Mr. Brown clapped his hands demanding everyone's attention.

"Alright guys you heard the announcement. Everyone head down to the gym in an orderly fashion," he said.

There were a few collective sighs in the room as everyone packed up and headed for the door.

Rick flung his backpack over his shoulder and grabbed Autumn's hand, lacing his fingers through hers before kissing her gently on the cheek. Mandy approached dressed in a blue tank top, and skinny jeans. With her pixie cut slicked behind her ears, she reminded Autumn of a fairy.

"So love birds, do you want the good new or bad news first?"

"Bad first always," Autumn replied.

"Nathaniel took off without us."

"The good news?"

Mandy smiled. "We *can* find him, equipped with weapons and whoop his sorry ass for abandoning us."

Autumn stared at Mandy in disbelief. "Are you two really a couple?"

They continued moving slowly and steadily through the flow of students, keeping close to their homeroom as best as they could. Surrounding them was a solid stream of chatter as students discussed their summer plans.

Listening to them, Autumn realized she had no idea what she wanted out of life. She had applied to the community college that was a half-hour away but she wasn't sure she wanted to go there. If she did, she would be studying literature. Aunt Katherine had given her the idea. She knew Autumn wanted to stay close to home and Rick. Her father wasn't pleased with her choice, even though he accepted it was hers to make. He had encouraged Autumn to attend university, schools that were out of the country, schools that would surely take her because of her excellent grades.

Though she hadn't intended to let her father down, Autumn couldn't please everyone. How could she when she didn't even know what she wanted for herself? Her future was a gigantic black hole of uncertainty and mystery. It was scary and thrilling all at once.

"Pssst hey." A hushed voice came from behind a cluster of lockers.

"What the hell was that?" Mandy asked as she ventured behind the lockers.

"You son of a bitch! I knew it!"

Mandy stepped out with Nathaniel in tow. Dressed in baggy jeans and a ripped t-shirt, he ran a hand through his ginger hair and grinned mischievously.

"Rejoice everyone because your savior is here!" he announced.

Mandy scouted around exaggeratingly.

"All I see is a giant moron who hides behind lockers to avoid school assemblies."

"Sorry babe," Nathaniel said, planting a kiss on her forehead affectionately. "I didn't want to draw attention."

"Because the *loud* whispering wasn't a dead giveaway?" Mandy rolled her eyes. "If there is a zombie apocalypse you won't be planning *anything* Nathaniel."

"So was there a reason you came back for us?" Autumn asked, trying to change the subject. She had witnessed the way gentle teasing morphed into a full-blown fight with Mandy and Nathaniel. She wanted to avoid *that* at all costs.

"I came to help you escape the assembly," Nathaniel said. "Unless you *want* to spend the next two hours staring at Mr. Steel's new breakup goatee."

"I cannot just bail," Autumn crossed her arms defiantly.

"Come on Aut. It is our last two weeks before graduation. What are they going to do? Give us detention? Fail us?" Nathaniel snorted. "Face it. They are utterly helpless."

"I can't skip this Nate! I am the school valedictorian. What will people think?"

"That you are awesome!" he said, grinning impishly.

Mandy placed a hand on Autumn's forearm.

"I don't want to be the devil on your shoulder," she began.

Autumn sighed. "Yes you do."

"But Nate has a valid point," she went on. "Should we really be spending our last days as seniors crammed into a crowded, stuffy gymnasium that reeks like sweat and Limburger cheese?"

Autumn wrinkled her nose in disgust. "That sounds absolutely repulsive."

"It is. So please. Come with us," Mandy urged.

Autumn had *never* skipped classes. Still, the thought of doing something a little wild, though most people would consider ditching an assembly rather tame, made her heart skip a beat.

"Fine," she relented. "Lead the way Nate."

Nathaniel led them to a secluded hallway and out a relatively unused side door.

A couple of guys followed them out. Autumn recognized them. They were also seniors.

"Where are we going?" the dark haired boy asked, looking back at the school anxiously.

"To the park," the other boy replied shortly. "I stole cigarettes from my mom's purse this morning. We can go smoke them."

When the two boys were out of earshot Mandy snorted. "Those guys are so badass," she said sarcastically.

"It doesn't get much worse than stealing from your own parents," Rick muttered as the two seniors faded into the distance.

"So where are *we* going?" Mandy asked Nathaniel as they trudged through the grass. Autumn could see a small forest area a mile ahead. She inhaled deeply, a mixture of campfire smoke and pine scents invading her nostrils.

"The forest," Nathaniel said. "We can go chill there until the assembly finishes."

"Hey guys! Wait up!"

Eric came striding towards them, dressed in dark jeans and a white linen dress shirt, his dark hair hanging messily in his eyes.

"Did my invitation get lost in the mail?" he joked as he caught up to them.

"Shouldn't you be somewhere polishing that new car of yours?" Mandy shot back, a mischievous grin on her face.

As soon as Autumn saw Eric she remembered the coffee shop kiss and like he could read her mind, he began grinning at her like a fool.

"Morning Autumn," he said before leaning in and whispering into her ear: "Are you thinking about that sweet kiss too?"

Autumn shot him a deadly glare. "No!"

Eric grinned, his perfect teeth bright white against his tan skin. "Aw, you are blushing sweetheart."

"No what?" Rick asked, looking at Autumn, perplexed.

"Nothing," Autumn muttered as they reached the opening to the forest.

She inhaled deeply, relishing the scent of pine, lilacs and fresh cut grass. The school grounds were meticulously maintained and the grass had just been mown this morning as Autumn was coming in.

Autumn knew she wasn't the most coordinated, so she moved carefully as though avoiding landmines when she walked. She watched her feet maneuver around large jagged rocks and other debris embedded in the mud.

It took her a moment to register the paleness, stark against the dirt and pine needles that littered the ground. She bent over and picked the object up.

It appeared to be the backside of a photo. It looked tattered and weatherworn. She flipped it over to examine it.

"Holy shit!" she exclaimed.

Rick and the others stopped, looking over their shoulders.

"What is it?" Rick asked, moving beside Autumn.

He looked at the photo then groaned in frustration.

"Seriously? We can't even escape him in the woods!"

7

"Escape who?" Mandy asked curiously as everyone crowded around Autumn.

"It's a picture with a half missing piece," Autumn said, clutching the tattered snapshot.

Mandy stared at the photo as realization came over her face. "Is that Mr. Garrison?"

Autumn nodded slowly. "I think so."

"Dude! Geezerson actually looks young there!" Nathaniel said as Eric looked at him, perplexed.

"He's not *old* Nathaniel. I would guess early twenties maybe mid."

Nathaniel rolled his eyes. *"Exactly.* He is practically geriatric dude."

"Who are those other people with him?" Eric asked, ignoring Nathaniel.

Autumn studied the photo. Mr. Garrison was smiling widely, dressed in a plaid button-down shirt and ripped loose fitting jeans. His brown hair was messy and wild yet much shorter then he wore it today.

Beside the handsome Mr. Garrison stood a tank-like man with olive skin, jet black hair and piercing dark eyes. His face was set in an arrogant grin, his chest puffed out like a proud peacock.

Beside him there *was* someone else but the tear in the photo made it impossible to tell *who*.

She flipped the picture over, hoping for clues but whatever words were written on the back had been washed away either by time or weather.

Autumn shrugged her shoulders. "I'm guessing they're friends of his."

"Garrison has friends?" Rick muttered sarcastically.

Eric sighed loudly, clearly frustrated. "What's with the two of you?" he gestured to Rick and Nathaniel.

"They hate Mr. Garrison," Autumn confirmed.

"Hold on. I *never* said anything about hating him," Nathaniel protested.

Mandy stared at the photo pensively. "He is so handsome. I bet he could've been a model."

"Okay *now* I hate him," Nathaniel grumbled.

"Wake up guys!" Eric snapped. "He's an adult. I'm sure he has a life of his own *and* a girlfriend. I don't think he's after either of yours." He looked at Rick and Nathaniel pointedly. "He might even be married."

"For the record," Mandy said. "Garrison is sans ring. So *if* he's married he obviously doesn't care enough about her to wear his shackle to work."

Eric gave Mandy a look of disapproval. "Trust me. My opinion, as a man..."

"A man?" Mandy snorted.

"Yes, a *man*," Eric recovered, sitting on a huge boulder near a cluster of trees. "He probably isn't going to hook up with girls your age."

"Don't hold back or anything Eric," Autumn said sarcastically.

Mandy shrugged. "Maybe not me per say, but I have seen the way he looks at *her*." She pointed at Autumn, smiling impishly.

Autumn buried her face in her hands. Mandy loved getting Rick going. Autumn noticed that lately it wasn't so difficult a chore. Rick's temper was flaring more often than not.

"See! I knew it!" Rick roared, his face reddening with anger.

"I give up." Eric shook his head hopelessly.

Autumn touched Rick's shoulder and rubbed it soothingly.

"Sweetie, Mandy's just *teasing* you. You fall for it every time. You know that right?"

"Dude, she loves pissing people off," Nathaniel confirmed, plopping onto a patch of grass near Eric's boulder. "Why do you think my mom hates her so much?"

Mandy scowled at Nathaniel as Eric set his backpack on his lap and opened it, pulling out a cigar.

"So is anyone else questioning *how* that picture got in the woods in the first place? Or am I alone here?"

"Dude!" Nathaniel gestured to Eric's cigar animatedly. *"Dude!"*

Eric sighed. "I am fluent in Mandarin, French and Italian but I do not speak *Nathaniel*."

"None of us *really* do," Mandy added, sitting next to her boyfriend.

"Cigars dude! Send one this way!" Nathaniel said.

Eric handed him one reluctantly. "Smoking is bad for the lungs my friend."

"Says the guy about to light up a big fat cigar," Autumn said disapprovingly.

"Ah but it's my lot in life as a wealthy man," Eric said outstretching his legs in front of him. "Live fast and die young and all that jazz."

"Aren't you just a ray of sunshine on a cloudy day?" Autumn said sardonically as she found a seat on a rock opposite Eric. Rick sat beside her, sliding his arm around her.

"I am entirely disappointed in you guys," Eric went on, puffing the cigar lazily. "Whatever happened to teamwork? The need to sleuth? Hunting things that go bump in the night?"

"Garrison isn't a hideous deformed cave monster," Mandy said shortly.

"That we *know* of!" Rick piped in. Autumn nudged him sharply. "Ow!"

"So no one finds it odd that there is a random picture of the guidance counselor and his buddies lying around in the school forest?" He looked at Autumn who was still studying the photo intently. "Except Autumn apparently."

"I think it's weird," Rick admitted. "But truthfully, I don't like the guy. So I don't give a shit about his life."

The sound of branches crunching nearby caused them all to fall into silence. Through the brush stepped out a girl, with brown eyes and long straight chestnut hair. Autumn recognized her from math class.

"Hey Allison," Autumn said, stuffing the photo into her pocket.

"Hi there Autumn," Allison whispered. She appeared to be out of breath, her dark eyes wide like saucers. "Sorry to interrupt your party," she apologized. "I came here to meet a friend."

Allison smiled at Autumn but something wasn't right about her. Much like Autumn, Allison was polite and studious. She was quiet and kept mostly to herself. Autumn didn't know her too well, but something about her smile gave Autumn a bad feeling in the pit of her stomach.

"No problem," Autumn replied.

Eric watched Allison carefully, his eyes never leaving her. He smoked his cigar, appearing to be without a care in the world, but Autumn knew better. He was profiling her, studying her.

He could sense something was awry too.

Autumn was about to ask her if everything was copasetic when he appeared. A blonde boy with piercing blue eyes. Tall and built like a football player, he stepped out from the brush and approached Allison, smiling.

"Allison. I was looking for you." He glanced at the others. "Hello." Everyone greeted him and he turned back to Allison, kissing her gently on the neck.

"I don't want to be rude but I thought it was just going to be *us.*"

Allison giggled. "Of course Matt. I was just saying hi. We can go."

She waved to them and trotted off with Matt, disappearing into the sea of trees.

"I always thought Allison Kendall was a goody-goody," Rick said, looking somewhat scandalized. "The girl won't even go on a date."

"Says who?" Mandy asked.

"Nathaniel after she rejected him last year."

Mandy crossed her arms over her chest, looking unimpressed. "Tramp."

Eric took another drag from his cigar. "Something wasn't right about that girl. Her aura was dark."

Autumn looked at Eric. "You noticed it too? I mean, not the aura thing but the Allison acting strange thing."

Eric nodded. "Arabella taught me some magical aura reading. I can see it. Something is in her."

Mandy snickered. "Far too easy."

"Not what I meant," Eric said as he exhaled smoke. "She's possessed. Or being puppeted. I don't know which yet."

Autumn wanted to help Allison. Because she was her classmate of course, but also because this was what they signed up for. They were supposed to aid people. The people that knew nothing of the darkness that surrounded them, the people who took the world at face value.

Eric, however, didn't think either Allison or Matt were in any immediate danger. He thought they were harmless.

"Allison isn't herself, but that doesn't mean she will hurt anyone. She just might act a little more," he paused, looking for the word. "Uninhibited."

Autumn wasn't convinced. Even though Allison and Matt were long gone, her heart still pounded like a hammer and sweat trickled from her neck and down her back.

Her body was sending her all the signals that danger wasn't far off.

Autumn stood up abruptly and Rick jumped up, startled. "Aut? What is it?"

"I'm getting a bad feeling," she murmured.

Nathaniel and Mandy exchanged worried looks. Mandy stood up, dusting off her clothes.

"I really hate when she says that."

"*I* hate that she is *never* wrong when she does," Nathaniel added.

Autumn took deep breaths as Rick coaxed her, trying to calm her down

Autumn grabbed his arm, squeezing it tightly. "We need to go. *Now*."

Eric might have deemed Allison harmless, but even he knew Autumn's intuition was rarely flawed.

He put out his cigar, standing up immediately. "You heard the girl. Let's go! Don't dilly dally now!"

Everyone grabbed their bags and headed back towards the school. As they walked, Nathaniel looked at his phone.

"Dude, I just got a text. The assembly isn't even close to over yet. We are so getting caught."

"I think Principal Steel's wrath is not nearly as frightening as whatever we are running from Nate!" Mandy snapped.

As they made their way back to the school, Autumn's heart rate stabilized and her breathing returned to normal. The cold chills she had been experiencing subsided. Rick held her hand firmly in his. He was her pillar of strength.

"So have we figured out *how* we are sneaking back in *without* getting caught?" Nathaniel asked. "Or are we winging it?"

"Do we ever have a plan?" Mandy retorted.

"I wouldn't worry about it," Eric said, as they strode towards the side door they had escaped from.

"Every year I skip the closing festivities and every year nothing happens. They expect people to bail. Especially seniors."

"And the valedictorian?" Autumn asked, looking hopeful.

Eric shrugged. "I think *you* might be in trouble."

"Wonderful," Autumn said sarcastically as Eric held the door open for her, grinning widely.

She rolled her eyes and stepped inside. She wasn't afraid. After facing the wrath of hell beasts, teachers were a piece of cake.

"Well, well. What do we have here?"

Dressed in a grey dress shirt and crisp black slacks, Mr. Garrison stood leaning against the wall, eating his trademark apple nonchalantly. He took a bite and beamed at the five of them.

"Look what the cat drug in." He paused. "A gang of truants."

"Actually for a *cat* to drag in five teenagers would be physically impossible," Eric quipped.

Mr. Garrison gave him a small, indulgent smile. "That was a figure of speech. Something I'm sure you are familiar with Mr. King. But please, no need to deflect. Where have you all been?"

Rick threw his shoulders back and looked at Mr. Garrison defiantly.

"We went for a walk."

Mr. Garrison nodded slowly.

"No need to get testy Mr. Jacobs I just have a few questions." He took another bite of his apple. "Where did you walk to? Did you walk the perimeter of the school grounds? You do realize being off school property during school hours is a violation of the rules."

Everyone stared at him, unable to speak.

Mr. Garrison smirked. "Aren't you guys supposed to be at the assembly?"

The five nodded in unison. They weren't getting out of this easily. They had been caught red-handed. Even Eric's smooth silver tongue and bulging wallet couldn't help them now.

No one said anything. It was Mandy who finally stepped forward and spoke up.

She batted her dark eyelashes, a hangdog expression on her face.

"Mr. Garrison, would you like the truth?"

"Well I certainly don't want a lie," he said, arms crossed over his chest.

"Fair enough. We skipped the assembly," Mandy admitted. "They are boring. Mr. Steel prattles on and on. Jocks like Ben Mills get awards for throwing a football really far. The cheerleaders *cheer*. It is all so irritating and cliché."

"Ladies and gentleman, the perpetually blunt Mandy," Eric grumbled, rubbing his forehead in frustration.

Autumn looked at Mr. Garrison, her green eyes wide. For a moment, she thought Mandy's candor might get them into more trouble but she could swear Mr. Garrison appeared to be stifling a smile.

"I can't say I blame you Ms. Jensen," he said finally. "Assemblies can be rather dull."

"Mr. Garrison you rock!" Nathaniel jumped in.

"Still, I can't condone you guys skipping. So let's make a deal." Mr. Garrison went on.

"With the *devil*," Rick muttered under his breath and Autumn gave him a sharp nudge in the side.

"I have been called many things Mr. Jacobs," Mr. Garrison said, not missing a beat. "But the devil? *That* is a new one." He gestured with his hand towards the vacant hall. "Now follow me."

Rick grunted his disapproval as they followed the handsome counselor through the desolate hallways. There were no stragglers no students lingering by lockers. The halls were actually empty. The silence was deafening, only broken by the sound of their footsteps on the floors resonating in a strange rhythmic pattern.

Autumn saw the gymnasium up ahead. The huge looming doors were shut. It was odd. The doors were always left open, especially during large gatherings. The amount of bodies packed into the gym, like sardines in a can, made it particularly stuffy and sweltering inside if the doors were closed.

"Weird the gym doors-" Autumn began but she stopped when she noticed the flickering of the schools overhead lights.

Was there a storm? A power outage? Autumn looked out the closet window.

Sunlight spilled through the glass, bright and inviting.

Mr. Garrison ran a hand through his dark hair, looking warily at the doors ahead.

"I was going to walk you guys into the assembly but why don't we step into my office instead?"

"But aren't we already late?" Autumn asked.

"I can write you all notes."

Autumn exchanged puzzled looks with the others as they approached the guidance office. Ryan held the door open for them and they went inside.

Autumn observed the empty and eerily silent office. Even the secretary, Mrs. Sanderson, was nowhere to be seen and the other counselor's office doors were shut tightly. The whole scene had a very "after school lights out" quality about it that made Autumn cringe with discomfort.

Mr. Garrison pulled out his key and unlocked his office.

"Go on in."

They all followed his instructions and once they were inside the small yet cozy office, Mr. Garrison, went to the main door and latched it tightly.

Autumn knew it then.

Something was up. Why else was he locking the door?

She felt her heart rate escalating, and beads of sweat began forming on her forehead.

Mr. Garrison followed them into the office and locked the door behind him, trying his best to be nonchalant. Autumn realized the others weren't paying much attention. Mandy and Nathaniel were jabbering about a movie they wanted to see on the weekend and Rick was lost in his own world. Only Eric met her eyes. He seemed to be aware that Mr. Garrison was acting odd.

Autumn's vision began blurring. Everyone around her began fading and her heart banged inside her chest like a drum. Her breaths were shallow and she heard Rick calling out to her, his voice panicked and desperate but his words made no sense.

She knew what was coming next. She tried to move towards a chair, tried to hunker down but it was in vain.

The blackness swallowed her whole.

8

Autumn felt cool dampness on her forehead. Her eyes felt heavy but she forced them open. In a circle kneeling over her was Mandy, Nathaniel, Eric and Mr. Garrison. Rick was cradling her head and pressing a wet cloth against her forehead.

She had blacked out.

"Autumn, are you alright?" Rick asked, his face tight with worry.

"I think so," she replied softly.

She started to sit up but Mr. Garrison pressed a firm hand against her shoulder.

"Stay put. Give it a few more minutes," he instructed.

"Did I hit anything on the way down?"

"Nope. I caught you. Just in the nick of time," he said.

Rick scowled but said nothing.

"Mr. G was like a freaking superhero!" Nathaniel piped up. "Considering how little reaction time he had, it was pretty epic."

Rick shot Nathaniel a glare of disapproval.

"Rick totally *could've* caught Autumn though."

"Do you black out often Ms. Kingston or do you just enjoy making me sweat?" Mr. Garrison wore a grin on his face.

"Not often. I just didn't eat breakfast today," she lied.

She had always had remarkable intuition, even when she was younger. Once, when her sister Audrina went to a dance, Autumn had warned her mother something bad would happen to her. An hour later she came home with her date. She had sprained her ankle dancing.

Still, she wasn't about to tell her guidance counselor she had a bad feeling after she saw him locking doors. Clearly, he *wasn't* the cause of the anxiety but the feeling of impending doom lingered in the air though it wasn't overpowering her anymore.

"You should *always* eat breakfast young lady," Mr. Garrison scolded her. "You aren't partaking in one of those crazy fad diets are you? Because nobody should live on cayenne pepper and maple syrup for a month."

"No fad diets here," Autumn promised. "Just an off day."

Rick looked at her, perplexed. He had seen the massive plate of food she had eaten before school. He knew she was lying to Mr. Garrison.

"Don't ever scare us like that again Kingston," Eric teased as Rick and him helped Autumn into one of the office chairs.

Mandy leaned into Autumn.

"It was worth it to see Mr. Garrison catch you," she whispered.

When everything settled down and the commotion had passed, everyone continued to stand around, with the exception of Autumn who sat drinking water from Mr. Garrison's office water cooler. He went about his business, working on paperwork at his desk, until finally Eric spoke up.

Mr. Garrison glanced up from his work. "Can I help you Mr. King?"

"I was just wondering why we are still here?" Eric asked. "Shouldn't you be taking us to the assembly now?"

"No he shouldn't!" Nathaniel said before elbowing Eric sharply in the ribs. "Don't give him any ideas King!"

Mr. Garrison sighed while rubbing his temples. "Honestly, to bring you guys in there so late, you would all be in immense trouble. So instead, I will keep you all in here under my supervision until the assembly is over."

"And what exactly are we supposed to do in this cramped little office?" Mandy asked as she leaned against his desk. "I know. We can play truth or dare and I'll go first. Mr. Garrison, truth." She grinned. "Are you married?"

"Mandy! You can't just ask him that!" Nathaniel barked.

Mandy rolled her eyes. "Why not?"

Eric looked at her with incredulity. "Unbelievable Jensen."

"Ms. Jensen, that is a very personal question that I will not answer but please feel free to talk amongst yourselves." Mr. Garrison said, going back to his paperwork.

Only twenty minutes had passed when Autumn noticed the lights above her head begin to flicker ominously. Mr. Garrison looked up from his work, watching the lights steadily, as if in a trance.

They gave one last feeble flash of protest before going out completely.

* * *

Everyone was quiet. Autumn looked around the unfamiliar office, eyes darting frantically. The only light came from a small square window that was covered by blinds.

She was surrounded by all-encompassing blackness. She felt Rick's hand grasp hers. She squeezed it tightly.

"What the hell is going on?" Mandy's voice came from the silence.

"The lights are out," Mr. Garrison said flatly.

"No shit Sherlock," Rick said curtly.

Mandy kicked Rick in the shin sharply.

"Ow!" Rick yelped.

"You can't say those things to him. He's faculty!"

Mr. Garrison sighed. "Not to worry Ms. Jensen. Many student and faculty rules seem to be getting broken today. I'm pretty sure I'm not supposed to be aiding and abetting truant students yet here I am."

Autumn's eyes began adjusting to the darkness. She heard rustling as Mr. Garrison began searching through his desk drawers. He pulled out a small flashlight.

She observed him. He didn't look the least bit surprised by this turn of events. In fact, the expression he wore was one of utter and total calmness.

Eric, who was sitting, propped his feet up on Mr. Garrison's desk. He sighed, looking bored out of his wits.

"So now what?" he asked, sounding completely blasé.

Mr. Garrison looked at Eric's feet disapprovingly.

He grunted and removed them from the desk. "Can we leave now?"

"We get to go home!" Nathaniel lit up like a Christmas tree at Eric's suggestion.

Mr. Garrison was quiet but his brow was furrowed in thought. Autumn couldn't put her finger on it, but something about his demeanour was odd.

"It is probably best we evacuate the school immediately," he began.

"It is just a blackout," Mandy said, looking perplexed. "Not anything serious."

"It is just a precaution Ms. Jensen. You can never be too careful."

Rick leaned towards Autumn, whispering into her ear.

"I don't think it's *just* a blackout," he murmured.

Eric got up, looking completely exasperated. "So we *are* going then?"

Mr. Garrison held up a finger, indicating he needed a moment. He went to his desk, opened the top drawer and pulled out a booklet. He used his flashlight and began flipping through pages until finally he came to what he was looking for. He read silently, eyes skimming the pages, and then he put the booklet back in the drawer.

"According to the code of conduct, we should evacuate the school until they figure out what the issue is and if it is safety related."

Autumn listened carefully. She heard nothing. No sounds of movement or voices in the halls. In fact, it was eerily silent. It was like the world around them had come to a screeching halt.

"What about everyone in the gym? Are they evacuating too?" Rick asked.

"I have no idea what is going on in there but you guys are my responsibility. So we are doing what the book says. We are going."

Rick opened his mouth to argue but Eric gave him a threatening look. He wanted to get out of the guidance office and go home just like the rest of them.

"They have plenty of teachers with them Rick, they will be fine. Let's just go," Mr. Garrison said with urgency. "Everyone just follow me and stay close."

Mr. Garrison opened the door, letting them all go through. They stood in the waiting area as he locked his office up. Then he walked to the main door and opened it, ushering them through and out into the dark and silent hall. Autumn felt her cell vibrate. She pulled it out hastily.

Something is very wrong here. It was Eric. Autumn looked up at him and nodded. Then she texted back:

I know.

When Mr. Garrison was done locking up the main office, they headed down the hall. The silence surrounding them was unnerving. Autumn was tempted to talk just to make noise but she didn't.

"Do you have any idea why the lights would suddenly cut-out Mr. Garrison?" Mandy asked after a minute. "It isn't storming out right?"

"No. It could be anything. A short in the electrical system or power failure..." he trailed off.

As they navigated the halls that were only illuminated by the small streaming of light from various windows or doors, Autumn took in the emptiness around her. A sudden crackling sound caught her attention, followed by the backup lights humming to life.

"The generator must've kicked in," Mr. Garrison explained.

Autumn scrutinized him. He still seemed unfazed. Perhaps it was just his way. Most adults seemed innately capable of staying calm in the most stressful circumstances. And being a guidance counselor meant he was probably trained in remaining cool, no matter what the situation.

Mr. Garrison caught her gaze suddenly, like he was reading her mind. She looked away quickly.

They were walking past a fleet of ugly sage colored lockers when they heard it.

A blood curdling scream followed by echoes of chaos and commotion coming from the gymnasium.

The scream gave Autumn chills.

"Did you guys hear that?" Mandy stopped dead in her tracks.

Rick stopped beside her. "Who wouldn't?"

"Guys we cannot stop!" Mr. Garrison said firmly. "We keep moving."

Despite his specific instructions, no one budged. He sighed, looking exasperated. "I have tried to be pleasant and I'm sure you would all agree. I have been more than patient but this isn't a request. We are going *now!*"

"Someone was screaming bloody murder! We can't just ignore that!" Rick snapped.

"I *can't* let you guys go back. If there really is any possibility of danger, I need to get you all out safely. Then I will come back and check on everyone in the gym."

Autumn looked at Rick. His hands were balled into fists, his body tensed. She put a hand on his shoulder, trying her best to quell his rage.

"Rick. I think Mr. Garrison knows what is best," she said softly.

"He doesn't *know* anything! He doesn't realize that whatever is behind those gym doors we can handle no problem."

Autumn winced. Rick was treading on thin ice with Mr. Garrison already. He had been mouthy and disrespectful. Autumn knew Mr. Garrison wasn't Rick's favorite person, but lately his temper was out of control.

Mr. Garrison looked at Rick indulgently.

"Rick, I never said you *couldn't* handle it but it is proper conduct for me to get you guys out of here. If I fail to do so, my job will be on the line. I assure you, whatever is going on, the other teachers are more than equipped to deal with it. So please, we don't need a vigilante."

The last comment about vigilantism pushed Rick over the edge. His face flushed with fury and he opened his mouth, ready to unleash but Nathaniel stopped him.

"Dude, let the guy do his job," he urged. "I don't want to see Mr. Garrison fired. I mean, he could've turned us in today but he didn't. That was pretty epic."

Rick considered this. He looked to Autumn, who gave him her best imploring look.

"Let's go," Rick said, defeated.

They began moving again and Autumn beamed at Rick.

"I'm proud of you," she whispered into his ear. Their eyes met, his ice blue ones sparkling.

"Why is that?" he asked as they trekked towards the nearest exit.

"You didn't fight with him," she said and kissed him on the cheek. "Thank you."

"I just want to help those people," Rick murmured.

"I know," Autumn whispered. "I do too. But we have no weapons and no strategy. We would be jumping in blind. Not the best idea."

They walked for a few minutes, passing many exits along the way. Mr. Garrison was adamant. He knew the best way out. He informed them of an exit located behind the stage in the drama room that most students weren't aware of.

Autumn didn't understand why he was so determined they use the secret exit. With so many ways to escape the school, why was this one so special? It made her think Mr. Garrison knew *exactly* what was happening in the gym, why the lights went out and what kind of danger they were in.

She had questions and she would get answers eventually. At the moment, she put everything on the backburner and followed everyone through the door that led outside.

The sunlight hit her eyes, momentarily blinding her. When her eyes adjusted, she saw they were in the back parking lot. She looked at all the parked vehicles. All machines, no people. The area was deserted.

Autumn and Rick stood in a cluster with Nathaniel, Mandy and Eric, awaiting further instruction.

"So what is the plan now?" Eric asked, sounding genuinely intrigued.

Sharp movement in the corner of her eye caught Autumn's attention. She turned to get a better view and saw two men, no one she recognized, standing by the gyms exit doors.

She scanned them quickly, taking in details like she would when analyzing monsters or any other form of imminent danger. Both men wore crisp black suits despite June's heat and both wore sunglasses. One man was broad and dark skinned with a shaved head and the other was tall and wiry with curly blonde hair. Autumn nudged Rick gently in the side.

"Check that out," she whispered and he looked over.

Rick shook his head. "I *knew* Mr. Macpherson was an alien. The agency has finally come to grab him."

Mr. Garrison looked at Rick, confused. It didn't take him long to piece it together.

He saw the strange men and grimaced. "Wonderful."

And like clockwork the suited men noticed them too. They exchanged glances and began moving in their direction. They weren't walking. They were running, charging towards them like football players on the field.

"Mr. Garrison?" Autumn's voice came out panicked. Her heart was racing now. These guys were seriously bad news.

"Are those dicks coming for us?" Mandy asked, her body assuming a defensive stance.

"I think so but it's obviously a case of mistaken identity," Mr. Garrison replied. "Either way, let's just get out of here. They look rather dangerous. My car is over there."

"I hate running!" Nathaniel muttered as they all began sprinting towards the vehicle.

They stopped in front of a beaten up black car. Its paint was chipped, the doors rusted. The bumper looked like it had seen better days. It was definitely a clunker.

"What the hell is this?" Eric asked, mildly disgusted. "It's hideous."

"It's my car and it is a classic," Mr. Garrison sounded annoyed, as he unlocked it.

"That's generous of you," Eric muttered.

"It doesn't matter what it looks like Mr. King, what matters is I get you all out of here, safe and sound. So everyone get in!"

"Shot gun!" Nathaniel called out as he headed towards the passenger side.

"I don't care if you ride in the trunk! Just hurry!" Mandy barked.

Autumn glanced behind her. The men were closing the gap between them fast. As she watched them, entranced, she saw they were holding something in their hands.

They had guns.

Autumn felt like she might collapse but she forced herself to run faster. Mr. Garrison began shepherding everyone into the car. Rick was the last one to get in and right before he did, Autumn heard a shot go off.

Rick jerked and all the color drained from her face.

"Rick!" she shrieked as she yanked him into the car.

He managed to pull the door shut as Mr. Garrison looked back in the rear view.

"Rick!" Autumn looked him over, searching for blood. "Where did it hit you? Are you alright?"

"He was hit?" Mandy was panicked. Even Eric, who always managed to appear composed, looked shaken.

"What hit him?" Eric asked, his voice unwavering.

Autumn forced air in and out of her lungs. She had to stay composed. She had to help Rick.

"They had guns! He was shot!" Autumn said frantically. "Rick? Talk to me!"

"It doesn't hurt," Rick said, pulling up his pant leg. Autumn saw a strange looking dart sticking out of his leg. "But I do feel a little woozy."

"That's because they shot you with a tranquilizer dart," Mr. Garrison said rationally. He started the engine, which roared noisily to life and began pulling out.

Autumn met his eyes in the mirror. "A tranquilizer dart?" She was relieved.

He nodded matter-of-factly. "You think I would've remained calm if he had actually been shot?"

Autumn looked out the rear window as they sped off. The men hadn't given up. They were chasing the car, still determined to catch up to it. She thought they would never stop until someone came out of nowhere and jumped in front of them.

She watched as the stranger punched out the blonde while dodging a kick from the man with the shaved head. The blonde hit the pavement and shaved head shot at new guy. New guy dodged again before clocking shaved head in the jaw, putting him on the ground next to his friend. Autumn felt relief wash over her. They were safe now.

She looked at the man, their saviour, convinced she knew him from somewhere.

It took her a moment to place him.

He had aged but still had the same brawny build, olive skin and jet black hair. It was the man from the picture found in the forest.

The man who was standing beside Ryan Garrison.

9

The car let out a booming squeal and backfired as Mr. Garrison navigated it through the parking lot. He turned sharply onto the main road and accelerated as Autumn gripped the door handle tightly.

The car backfired one last time as Eric rubbed his temples wearily.

"If anyone sees me in this hunk of junk..." he trailed off.

"It would be an honor Mr. King," Mr. Garrison finished for him. "Now where did you want me to drop you guys off?"

"My house is fine," Nathaniel replied.

He was wedged in the passenger seat with Mandy and Mr. Garrison. Rick, Eric and Autumn were piled together in the backseat.

Autumn looked at Rick. His eyes were half-shut and his muscles limp. The sedative was finally in effect and she assumed it wouldn't be long before he was out. She ran her fingers through his hair softly.

"Ricky," she whispered. "I'm here. We are safe now."

He looked up at her drowsily, resting his head on her shoulder.

"Safe?" he muttered. She nodded. "Mmm hmm."

"Good. I am going to sleep now. Nighty night."

He closed his eyes and sighed as Eric looked over. "Did he just say *nighty night?*"

Mr. Garrison glanced quickly over his shoulder. "How is he doing Autumn?"

"I am *frine*," Rick slurred, eyes still closed. "Eyes on the road Mr. *Harrison.*"

"Should I be worried Mr. Garrison?" Autumn asked.

He shook his head. "No. He should be fine. He'll be knocked out for about an hour, maybe two. Though I have to say, he's fighting it. Most people would be zonked out by now."

"You got that right. I fight monsters. I'm a superhero," Rick muttered. A moment later, Autumn heard him breathing deeply. He was finally asleep.

"Superhero? I wish *I* was shot by that tranq gun," Mandy joked nervously.

Mr. Garrison was unfazed and completely focused on the road ahead of him. "Just make sure he stays hydrated and eats something substantial when he wakes."

As the car raced down the road, Autumn stared out the window, Rick's head nestled in her lap. She wanted to know who the men at the school were and why they were armed with tranquillizer guns. The man in the picture, the one that saved them, he was a mystery too. Obviously Mr. Garrison knew him. She had so many questions, but it seemed like an inopportune time to ask them.

The men with the guns, the mysterious dark-haired guy, Mr. Garrison acting like he knew more than he was letting on. The puzzle pieces were there, Autumn just needed to put it all together.

And she wasn't going to stop until she did.

* * *

The door flew open, waking the boy from his restless, fearful sleep. He looked up and saw a different guard hovering above him.

"Last guard told me you haven't been compliant," he said, staring at him with malice. "Says you refuse to do what you did in the forest that night."

"I don't know what you mean," the boy stammered.

He was lying. He knew exactly what the guards wanted. The problem was, he *never* wanted to become that beast again. Also, he had no idea how the change had come to be.

"Don't play coy with me you insolent little fool!" the guard spat. "We saw you that night. We know what you are! You freak!"

The boy went white. He didn't think anyone had seen him that night. After it was over, he was disoriented and terrified. He never lost himself to rage but that night it was uncontrollable, his need for violence insatiable.

The guard smiled, a cruel grin that sent shivers down his back.

"That's right boy. We have been tracking you for some time now. Did you really think your capture was just a fluke? It was well-planned."

"What do you want from me?"

"We want to see you do it! Right here and right now!" the guard encouraged, his eyes gleaming. "It happened once boy. It can happen again."

That was just it. He didn't *want* it to happen again. He was scared of himself when he was like that. His quivering hands, his muscles that twitched as his body morphed. The rage in his belly that burned like a spark doused in gasoline.

The truth was, he didn't know *what* triggered his change. It was impossible to replicate.

"I don't know how to!" the boy snapped.

The guard, with his hat dipped so low the boy could barely see his eyes, snorted.

"The funny thing is, I believe you kid," he snarled. "It's quite common actually. The problem is, you got no choice. You either do it or we induce it and that can be," he paused. "Mighty unpleasant for *you*."

The boy's eyes went wide. He wasn't delusion. He never deemed this place safe, but he didn't think there was any threat of immediate danger.

Until now.

"I can't do it," the boy said firmly.

The guard glared at him as he reached into his utility belt, pulling out a syringe.

"Pathetic," he said bitterly. "I guess you need some motivation boy. Maybe we can bring your mother in to help us out? Or your father? Saw 'em on the news. They seem like nice folk. Would be a shame to have to hurt 'em."

The guard curled his lips into a sneer. He was taunting him. The boy felt the anger pulse through him. His body started trembling.

If *anyone* laid a finger on his mom and dad, they would be sorry.

"No!" the boy shouted, feeling the familiar feeling wash over him. "No! Stop!"

"That's it boy!" The guard urged. "Your parents seem like the loyal kind. I am betting they would need some persuasion to get 'em talking but here at DSI we specialize in torture. Wouldn't take long before they cracked!"

"LEAVE THEM ALONE!" The boy spat, shaking even harder now. He could feel the rage taking him over, the same way it had before.

The guard pushed him, egging him on until he couldn't take it anymore. He was pushed over the edge, too far gone to return. The anger swelled though his veins and his blood pumped rapidly. His muscles ached, welcoming the change. He took deep breaths, trying futilely to subside it.

His bones began cracking. The pain was excruciating. He screamed in agony but his cries sounded like yowls. Tough hands grabbed him. He felt a sharp stab and as he drifted away he heard the guard speak.

"Good job Andy. Let it take over. We got you now."

* * *

Autumn had been to Nathaniel's house a handful of times since moving to Whitan. It was quaint and cookie-cutter, much like Rick's home. The typical suburban dream house. Three huge bedrooms and two and a half bathrooms. The only thing missing was the white picket fence.

The car let out a backfire of protest as Mr. Garrison pulled into the driveway. He cut the engine and turned around in his seat.

"So you kids will be fine?" He sounded unsure.

"Why wouldn't we be?" Mandy asked casually as she unbuckled her seatbelt. "Everyone is safe and sound." She glanced behind her at Rick. "For the most part."

"It has been quite the day," Mr. Garrison said rubbing his brow.

Autumn saw the apprehension in his dark eyes and suddenly understood how he ended up with grey hair at his age.

"We can hold our own," Eric said, flashing his trademark confident grin. "We will be fine Mr. Garrison."

Autumn gently adjusted Rick, moving his head from her lap and slowly pulling him upright. He was snoring now, a soft steady rhythm that assured her he was still breathing.

"Let me and Nate get him Aut," Eric insisted. "You and Mandy get inside."

Mr. Garrison offered to help them, but Eric convinced him they were good. They took turns thanking Mr. Garrison for getting them home safely and headed towards the house.

"Autumn!" Mr. Garrison called out his window before pulling out of the driveway. "Can I have a word?"

"Sure." She saw the devilish grin on Mandy's face as she walked over to his car.

She leaned in through the open window. "Is everything alright?"

"Take this," he handed her a crisp business card. "It has my cell number on it."

"Your cell number?" she said, feeling her cheeks heating up.

There was no way in hell Mandy had been right about him *liking* her... had she?

Mr. Garrison had the ghost of a smile on his face. "I know it seems unprofessional, but you may need it soon. What happened today wasn't a coincidence."

"I knew it!" she exclaimed, feeling vindicated. "I knew something was up!"

"I am not surprised. Your instincts are usually spot-on," he said. "Still, I can't tell you much more than that Autumn. What I can say is, whatever happens you need to stay vigilant. Not matter how difficult things get. All of you, your friends, Rick, you have to stick together and be very careful who you trust."

Mr. Garrison was warning her. He sounded grave and ominous. The whole thing was unnerving and her legs felt like jelly. She wobbled slightly, feeling as though she might fall over. She placed both her hands against the car roof for support.

"Is Rick in danger?" she whispered. She was afraid of the answer.

Mr. Garrison looked at the others quickly before turning back to her.

"Yes he is. In fact, you all are."

10

The others were gone when Autumn finished her conversation with Mr. Garrison. She looked at the card in her hand.

Ryan Garrison.

She placed it inside her pocket and went inside.

Autumn remembered Nathaniel saying his parents were away at their family cottage for the week, preparing it for summer vacation. She sighed, thankful she wouldn't have to explain anything to anyone.

She looked around, taking in her surroundings.

Wood paneling decorated the entrance way walls along with lush and vibrant plants placed sparingly around the room. Above a long winding staircase was a family portrait. Nathaniel, his brother Conrad and his parents, posed together in a studio, smiling.

She heard faint chattering coming down the hallway. She followed the sound and found everyone in the living room. Nathaniel, Mandy and Eric lounged on a couch while Rick lay unconscious on another.

In the corner, in a plush recliner, sat Nathaniel's brother Conrad, drinking a beer. Autumn would've doubted he was a ginger, if she hadn't seen the portrait in the hallway. Conrad had the fair skin, freckled cheeks and hazel eyes, but his hair was sandy blonde. Nathaniel said he first dyed it when he was sixteen and never looked back.

"Finally back are you?" Eric teased when Autumn appeared. "We were getting worried in here."

"Speak for yourself," Mandy said, grinning like the cat that caught the canary. "I was hoping she and Mr. G were up to something seriously naughty."

"Really Mand? In front of her comatose boyfriend?" Conrad grumbled.

He smiled at Autumn. "Autumn, always a pleasure. It is *nicer* to see you while you're wielding your scythe but I'll take what I can get."

"Conrad, how are you?" Autumn asked, sitting beside Rick. She raked her fingers gently through his curls. He didn't even stir.

"Ah, not bad. Enjoying my day off." He held up his beer bottle proudly.

"You don't work man," Nathaniel muttered.

"Not per say. But those of us working in the field I so generously call *miscellaneous* need a break too little brother."

"Miscellaneous or crimes seedy underbelly," Mandy cracked. "You say potato."

Conrad studied Rick while taking a swig of his beer.

"I wasn't going to ask but I am curious."

"He was shot. Tranquilizer gun," Autumn said. "Our school was under siege."

Conrad kicked his feet up on an ottoman. "Seriously. There is one for the PTA meeting."

"We didn't stick around man. We hauled ass," Nathaniel admitted, looking embarrassed.

Autumn knew how much it meant to Nathaniel to be brave and tough like his older brother. Admitting he bailed out couldn't be easy for him.

"Not by choice," Mandy corrected him. "Our guidance counselor forced us evacuate. Protocol and all that."

"So you guys have no idea *why* you were evacuated?" Conrad asked.

The four of them shook their heads. Mr. Garrison clearly knew something. Autumn understood this now. Still, she wasn't going to mention it to the others. Not yet anyway.

"I swear Whitan only gets weirder," Conrad muttered.

The TV hummed in the background quietly, when Eric saw an image of Whitan High flash across the screen with the banner BREAKING NEWS trailing underneath it.

"Hey man, can you turn that up?" Eric asked.

"Sure." Conrad grabbed the remote and raised the volume.

On the screen was a middle-aged male newscaster with grey hair and perfect white teeth.

"According to sources, the lights went out during a regulated school assembly. During the blackout, chaos ensued. Order finally returned when the generator kicked in. That was when the students and faculty alike reported seeing a variety of armed men blocking all exits of the Whitan High gymnasium. The men were masked, prepared and announced they were looking for someone, though they didn't specify who. Only that whoever it was wasn't there."

"No students were injured during the attack but five students that were accounted for during the assembly have gone missing. It was reported that they were taken when the lights were out as no one actually saw them get snatched though some commotion was heard. Our hearts go out to those parents whose son or daughter is missing tonight," the reporter went on.

"Assassins?" Conrad offered, muting the TV.

Eric looked at him. "At a high school? Seems strange right?" He paused. "Though an effective way to make us do homework."

"We *have* seen stranger," Mandy piped up. "I wonder who or what they were looking for."

"Definitely *who*," Autumn said, remembering the newscasters report.

"Those guys weren't just run-of-the-mill street thugs though," Nathaniel said, brow furrowed with concern.

"How do you know?" Mandy asked.

"Because I live with one," he gestured to Conrad. "No offense Con."

Conrad shrugged. "None taken. It isn't like I'm curing cancer or anything like that. If they were wielding tranq guns *and* took five students in the blink of an eye, they are playing in the big leagues. No doubt at that. That attack was clearly planned out."

"But they didn't find someone specific they were looking for," Eric rationalized. "Obviously they wanted *certain* students."

Autumn looked at Rick. She had a nagging feeling when she looked at him, lying there in his sleepy coma. He was mixed into this somehow. Mr. Garrison's words had confirmed her suspicions. They were all in danger.

It wasn't a coincidence that they were chased or that Rick was tranquilized.

It wasn't a fluke Mr. Garrison had rushed them out so frantically.

Somehow Rick was tied into this. Perhaps they all were.

She wasn't sure exactly.

All she knew was her eyes were open now.

She would have to be ready for anything.

11

Autumn's fists struck the bag and it swayed, moving to and fro, as she stepped back. She punched again, harder this time, rattling the chain the punching bag hung on. She jumped up, kicking the bag with her right leg. She landed strong, her hands in fists protecting her face, breathing hard.Her face dripped with sweet, her heart raced.

She hadn't felt this fit in a long time.

"I kinda feel sorry for the punching bag," Eric joked, as he walked into the training room. He handed Autumn a bottle of water and took a seat on an exercise bench.

"You look great though. Your form is impeccable." He grinned wickedly at her.

"Thanks Er," she said, opening the water. She took a deep swig from the bottle.

"With all the training you've been doing, I'm surprised you had time to finish your valedictorian speech," he said outstretching his legs.

Ever since she had figured out Rick was being hunted, she had begun training every day. She was determined. If anyone or *anything* came for Rick or anyone else, she would be ready.

"It hasn't been easy," Autumn admitted. "Sometimes I actually *forget* what sleep feels like."

Eric observed her carefully. She was still beautiful, of course. Upon closer inspection however, he could see her eyes looked tired.

"You aren't in this alone Aut. I told you. This whole thing with Rick, it isn't just your burden to bear. You have me. And the others," he said softly. "Though I must admit, I do enjoy seeing you prance around in those tight yoga pants."

Autumn rolled her eyes but couldn't hide her grin. "I don't prance King."

"In my mind, you are prancing," he said, smirking. "Very seductively, may I add."

"So how is Rick taking the news? It can't be easy walking around with a giant bullseye on your back."

"He is being Rick," Autumn said matter-of-factly. "He's training, skateboarding, spending time with me. Normal stuff given the fact that he was tranquilized and hunted down by a bunch of armed men just days ago."

"That dude is laid back," Eric said with incredulity. "It's not bothering him at all?"

Autumn knew better. If it was troubling Rick, he wouldn't let on. He didn't want to worry her. He prided himself on being manly and strong. He couldn't take care of her if he was petrified.

"I'd say he is shaken up by it all," Autumn confessed. "But he would never admit it."

Autumn heard the faint ringing of her cell phone in her purse. She grabbed it. The screen read *Mandy*.

"Hello Mand."

"Hey! Are we still on for tonight?"

"You bet," Autumn said. "Unless... Are you having second thoughts?"

Mandy chuckled. "When it comes to Ryan Garrison, I only have one thought. That's of me on top of him."

Autumn grimaced as Eric looked at her, perplexed.

"You have a boyfriend remember?"

"I do?" Mandy asked, innocently.

"The ginger guy who *adores* you."

"Relax. I am only teasing. I know Garrison likes *you*," Mandy said. "The guy called you over to his car for a private chat."

"Yeah and the whole 'You guys are in grave danger' spiel he gave me? Totally hot," Autumn said sarcastically.

"And need I remind you? Tonight isn't about fun. It's about finding out what he is up to."

Eric raised an eyebrow, looking intrigued.

"I know. I am in on the plan, remember? We trail him after the staff meeting at school tonight."

After Autumn was off the phone with Mandy, she sat with Eric explaining their plan. They were going to tail Mr. Garrison and see exactly *what* he was hiding from them. He concurred that Mr. Garrison was not your average guidance counselor and offered to help them do reconnaissance. Autumn told him if they needed assistance she would call but the less people shadowing Garrison the better. She thanked Eric for letting her use his training room then she headed home to shower and get ready.

After she was showered and dressed, she found Rick, who had been out skateboarding with Nathaniel, sitting on her bed, studying for his math exam.

He looked up from the textbook as she entered the room.

"Hey sweetheart," he said, jumping up and kissing her.

Autumn embraced him tightly.

She wished she could tell Rick what she was doing tonight but she didn't want him to get jealous. Mr. Garrison was a touchy subject, especially if Rick knew she was spending the night tracking him.

Still, she felt terrible keeping secrets.

Rick held her close to him, his eyes fixed on hers. "How was training?"

"Intense," she admitted, kissing his cheek softly. "Tension relieving."

"There are better ways to relieve tension." He ran his fingers through her dark hair. "Mom and dad are still working."

Autumn didn't want to talk.

She gently pushed Rick onto the bed and climbed onto his lap, as they continued kissing. She was losing herself in the kisses, in him, and nothing else mattered. Tailing Garrison, hunting monsters, supernatural secrets. All those things were forgotten. She was with Rick now: safe and enthralled.

By the time they were done, Rick was on top of her, and they were breathless. They stopped for a moment and Autumn glanced at the clock. She was losing track of time. Mandy would be meeting her in twenty minutes.

"Rick," she whispered, sitting up slightly. "I have to meet Mandy soon."

"Chick night. I totally forgot," Rick said, breathing hard.

The sudden slam of the front door, followed by Aunt Katherine announcing she was home startled them both.

Autumn began smoothing out her hair and clothes. Rick sat up, pulling his text book onto his lap as he pretended to read.

There was a soft rap on the door.

"Autumn? Can I come in?"

"Sure." Autumn huddled in close to Rick like she was helping him study.

The door opened and Aunt Katherine stood there. She was dressed in a crisp white blouse and a grey pencil skirt, her dark hair, which had grown out to her shoulders, framed her face. She smiled, her pearly white teeth even whiter against her red lipstick.

"Hello, you two. How was your day?"

"Rather uneventful," Autumn said. There weren't any armed men shooting at them in the parking lot, after all.

"How about you?"

"It was a busy day at the office. The change in the weather means there are numerous people with colds," she said, her hands on her hips. "Any news on the missing kids from your school?"

Rick shrugged, looking up from his text book. "Nope. The security at the school is crazy now. They have guards at the exits. It is worse than the airport."

"That is actually a relief," Aunt Katherine said. "I know school is almost finished for you both, but I like knowing while you *are* there, you are safe."

"So, dinner is going to be a little late tonight."

"Late?" Rick grimaced. "What's for dinner?"

"Spaghetti and homemade meatballs," she said. "Are you and Mandy still going out tonight Autumn?"

Autumn nodded. "She will be here soon to pick me up."

Aunt Katherine smiled. "Is she staying for dinner?"

"Oh no. I think we are going to grab something while we are out."

"Well, I'll be sure to save you some leftovers, if Rick leaves any." She winked. "Well, I better get to it. Rick, keep up the studying. Autumn, if I don't see you on your way out, say hi to Mandy for me and have fun."

"Will do," Autumn said.

* * *

"Garrison is going to be the last one to leave isn't he!" Mandy sounded frustrated as she changed the radio station.

The soft hum of music played over the speakers, creating comforting background noise. They sat parked in Mandy's Jeep, awaiting Mr. Garrison's grand exit from the school. They watched teachers and other school personnel, filtering out.

"I just hope he showed up," Autumn said, looking at Mandy through the dim radio light. "It would be a complete waste if he ditched."

Mandy nodded. "Let's hope that doesn't happen."

A few minutes later, a man emerged from the school. Dressed down in jeans and an undone plaid button up with a t-shirt underneath, he strolled down the concrete stairs towards the parking lot.

"There he is! Mr. Garrison!" Autumn announced.

"We are stalking him now. I think *Ryan* is more appropriate, don't you?" Mandy offered.

Mr. Garrison walked to his beat up car, parked a few cars over from their Jeep. He got inside and Mandy looked at Autumn with delight.

"This is so exciting. It has been so long since I tailed someone."

Autumn stared at her as she started the engine. "You have done this before?"

Mandy nodded as she pulled the car out slowly, letting another car fall between hers and Mr. Garrison's.

"What can I say? I have a," she paused for effect. "Colorful past."

Autumn nodded, her eyes fixated on Mr. Garrison's car up ahead.

"Okay. Are we talking like a few splashes of vibrant color here and there or like a full-on rainbow Mand?"

Mandy chuckled lightly as she followed the cars out of the parking lot.

"I am talking every color in the crayon box sweetheart."

They followed Mr. Garrison's car closely while remaining as inconspicuous as they could.

They drove for about ten minutes when Mr. Garrison turned onto a small court on the right. They turned onto the court but stopped in front of the community mailbox. Mandy cut the engine. Autumn looked around. The homes, all rather large and relatively modern, made up the small cul-de-sac.

Mr. Garrison eventually pulled into a driveway at the far end of the court.

"Can we get a little closer?" Autumn asked.

"Thanks to my tinted windows, yes we can," Mandy said, starting the engine. They pulled up just in time to see Mr. Garrison getting out.

His house was white with russet trim. The grass was green and well-kept, the flowers and bushes immaculate. It made Autumn wonder: Maybe there *was* a special someone in his life?

An hour passed by and dusk was settling in. There had been no sign of Mr. Garrison and Mandy was getting impatient.

She sighed, rubbing her temples in frustration.

"Great. So we came all this way to watch the outside of his house!"

And just like fate had heard her, the front door swung open.

12

The door opened and Mr. Garrison emerged from his house with a beautiful woman in tow. Tall and slender, she had long black hair and deep caramel skin. They headed towards his car, where he held the door open for her as she got in.

"What a gentleman." Mandy said ruefully. "Who is that?"

Autumn felt her stomach knotting up as something came over her. A feeling that was crushing, tactile, and strangely familiar: Jealousy.

Like Mandy was reading her mind, she looked at Autumn's troubled face.

"Jealous?" she offered as Mr. Garrison's clunky car pulled out of the driveway and zipped past them. Mandy let them get a head start before pursuing them.

"I am not jealous!" Autumn snapped.

"We thought he was single but it turns out his girlfriend is a leggy lingerie model. It stings. I get it."

"I am fine!" Autumn insisted. "Are we following them or what?"

"Yep. I was just letting him get ahead of us. I don't want him getting suspicious."

Autumn wasn't jealous was she? Over Ryan Garrison? It was ludicrous. He was her guidance counselor *and* she was in love with Rick.

Why was she so shocked then? Maybe she wasn't expecting him to be with anyone. Not like he would tell her if he *was* and rightfully so. It wasn't any of her business who he dated.

After tailing Mr. Garrison for another ten minutes, he finally arrived at his destination: A conservation area on the outskirts of Whitan that boasted the most beautiful trees and foliage. Night had come and Autumn felt less exposed under the cover of darkness as she watched Mr. Garrison getting out of the car with the mystery woman.

"If he is on a date and we have to watch them kiss... or worse," Mandy trailed off.

Autumn cringed. "You think they came *here* to do *that*?"

Mandy pulled out two pairs of binoculars from the backseat, handing Autumn one.

"Let's find out."

After walking for some time, the pair sat down on a picnic table in the conservation dining area. Autumn and Mandy lost their clear view of the couple as they were swallowed by the mass of trees.

"I can't see anything now," Autumn grumbled, putting down the binoculars in frustration.

"We need to get out. If we can stay hidden, we can eavesdrop and find out exactly what those two are doing here."

Autumn thought about it. They had come all this way and really, what did they have to lose?

"Fine. But whatever they *are* doing, they better be wearing clothes."

They got out of the Jeep and walked towards the dining area, looking for the best place for concealment. They eventually found a clustering of Evergreen's that were adjacent to the picnic table Mr. Garrison sat at. It was close enough to get a decent view and hear snippets of conversation, if Mr. Garrison and the mystery woman spoke particularly loud.

"Perfect. We are set," Mandy whispered, pulling out the binoculars again.

"Do we really need those? We are 30 metres away," Autumn murmured.

"Sorry," Mandy apologized. "They make me feel like a real detective."

"My bad. Next time I will bring my monocle and pipe," Autumn said shortly.

Mandy turned to her, a mixture of shock and amusement on her face.

"Did you just snap at me?"

"I guess I did."

"You never snap at *anyone*," Mandy said, grinning.

Autumn shrugged. "That's not true. I snap at my sister Audrina all the time."

"But not me," Mandy said. "So what's *really* grinding your gears tonight Aut?"

Autumn rolled her eyes. She knew exactly where this was going.

"Mandy, don't bother. I am just tense. With my speech coming up and all of us being in danger…"

"And Mr. Gorgeison being on a date with *legs* over there," Mandy added.

"This has nothing to do with Ryan." Autumn frowned.

"Ryan? On a first name basis are we? I like this," Mandy teased. "Just admit it Aut. You are *jealous*."

"I am not jealous!" Autumn shot back.

"The lady doth protest too much, denial is not just a river in Egypt," Mandy said, unwavering. "Shall I go on with the platitudes?"

Autumn sighed, rubbing her temples. "I am tired and perhaps, a little cranky but it has nothing to do with him. He can date whoever he pleases, even *legs*. I happen to have a boyfriend, in case you forgot that part."

"Just remember, if you ever want to talk about, *not* being jealous of Ryan and legs, I am here to listen."

Autumn felt a rush of affection for her friend, despite her teasing. She reached out and hugged her tightly.

"Thanks Mandy."

"Anytime," she said, squeezing Autumn back.

* * *

The next half hour passed by without much excitement. Autumn and Mandy were barely awake when he arrived. Average height and build, with a bushy brown beard and chocolate eyes, Autumn recognized him right away.

She nudged Mandy gently. "It's Stuart."

Mandy, who had been nodding off, perked up. "Stuart?"

"The homeless man Rick and I see around town."

Mandy peered through the trees. "Well that date just got really awkward."

Stuart sat down with Ryan and the mystery girl. Autumn strained to hear what they were saying, but couldn't make out anything through the din of the outdoors. Eventually, the three stood up and Autumn thought they might be leaving.

"Are they going finally?" Mandy murmured, eyes barely open. "They are putting me to sleep over here."

Autumn watched as they strolled away from the picnic table and stood together in a circle. The woman crouched down and took something out of her bag. Autumn squinted. They looked like ordinary stones. She began placing them on the ground in a ring. Next, she took her finger and drew symbols in the dirt.

"I have seen symbols like that before," Autumn whispered. "In one of Eric's magic books. They're called runes."

Mandy's eyes shot open. "Do you know what they mean?"

Autumn shook her head in response. She made a mental note to ask Eric about it later.

When the woman was done drawing the runes, she stood up. She held out her hands and Ryan took one and Stuart the other. She closed her eyes and began chanting in a foreign language.

Mandy continued watching, astonished. "This *date* just keeps getting creepier."

"It's an incantation of some kind," Autumn said, enthralled.

Suddenly, the stones on the ground began glowing, a white light pulsating around them. The breeze began picking up, like a wind tunnel surrounded the area. The chanting stopped and the woman spoke again, in English this time.

"Goddess of light and protection, we implore thee to watch over the one born of stars. Shall he be safe under our watch and we ask that you apprise us if danger befalls him or his kin."

Her voice boomed into the night as her eyes fluttered open, and her once chocolate colored eyes were as pale as the glow encompassing the stones. Her hair had morphed from dark to light, her body levitated. She looked ethereal.

Mandy inched closer. Autumn followed behind, cautiously.

"Don't get too close. It could be dangerous," she warned.

The stones continued to pulsate and glow, like beautiful orbs of opaque light. Autumn was hypnotized by their beauty.

"Goddess who stands before us now," Ryan spoke. "Will you aid us in our time of need?"

"She's a *goddess?*" Mandy whispered. "I thought lingerie model was stiff competition."

"Focus, please," Autumn grumbled. "I think she is channeling a goddess, not actually one."

The woman spoke, her voice so melodic and beautiful it gave Autumn goosebumps.

"You came to me, seeking my assistance for the one among the stars. The one who brings change, who turns tides, who is the key to salvation. I will abide this and watch over him and his. Let it be known, if the fates want him to face trials, I cannot interfere. These trials will inevitably lead him on the path to becoming the man he's been foretold to be."

"Of course, my goddess. If the fates require this of him, or *anything* of us, we too shall abide it," Ryan said, hand on his heart.

"I shall inform you of the one among the stars whereabouts and any danger that may befall him in the days to come. You only need use the stones of light to call on me and I shall be here, by your side. Any questions you have may be answered then."

Neither Mandy nor Autumn dared to move. Both were transfixed, watching Ryan speak to the lovely goddess.

"We thank you so much for your patience and guidance goddess," Ryan said.

"Is there anything else I can assist you with? Or shall I leave this vessel?"

"You may leave, in peace and harmony," Ryan said.

There was another gust of unnatural wind and bright silver light encompassed the area. It was almost blinding and Autumn and Mandy shielded their eyes until the light disappeared.

Moments later, the darkness returned and the stunning glow of the stones faded until they looked like regular rocks.

Ryan's enigmatic friend floated down the ground, softly like a feather. When she opened her eyes this time, they were brown again, her hair was black, and the luminosity around her had disappeared.

Autumn and Mandy waited around until Ryan, Stuart and the woman had left. Nothing happened after the appearance of the goddess and both girls decided to call it a night.

As they headed home, they discussed what they had seen. The whole point of the evening was to answer questions they had about Ryan and whatever dangers they were facing.

Instead, they were left with no answers.

Only more questions.

Who was *the one among the stars?* Why did they need protecting and from whom? How did Ryan and Stuart know each other and how were they tied into all of this?

Autumn and Mandy both agreed, they were too tired to piece it together tonight. Still, when Mandy dropped Autumn off and she went to bed, she just lay there, thinking of everything she had seen and heard.

The last thing she thought, as she was dozing off, startled her. So much so, it shook her wide-awake.

Was Ryan *really* their ally? Or was he just a wolf in sheep's clothing?

13

The last day of school arrived and Autumn was delighted. Part of her would miss school. The routine, her favorite classes, even her teachers but the idea of starting a new chapter in her life was exciting. She couldn't wait to figure out what she wanted to do next.

Rick drove in that morning, which meant they got to school at least ten minutes later than Autumn did when she was behind the wheel. Rick drove the speed limit, sometimes less, and managed to piss off many motorists on the road who were in a sputtering rush to get wherever they were going.

Unable to hide what Mandy and her saw at the conservation area Saturday night from Rick and the others, Autumn came clean. At first, Rick was livid. She *had* lied to him. When she explained *why* she couldn't tell him the truth, he admitted when it came to Ryan, he was definitely irrational.

Autumn told Rick everything. About the mystery woman who acted as a vessel for the goddess, Stuart the bum knowing Ryan, rather well it seemed, and *the one among the stars.*

The morning went by so fast Autumn could hardly believe it when lunch rolled around. To commemorate their last day as high school students, her and Rick were going to eat lunch outside. Autumn and Rick headed to the wooded area by the school to meet up with Mandy, Nathaniel and Eric who were joining them.

As they strolled through the hall, they passed Ryan, who was talking with a student. He waved at them absently as they passed. It was just as well. Autumn could barely *look* at him after Saturday night, let alone speak to him.

The mornings grey sky had lifted, revealing a beautiful blanket of blue with a hint of sunshine peeking through. They had only been walking a minute when Rick looked at Autumn.

"That was weird right?"

She looked back at him, perplexed. "What was?"

"The way Mr. Garrison waved at us. It was like he was brushing us off," Rick said, agitated. "Normally the guy will take any chance he can get to talk to you."

She scowled at him. *"Rick."* Her tone was warning.

"Okay, *fine.* To talk to *us,*" he corrected.

Autumn smiled, satisfied. "Better. And I don't think it was odd. He was busy with another student. His job doesn't revolve around us."

"*Today,*" Rick said, sarcastically.

Autumn was relieved to see Mandy, Nathaniel and Eric waiting for them in the clearing. Their appearance was a welcome distraction. She didn't want Rick dwelling on Ryan or his *weird* behaviour.

"You lovebirds finally made it," Nathaniel teased, his arm around Mandy's shoulders.

"Shall we?" He gestured to the masses of trees behind him.

It didn't take them long to reach their destination, a place with numerous boulders to sit on, surrounded by trees, foliage and bushes that offered them some semblance of privacy. They all found seats and began unpacking their lunches. Autumn was about to dig into her chicken wrap when a noise caught her attention. It sounded like ragged breathing and it gave her chills.

She nudged Rick, who had already devoured half of his BLT sandwich.

"Did you hear that?"

"It would be hard to hear anything over his loud chewing," Eric grumbled.

"Listen."

Everyone went quiet.

A minute passed before they heard anything. This time it was groaning, like someone was in agony.

"I'll go check it out," Eric offered, standing up.

Autumn got up as well. "You aren't going alone Eric. I'll come with."

Rick frowned, clearly not liking Autumn's proposal. Still, he knew better than to argue.

"Be careful," he warned her and she nodded.

"Always."

She and Eric followed the path, keeping a watchful eye. Training wasn't just learning how to fight. It also meant being mindful of your surroundings at all times and never letting anyone get the jump on you.

The moans were getting louder until it was apparent that whoever was hurt was nearby.

Autumn saw it first. A figure, a few feet away, crumpled on the ground.

"Eric," she whispered. "Look."

"Oh shit."

When they got closer they saw it was a girl. She was lying on her back, eyes closed. Her clothes were torn, like she had been attacked and her hair was a tangled blanket under her head.

Her right eye was swollen, her left cheek bruised. It took Autumn a moment to recognize her.

"It's Allison Kendall," she said, kneeling beside her. She was still breathing. Autumn looked down. She saw blood. Allison's leg had a large gash under her knee. It looked deep.

"The girl we saw out here last time?" he said. "With the guy?"

Autumn nodded. "We need to stop the bleeding." She pulled her scarf off, thankful she had worn it today, and began wrapping the wound up.

"That should do for now. Go get Rick and the others and get help."

* * *

Allison's eyes darted open and she groaned loudly, the same noise that had alerted Autumn of her presence in the first place. It took her a moment to focus and recognize her surroundings. She looked up at Autumn.

"Autumn? Is that you?" she said, her voice barely audible.

"Yes. Just relax for now. Don't try to move."

Autumn's heart swelled for this girl. Whatever she had been through, whoever had done this to her, this would probably traumatize her for life.

"Where is he?"

"Don't talk," Autumn said softly. "Eric went to get help."

"Matt," she whispered, her eyes filling with fear.

Matt was the guy Allison was with the last time they came out here.

Autumn grimaced. "What about him?"

Allison was quiet for a moment, like she was debating whether or not to tell Autumn the truth.

"He is the one that did this to me," she said finally.

Autumn stiffened. "He hurt you?"

She nodded slowly. "He changed..." she trailed off. "Forget it. You won't believe me. You will think I am crazy."

Autumn reached out and took her hand. "No Allison. I won't think that."

"Why not?" she scoffed. "I do."

"Allison, you need to tell me exactly what happened. What did Matt change into?"

Something supernatural was afoot and Autumn had to know what. If Allison withheld pertinent information, Matt might never be found and he was far too dangerous to be roaming the streets.

Allison adjusted slowly, trying to sit up. "He was normal, at first. He was kissing me and it was beautiful," she said, looking anguished. "I opened my eyes for a second and his face was *different*. It was scaly and ridged. He looked like a *monster*."

Autumn squeezed her hand gently. "Then he attacked you?"

She nodded. "It all happened so fast. I can hardly remember what he did to me."

"Don't worry about that now," Autumn said gently.

Autumn remembered Eric telling her that some people that went to the caves, when it was tainted, ended up possessed. She couldn't help but wonder if Matt was one of the unlucky few.

"Aut!" Mandy was racing through the bramble, with Nathaniel and Eric but no Rick.

"Where is Rick?"

"He went to get Garrison," Nathaniel said.

Autumn looked at Allison. She was still clutching her hand.

"Did you hear that Allison? Help is on the way."

"What if I die?" she whispered.

"You aren't going to die."

Mandy, who had been assessing the damage, looked at Allison.

"I have seen worse. You'll live."

A few minutes passed before Rick arrived with Mr. Garrison trailing behind him. Allison had closed her eyes but her breathing was much more relaxed now. Autumn relinquished her hand, wanting to give Ryan space to do whatever he needed to.

Ryan took in the scene, remaining calm and collected, as usual.

He knelt beside Autumn and his eyes met hers. He forced a small smile.

"Was she coherent at all before I arrived?"

Autumn nodded. "She was talking and explaining everything. Though she seems to only remember fragments of what happened."

Mr. Garrison looked at the others. "You guys should head back to the school."

He turned back to Autumn, who was kneeling beside Allison, her brow furrowed with worry. "You too Mrs. Jacobs. I can take it from here."

Autumn said nothing but stood up. She dusted off her clothes as Mr. Garrison proceeded to pick Allison up and carry her with ease.

As they headed back, Autumn wondered where Matt might be hiding. Was there a new hangout where the evil and possessed folks of Whitan congregated?

She certainly didn't know but she knew someone whose eyes were always watching the streets. And he might have the answers she was looking for.

14

"You think Stuart might know where that jerk Matt is?" Rick asked.

After Ryan took Allison, Autumn hadn't heard anything about the incident. She assumed Allison was sent to the local hospital but if an ambulance had shown up at the school? That gossip would've spread like wildfire. By last period, *everyone* would've known, but she hadn't heard a word.

"Stuart gets around. He might know *something* and right now anything can help."

Rick pulled his car into the lot. They were at the park Stuart frequented the most, the one nearest Rick's house.

"Maybe he's heard or seen something shady? We need some clues to lead us to Matt."

"I just can't believe what Matt did to Allison," Rick said, cutting the engine. "The guy is a menace."

Autumn unbuckled her seatbelt. "That is exactly why we need to find him. If he is possessed, which by her description of his face *changing,* I would say he is, we need to get him off the streets."

"And into a body bag," he deadpanned.

Autumn looked at Rick.

He was dead serious.

It didn't take much time or effort to find Stuart. The park wasn't huge and he was visible in the distance. Across the emerald field, nestled between two large trees, sat Stuart.

When he saw them approaching, he smiled, his familiar crooked grin.

"Hello there," he said. "Good to see you both on this fine evening."

"Hey Stuart." Rick smiled back. "How goes it?"

"Ah it goes," he said, standing up and dusting off his ratty shorts. "The day in the life of a bum." He grinned. "So what brings you two to my neck of the woods?"

"We'd like to ask you a few questions," Autumn said, getting right to it.

"Uh-oh," he said. "That is never good."

"Today, we found a girl in the forest behind our school," Autumn began carefully.

"Alive right?" Stuart asked.

Rick nodded and he sighed with relief.

"You might want to lead with that next time. Go on."

"She was attacked, beaten and stabbed. She told me the guy she was dating, Matt, he was the one that hurt her."

Stuart nodded his head slowly. "Jealous boyfriend or just off his nut?"

"We think he was possessed," Rick chimed in.

At the mention of this, Stuart looked up.

"I see. What do you think possessed the lad?"

"Evil cave spirits?" Autumn offered. "Eric figures a few of the possessed people were left wandering around, even after the caves were cleansed."

Stuart didn't speak for a moment. Instead, he paced back and forth, running a hand through his beard thoughtfully.

"We were hoping you might know if these possessed monsters have a den," Rick said finally. "We know you have your eyes on the streets and that you believe in the supernatural."

Stuart interrupted Rick with a hearty chortle.

"Kid, I don't just believe it. I've seen it all with my own eyes."

He stopped pacing and looked at them both seriously.

"What you guys did in those caves, from what you told me, wasn't easy. Taking the life of a demon doesn't weigh too heavy on one's conscience. But these people you are hunting down are just that. *People.* Not demons. Not monsters. They are human. And having to take a human life just isn't the same."

Autumn had already considered this. Matt was possessed. He wasn't an actual demon. There was still a person somewhere inside his corrupted soul.

"We want to save them," Autumn said, her eyes meeting his with determination. "There has to be a way to purify them. Eric is looking into it as we speak."

Rick sighed, clearly exasperated. "I tried to explain to Aut, we couldn't save Eric's cousins Renee and Caleb, so our chances aren't great."

"Because we never found them!" Autumn shot back. She refused to believe they were helpless. There had to be a way to save Matt and the others.

"I don't understand why you kids, so young with such bright futures ahead of you, would take it upon yourselves to save these people," Stuart said. "However, I do admire your bravery. Most everyday folk wouldn't risk their hides to help this town. Hell, most of them wouldn't report a robbery if they saw it with their own two eyes."

"That said, I may be just a humble bum, but I do have some secrets of my own," he smiled his crooked grin. "So I can tell you. If you guys can round up these people, I have something that can cure what ails them."

Autumn couldn't believe what she was hearing. Stuart knew how to save Matt and the others in Whitan who were possessed. Autumn looked at Rick. He looked almost as stunned as she did.

Stuart chuckled lightly. "Don't look so shocked. I believed you guys," he pointed at Autumn and Rick. "When you told me you hunted monsters."

"Are you a hunter too?" Rick asked hopefully.

Stuart shrugged. "I got my secrets. Like I said."

"So you are!"

Stuart grinned. "That's why they call them *secrets* boy. I won't be spilling the beans anytime soon."

"Let's just say, I know my way around a monster or two and from what I've seen, there aren't many possessed people left in this town. It sounds like you might be able to help this Matt kid. He left the girl alive, which indicates some humanity. There may be hope for him yet."

Stuart went on, telling Autumn and Rick of rumors that were floating around about a gang of cave worshippers that lurked around the defunct caves.

"I don't understand why the giant wolves never got to them yet," Rick said, looking puzzled. "From what I saw, those wolves meant business."

Stuart grimaced. "You ask me, those kids are lucky the wolves haven't found them yet. From what I know of wolves, they kill now and ask questions *never*."

The three of them sat on the grass talking more about the wolves, the missing kids and life in general. As they chatted, Autumn wanted to unload everything on Stuart. Over time, he had become a confidant for Rick and her. She wanted to tell him about Rick being chased and tranquilized by strange men.

She didn't.

Instead, as they were saying their goodbyes, Autumn looked at Stuart.

"Stuart, I know this may sound odd but do you know anyone but the name of Ryan Garrison?"

Stuart, who was counting some coins in his hands, didn't even flinch.

"Nope. I can't say that I do," he looked up at Autumn. " Why do you ask? Should I know him?"

Rick looked at Autumn. He knew what she was getting at but she didn't want to admit she had been tailing Ryan.

"I saw you. At the big fancy park near the newer houses."

"Oh yeah. I like that park. Lots of affluent people hanging around there," Stuart smiled fondly. He looked at Autumn. "You saw me and didn't say hello?"

Autumn felt her face getting hot. She wasn't great at lying, even small fibs. She either felt guilty and confessed or got caught.

"You were busy talking with Ryan. He is my guidance counselor."

Stuart nodded. "I think you may have mentioned him to me before."

He looked to Rick. "The guy you aren't so fond of?"

Rick threw his head back, groaning. "That would be him."

"Maybe I do know him? Honestly sweetheart, I see a lot of people in my travels. You need to be more specific."

You did a magical ritual with him and some gorgeous girl, summoning a goddess that used her body as a vessel! Is that specific enough? She wanted to scream.

But, again, she didn't.

Autumn managed to change the subject back to Matt and the possessed people. She told Stuart that Rick and her would recruit Mandy, Nathanial and Eric and try to locate Matt and the others.

"Perfect," Stuart said, sounding pleased. "Meet me here at 7 PM sharp Friday night. I will bring the remedy with me."

* * *

Exams flew by and Autumn was relieved when she realized she only had her English exam left. It was in the afternoon and she showed up at school an hour early with Eric. Dressed in a white button down and blue jeans, her long dark hair in loose waves, Autumn headed to the mostly empty cafeteria for some last minute studying.

Eric, who sat across from her, dressed in a basic black t-shirt and jeans, was engrossed his English notes. Autumn, however, couldn't seem to concentrate. She was thinking. Now that school was over, she would probably never see Ryan Garrison again.

She still had so many questions for him: about Rick, Stuart and the strange occurrences from the past few weeks. The last time they had spoken, he informed her that Allison was in the hospital. They examined her and along with her many wounds, she was severely dehydrated and traumatized. Her parents didn't want anyone causing her undue stress, so only family was permitted to visit, though they did send Autumn a card, thanking her for helping Allison.

Autumn tapped her fingers on the table absently.

"Autumn," Eric said, glancing up from his book, looking mildly frustrated.

Autumn, shaken from her reverie, looked back at him innocuously. "Yes?"

"Don't get me wrong. You are by all means, the best study partner a guy could ask for and the prettiest." He grinned. "But if you keep tapping, I will be forced to restrain you."

Autumn looked from Eric's brown eyes to her tapping fingers and stopped abruptly.

"Oh sorry. I didn't even realize."

"It's okay. We all have our quirks. Mine? Teasing hot girls about *theirs*."

He set his book down. "So what's bothering you?"

Autumn sighed. Eric had come to know her quirks extremely well.

"I want to go and see Ryan one last time."

Eric's lips spread into a grin.

"Are you finally giving into the magnetic attraction?" he teased.

Autumn couldn't stop her lips from twitching with amusement.

"I want to ask him some questions about Rick."

"So you are going to march into his office and demand he tell you everything he knows?" Eric sounded skeptical. "And you expect him to offer up the information *now*? Even though he's volunteered zero information yet?"

"Actually, I was planning on torturing him," Autumn said sardonically.

Eric nodded thoughtfully. "I have a better plan. Why don't you use what you have to your advantage?"

"You want me to pay him?"

"You are pretty Autumn. Use your feminine wiles, flirt. Butter Garrison up. *Make* him talk."

Autumn stared at Eric in disbelief. She could never flirt to get what she wanted.

Could she?

"I know. It is cliché male advice, but if you want to find out what he knows, just give the old guy an ego boost and bat your eyelashes at him."

Autumn crossed her arms, suddenly feeling defensive. Flirting with Ryan to get information was desperate.

"I don't need to flirt with him to get what I need," Autumn said firmly. "I will be direct and honest."

Eric shrugged as they both stood up. "Suit yourself. Just remember, even men his age have a hard time saying no to a pretty girl."

Autumn smiled, in spite of herself. "See you soon."

* * *

Autumn walked into the guidance office and saw the secretary, Mrs. Sanderson sitting at her desk. Dressed in a cream colored twinset, she looked up at Autumn appraisingly.

"Hello dear. Can I help you?" She smiled warmly.

"Yes. I would like to speak with Mr. Garrison." Autumn smiled back.

"School is finished for summer young lady. Only examinations now."

Autumn nodded. "I know but I would still like to see him if possible."

Suddenly, Mrs. Sanderson burst into a fit of giggles.

Autumn was taken aback. Her brow furrowed with confusion.

"Did I say something funny?"

The secretary had her face in her hands now, trying to stifle her giggles. When her laughter subsided, she took a deep breath, regaining her composure.

"Oh you girls," she said, shaking her head so vigorously her blonde ponytail bounced. "You think I don't see right through the act?"

Autumn blinked at her, even more confused now. "I'm sorry? I don't follow."

Mrs. Sanderson leaned in, her eyes twinkling with delight.

"All you young things make appointments with the handsome Mr. Garrison. He is the most popular guidance counselor, with the girls."

"Mrs. Sanderson, I *actually* need to see him," Autumn began but she was interrupted by the sound of a door opening behind her. She turned around and saw Ryan, dressed down in jeans and a white dress shirt, smiling at her.

"Mr. Garrison! This student is here to see you," Mrs. Sanderson said, a huge grin still plastered on her face.

Autumn gave a feeble wave. "Do you have a minute?"

"Maybe even two." He smiled. "Would you like to step into my office?"

She nodded and headed inside, as Mr. Garrison winked at Mrs. Sanderson, who flushed many shades of pink, before returning to her paperwork.

As soon as Autumn stepped into the office, she noticed how different it looked. The school year was over and Mr. Garrison had begun packing. A box filled with mugs, books and office supplies sat on his desk. Another was filled to the brim with paperwork.

Autumn wondered why he didn't have a picture of his gorgeous girlfriend, the dark haired beauty, in his office to show off.

"Have a seat Ms. Kingston," he said, sitting on the edge of his desk.

"My chair went home yesterday. I bring my own. The chairs they give us aren't chairs you want to spend ten hour days sitting in."

"It's okay," Autumn said, starting to fidget. Mr. Garrison was so close to her she could smell him. He smelt like cleanliness. Like he had just taken a shower and the soap scent was lingering on his skin.

"So what can I help you with today Autumn?" His words cut through her reverie.

She hadn't thought this through. She had no segue prepared. She would just have to wing it.

"I want to ask you something," she began.

Mr. Garrison smiled, welcoming her inquiry. "By all means, ask away. I just hope I have an answer for you."

You and me both, she thought.

"This might be overstepping my boundaries," she said, her eyes meeting his. "But I really need to know. The people that infiltrated the school during the assembly, were they after Rick?"

Mr. Garrison said nothing at first. He appeared to be unfazed by her question, like he had expected her to ask him about this sooner or later.

"Autumn, this really isn't the place to discuss this."

"I don't care!" she said sharply. "I want to know if those people would have taken Rick if they had gotten the chance. If we had attended the assembly, would his face be on posters plastered around town too? Those men saw *him* and started to chase us. They tranquilized *him.* They were aiming at *him.*"

Mr. Garrison sighed loudly. "They were."

"And I want to know *why!*"

"Autumn, I gave you fair warning. I told you Rick and the rest of you are in danger. I told you everything you need to know."

"You never told me who those people were or why they want Rick! You never told me why a bunch of armed men would come into a high school and start taking students randomly!"

"It wasn't random," Mr. Garrison said. "They knew what they were doing. That much I know. But I still don't know *why* they wanted those students, or Rick. Just that it was premeditated to abduct specific people."

This was no secret. Autumn heard the news report with everyone else.

The men were prepared and announced they were looking for someone, though they didn't specify who. Only that whoever it was wasn't there.

Rick. They wanted Rick.

Autumn glanced at the clock on the wall. She had fifteen minutes before her exam began. She wanted to keep prying, but she didn't have the time and whatever Mr. Garrison knew, he wasn't telling.

Eric had been right all along.

"I should go," she said, standing up.

"You should," he agreed. "You don't want to be late."

"So this is goodbye I guess?" she said quietly. She felt miserable all of a sudden, though she wasn't exactly sure why.

"Perhaps," he said, his lips curving into a smile. "But I wouldn't count on it. Whitan isn't that big. We are bound to run into each other eventually."

15

It was nearly seven o'clock on Friday night and Autumn, Rick, Nathaniel and Mandy were at the park, waiting for Stuart to arrive. Exams were finished, high school was done and Autumn had landed a job working part-time at a local bookstore. Stuart would be arriving with his concoction and Autumn and the others hadn't had any luck finding Matt yet.

Mandy, who was picking at the blades of grass absently, looked at Autumn.

"We graduate tomorrow night and you look miserable Auttie. What gives?"

"Yeah, Aut. Tomorrow is our day of emancipation," Nathaniel said before crinkling his nose. "Whoa, big word! Yuck."

"Speaking of *yuck*, Autumn got a job at the bookstore downtown," Rick said, sliding his arm around her.

"Gross," Nathaniel grumbled, sprawling out in the grass. "Labor. I do *not* look forward to that."

"I tried telling her we have all our adult lives to work," Rick said.

"It's only part-time," Autumn interjected. "I can still enjoy the summer."

"Man, when I work it won't be a typical 9 to 5 gig. Conrad said he'd hook me up with something if I wanted extra cash."

"Doing what dude?" Rick asked, looking skeptical.

"Something illegal," Mandy offered.

"I prefer, under the table," Nathaniel corrected her.

"Howdy strangers," Nathaniel was interrupted by Stuart. He looked around, perplexed.

"Aren't you missing someone? The fancy pants?"

"You mean Eric? His sister, Arabella, is in town," Autumn replied. "She's coming to graduation tomorrow night. So they are spending time together."

Stuart reached into his jacket pocket, pulling out a box.

"I just thought he might enjoy this, being into magics and all." He looked around, scanning the area for any onlookers. When he saw the coast was clear, he gave the box to Rick.

"There you go. That's the stuff that should return those kids to normal."

"Can I open it?" Rick asked hesitantly.

"Sure," Stuart said after taking another quick glance around the park. The box, which reminded Autumn of a small lock box, clicked open with ease. Inside it was a thinly minced brown substance.

"Dirt?" Rick looked flabbergasted.

"If memory serves, you were rather fond of eating it when we were young," Autumn said, grinning.

"They don't have to ingest it," Stuart said, obviously amused. "They just need to come in contact with it. Think fairy dust. Sprinkle some on the possessed and they will be cleansed almost instantly."

"Eric *would* be interested in this," Autumn admitted, observing the dust. "It really is right up his alley."

"I don't think I have to tell you, possessed people are unpredictable and dangerous. So please be careful."

"Thanks Stuart," Autumn said, smiling. "For the help and for looking out for us."

"Ah," he waved his hand, shooing the praise away. "You are all good kids. I wouldn't want to see anything bad happen to any of you."

"On a lighter note." He grinned. "So you guys are graduating tomorrow night."

"Even me," Nathaniel said proudly.

"Well congrats," Stuart said, sitting on a bench. "High school isn't easy. Especially when you are students slash monster hunters." He winked at them.

Autumn felt a sudden rush of affection for Stuart. He was easy to talk to and caring. She trusted him, though she hardly knew him. Without thinking, she rushed towards him and embraced him. He hugged her back, looking startled.

"Thanks again for your help. It's nice to have someone to talk to about this *stuff*. It's not something we can discuss with just anyone," she whispered.

"Anytime kid. You know that."

"Alright valedictorian. Let's get a move on," Rick said, clasping her hand into his.

"Valedictorian?" Stuart said and Autumn nodded.

He flashed his infamous crooked smile. "Well in that case, knock 'em dead sweetheart."

Saturday arrived and Autumn spent the day preparing for graduation: Editing her speech and awaiting her family's arrival. Her parents and sister would be spending the weekend at the house and were due to arrive any minute.

To kill time, she began researching the recent abductions in Whitan. She knew from the news that the students taken, including Andy Carson, had not been found yet. She also knew from her conversation with Ryan, that the abductions were planned and possibly linked.

Finally, after searching for about an hour, she found a blog. It was anonymous and belonged to a self-proclaimed *male conspiracy theorist*, located in Canada. She began reading. This man believed in many things she *knew* to be true: Monsters, hunters, magics. Autumn began reading some of his recent entries.

The news is indicating the student abductions in Whitan are "run of the mill abductions". I know better. I see what is happening. It's not a coincidence these teenagers were picked. They were handpicked for a reason. I think they must be gifted, special in some way.

Why else would armed men come in and snatch those students and be upset they missed someone specific? If it was random, they wouldn't have been so organized in their execution. The news even implied the abductions were premeditated.

I have been researching it, following leads and questioning sources. To the best of my knowledge, the abductors are independently funded with no government affiliation. The organizations name? DSI. I have no idea what it stands for...yet.

Every day I feel like I am getting closer to an answer and in turn I feel like I am in grave danger. Let it be known I will not be scared or threatened into silence or submission! We cannot stand by and let them tear down our towns and cities, taking our people hostage. We must be vigilant in fighting back, taking care of our own and looking out for each other. We must stand together.

Autumn went on to read his last entry, which was posted yesterday.

I have received many threats from people telling me they will find me and kill me for the words I write. Though the threats come anonymously and aplenty, I fear nothing. Though I too, remain a faceless stranger behind a computer screen, I feel like you are the cowards.

Threatening me for digging deep and revealing the truth? You wish to bury it, and me, like a secret never to be uncovered. People are going missing. People with bright futures ahead of them, with goals to accomplish and dreams to chase. Their lives are being stolen from them and DSI are the thieves.

To all those trying to find me, I do not blog from home. I don't shit where I eat. I'm not that stupid. To all the believers out there, hang tight, the answers are coming. The only question is: Are you ready?

Autumn stared at the screen, bewildered. This person was discussing the abductions without fear of consequence. More surprisingly, they knew about the supernatural.

DSI. Were they really behind the abductions? Were they the danger Ryan spoke of?

More importantly, were they after Rick?

Commotion downstairs pulled Autumn from her thoughts. She heard her parent's voices and jumped up from her desk with excitement. She couldn't wait to see them.

"Your parents are here," Rick was at Autumn's door. He stepped into her room, taking her in. Her dress, strapless with black lace, skimmed over her curves. Her long dark hair cascaded down her back.

"You look so gorgeous," Rick said, beaming. "I can hardly breathe."

"Thanks Rick." Autumn chuckled lightly. "My breathing tip? Inhale and exhale."

"Done."

He walked towards her and put his arms around her waist, pulling her close. The familiar scent of Rick overwhelmed her nostrils. He touched her cheek gently. He looked so happy she couldn't tell him about DSI or the blog. At least not tonight.

"You really do look stunning," he said softly. "I don't think I can let you out of the house tonight. You are going to steal too many hearts."

"You don't look so bad yourself there Jacobs," Autumn said, leaning in to kiss him.

"Sorry to interrupt. I would tell you both to get a room but alas you are already in one."

Autumn looked over Rick's shoulder to see her older sister, Audrina, standing in the doorway.

"Very Observant Aud. I told mom and dad you should've been a detective," Autumn teased.

"It doesn't take a P.I. to see what you two were working up to," she said, rolling her eyes.

She glared at Rick. "Do you think you can tear yourself away from her lover boy? I want to hug my sister."

Rick and Autumn shared a quick smile before they parted.

"Sure Audrina. You can *borrow* her."

Audrina walked past him, still scowling. "You never were good at sharing Rick."

She hugged Autumn, squeezing her tightly. As annoying as Audrina could be and as competitive as she was, Autumn shared a bond with her that was unique from any other. They were sisters. She would trust Audrina with her life.

Autumn squeezed her back and when Audrina pulled away, Autumn could see she was tearing up.

"My little sister is about to put on her cap and gown," she said proudly. "And she is the freaking valedictorian to boot."

Rick watched the scene unfolding in front of him and looked mildly traumatized.

"I don't think I have ever seen Audrina cry," he said, astonished. "I'm sorry to ruin the moment but it's like seeing a pig fly."

Audrina sighed exasperatedly, ignoring Rick's jab. She smiled at Autumn, her eyes glistening.

"I know we bicker sometimes Aut but you know I love you right?"

Autumn nodded. "I love you too Aud."

"I'm so proud of you. You have always been strong-willed and brave. What you went through with Nikki, most people wouldn't survive that but you did. You never let it change you or make you bitter. You are still the same kind-hearted, sweet person I grew up with," she said, taking Autumn's hand into hers. "You even managed to help Rick graduate. So miracles *can* happen."

"If they did, *you* wouldn't be talking still!" Rick shot back.

"Thanks Aud," Autumn said, wiping tears away with the back of her hand.

"Enough with the waterworks," Rick said, rubbing Autumn's back. "Shouldn't you guys be worried about your makeup smudging?"

"Whatever. I always look spectacular." Audrina grinned. "Mom and dad are dying to see you Aut. Come on." She grabbed Autumn by the hand and headed downstairs as Rick followed.

16

Autumn heard her parents in the kitchen. She missed the sound of their voices, in person. The phone, video calls, it just wasn't the same.

She walked into the kitchen and saw them both sitting at the table. Her mom, Erin, was dressed in a classic ivory sheath dress, her blonde hair in a chignon. Her father, Chris, was wearing grey slacks and a coordinating ivory dress shirt, his black hair, the same color as his Autumn's, was messy.

"My darling girl," her mother said, launching at Autumn before pulling her into a hug. She squeezed her for a long minute before letting go.

"You look so gorgeous," she said, taking Autumn's face into her hands. "You get more beautiful every day that passes. Doesn't she Chris?"

Autumn's dad, looking sentimental, nodded. "Our girls got some excellent genes, what can I say?" He walked over to Autumn and embraced her.

"My little girl is graduating with honors. I knew this day would come but not this soon. With me being so young and all." He chortled, his laughter loud and booming. "Seriously, I am very proud of you sweetheart." He kissed her lightly on the forehead before turning to Rick.

"Have you been treating my Autumn well Rick Jacobs?"

Rick smiled politely. "Always sir."

Autumn knew her father could be gruff and rather intimidating but Rick handled parents with respect and finesse, so she wasn't worried.

Audrina, back to her normal deadpan self, rolled her eyes.

"*Sir?* Did he rehearse this?" she muttered.

Mr. Kingston patted Rick's shoulder affectionately. "You are lucky to have Autumn and she is lucky to have you Rick."

"Funny. Last week Rick was, as you put it dad, a perverted little punk that wanted to deflower your precious Autumn," Audrina chimed in, grinning wickedly.

Mr. Kingston nodded in agreement. "I'll admit it. I was concerned about Autumn and Rick residing in the same house together, as a couple."

"What he really means is *sleeping* in the same house together, as a couple," Audrina whispered to Autumn.

"I expressed my worries to Katherine and James and they said there will be no hanky panky on their watch."

"And we are very diligent with the watching," Uncle James added in firmly.

"Though we really don't need to be," Aunt Katherine said quickly. "Both Autumn and Rick respect the rules and abide by them."

"What exactly are the rules around here?" Mr. Kingston pried, only to be interrupted by Mrs. Kingston's hearty chuckle.

"Alright Chris. Let's not spoil our family reunion with the third degree." She put her arms around her husband lovingly. "We are celebrating Autumn and Rick's accomplishment today."

"Besides, you have all weekend to grill Rick daddy," Audrina said, as she grabbed her jacket and headed for the door. "We are going to be late for the ceremony."

Autumn's mother checked her watch. "Aud's right. We should get there early so Autumn and Rick can get situated. Let's get going."

* * *

Autumn hadn't been nervous at all. Being the valedictorian was something she had strived for, it was an honour she had chased all through high school. Now, sitting on the stage in the schools packed auditorium, she wished the valedictorian was *anyone* but her. It was finally hitting her. She would have to speak in front of thousands of people. Her heart was racing, her knees wobbled, she was sweating profusely. She was nervous.

Mr. Steel was first to speak. Autumn watched as he walked up to the podium, looking relaxed and composed. He smiled, his trademark jovial grin, and began his speech.

Autumn tried her best to focus, but her mind began wandering. She glanced into the crowd and saw her family and friends. She saw Allison, who was just released from the hospital, with her parents. She saw Audrina staring dreamily at...Mr. Garrison?

Autumn blinked. She had no idea guidance counselors came to graduations. Autumn watched as her sister eyed up the attractive Mr. Garrison. But he wasn't Mr. Garrison anymore. He was no longer her guidance counselor. He was just Ryan Garrison.

Ryan caught Autumn's stare and gave her a reassuring smile and a wink. Autumn averted her eyes quickly, her cheeks heating up.

Mr. Steel's speech seemed to drag on. Autumn didn't mind. She was hardly paying attention when he finally introduced her.

"Ladies and gentlemen, please give a warm Whitan High welcome for our gifted and lovely valedictorian, Autumn Kingston."

The crowd burst into applause as Rick stood up, whistling loudly. Autumn's heart pounded, her hands trembled and her legs were like jelly. She stood up, plastered on her best confident smile and walked up to the podium. She was greeted by Mr. Steel, who shook her hand and wished her luck. Now she found herself standing in front of an ocean of people. They were all staring at her, awaiting her imparted words of wisdom.

She took a long deep breath. *Focus.* She thought. *You fight demons. This is nothing.*

When Autumn began her speech, her legs were shaking. So much so that her knees knocked together. She was thankful for the podiums cover and that she hadn't fallen over yet. Eventually though, her nerves calmed, and she began focusing less on the crowd in front of her and more on her family and friends.

Her mom, her eyes welling up with tears of joy, her dad listening intently, looking every bit the proud father. Rick, wearing a smile of encouragement on his handsome face. Her heart warmed and she felt safe in her cocoon of love and support. She had no fear, no reason to be anxious.

She was safe, surrounded by family and friends.

After Autumn's speech was finished, the crowd stood up and applauded. Mr. Steel came up and introduced the next guest speaker and Autumn went to join everyone else awaiting their diploma.

* * *

After spotting Ryan Garrison at the graduation, Audrina grilled Autumn about him. Who was the handsome older man? Was he a teacher? A parent? Was he single? Autumn told Audrina he was dating a gorgeous, statuesque woman and he was her former guidance counselor.

Audrina didn't bring up Ryan for the rest of the weekend.

When Monday morning came, Autumn was heartbroken to see her parents leave. She would even miss Audrina, who was uncharacteristically chipper most of the weekend.

"My darling girl. We will see you soon. You and Rick will be coming down to stay with us in August right?" Mrs. Kingston said, hugging her daughter tightly.

Autumn nodded, fighting tears unsuccessfully. "Of course mom. We are staying the whole month. I can't wait."

"Me either!" Rick chimed in.

Audrina rolled her eyes. "Suck up."

"Did I mention how proud I am of you?" Mr. Kingston was next to hug Autumn. "Your speech was amazing sweetheart. You brought the house down."

"Thanks daddy," Autumn said through sniffles.

Tears and I love you's abounded before the Kingston family left, leaving Autumn and Rick standing together at the front door. Autumn looked at Rick, and wordlessly crumpled into his arms. She sobbed into his shoulder, as he stroked her hair. She missed them so much already, but her father was right. Her and Rick were lucky to have each other.

17

Autumn's skin prickled with anxiety as she looked upon the cave mouth. Memories flooded her brain and she sifted through them hesitantly. Demons, rituals, oversized wolf men. Still, rationally she knew the caves were harmless now.

Though the moon cast a ghastly glow on its dark stone face, Autumn knew the evil inside had been banished. They hadn't come here to tonight to fight demons. They had come to save people *from* theirs.

Stuart gave them a tip after hearing rumors of teenagers hanging out inside the "forbidden caves". Autumn and the others decided the lead would be worth checking out, after graduation.

So here she was, with Rick, Eric, Mandy and Nathaniel.

The whole gang.

Rick clutched the box Stuart had given them tightly in his hands. Eric was looking through his vials for anything they could use because possessed people were unpredictable.

"Did you bring provisions sweetheart?" Mandy asked Nathaniel.

Nathaniel pulled out a shotgun, cocking it with a grin. "Do you even have to ask honey?"

Autumn and Rick exchanged concerned looks.

"You cannot shot Matt and the others," Eric said firmly. "They aren't *monsters* and that is what my potions are for, if the dust doesn't do the trick."

"We need to be prepared," Nathaniel said, still holding the shotgun.

"Fair enough but it will *not* come to that Nate. I have sedation potions with me," he reached into his satchel, pulling out syringes. "You stick them with the needle and its lights out."

"Or maybe they want help? Maybe they will come willing and get the cure from us," Rick said, his face hopeful.

Mandy let out a frustrated sigh. "Not bloody likely."

Autumn was listening to the conversation at hand but her body was staying alert by instinct. Her eyes darted around, her muscles tensed, and her ears perked up. Her senses were working overtime so when she heard *something* howling in the distance, she was hardly surprised. It sent chills down her spine and she looked at the others to see if they had heard it too.

Suddenly, they had all gone silent.

They definitely had.

"Did you hear that?" Nathaniel said, his lips curling into a smile. "The wolves have our backs."

* * *

The light from multiple flashlights danced on the caves walls as Autumn and the others moved through with caution. The rising temperatures of summer gave the cave a damp, musty smell but everything else looked the same as before. With the exception of the lack of blood thirsty demons, of course.

As they trekked along, even the slightest noise made everyone stop in their tracks. However, it was mostly silent, so quiet that Autumn was starting to think the rumor Stuart had heard might be false.

They had been walking for a while when Rick stopped abruptly, his eyes darting around searchingly.

"Did you hear that?" he asked, his voice barely a whisper.

Autumn looked around, feeling panic start to rise in her belly. She hadn't heard anything but if Rick had, it wasn't anything good.

"I can't hear anything over Mandy's heavy breathing," Nathaniel muttered.

Mandy nudged him in the ribs. "Or your flapping gums!" She grimaced. "What did you hear Rick?"

"Voices. Not far from here either," Rick said as he began walking again. "There are hidden coves all throughout this cave. We should check those out."

Everyone seemed in agreeance with Rick's plan, so they set off again, with Rick leading them through the maze of stone. Last time Autumn was here, she didn't notice the cave was so massive. Looking at it, without the mass of monsters inhabiting it, the cave was like a labyrinth. There were so many areas and tucked away spaces; it would take someone hours to thoroughly explore.

A sudden flash of red caught Autumn's flashlight, starling her. She slowly moved closer to the rocky surface to investigate.

There was writing on the cave wall, in dark blood-red spray paint. Each word was slightly smeared, with a tail of red paint dripping from the letters.

THEY WILL RETURN.

The others stopped, reading the ominous message before them.

"Any guesses on who *they* are?" Mandy said sarcastically.

Eric's eyes blazed with white-hot rage. "Those idiots are trying to reawaken the darkness."

The sound of voices, so loud and clear this time everyone heard them, echoed throughout the cave. It was obvious where the sound was coming from, so they continued on, making their way towards the chatter. They followed a long, narrow pathway, away from the main cave trail, until the voices got loud enough to distinguish words.

Autumn held a finger up to her lips. She wanted to hear what they were saying.

They edged in closer, hidden behind a wall of jagged rock.

Inside a cove, buried deep within the cave walls, a light radiated. Autumn didn't realize it right away, until she smelt burning embers. It was firelight she was seeing.

A female voice spoke, steady and determined. "We humbly come to bring you offerings of blood sire. I will begin with my blood, fresh from my veins, pulsating with life."

The sound of flesh being sliced resonated out and Autumn flinched.

A male voice spoke next. "I offer you the blood of my true love."

Each of them offered up blood and spoke of where it came from. Family, friends, lovers and strangers. Just the thought of it made Autumn's blood run cold.

"Please let these offerings be sufficient," the female said. "We have come to watch you rise and bring forth your hordes of demons, once more. Reign will be yours Queen Bianca."

Autumn looked to Eric. His body was tensed, his face contorted in rage.

He knew what was going on. They all knew.

These teenagers were trying to undo the cleansing. They were trying to revive Bianca, using blood magic. They were preforming a ritual.

Autumn didn't speak. No one did. If they wanted to get the jump on these people, they needed to be stealthy. Rick handed Autumn her scythe, his eyes trained on hers. She knew, without words, what he was saying. As much as they wanted to save these people, they might not be able to.

Autumn gripped the metal scythe in her hands. It felt familiar, almost comforting in her grasp.

Everyone was going in armed. Rick had his sword, Nathaniel his shotgun, Mandy a handgun. Eric even had an antique dagger that Arabella had gifted him for graduation.

"When I give the signal," Rick whispered. "We go in. Remember, no violence unless it is completely necessary. We want to save these people but if they attack-"

"We defend ourselves," Nathaniel offered and Rick nodded. "Exactly."

When everyone was ready, Rick gave the go-ahead. Together, they began moving into the cove, deliberately and cautiously. Autumn noticed, as they got closer, the burning fire wasn't the only source of light. Candles and torches were lit within the cove. They flickered, casting strange almost specter-like shadows throughout the cave.

She stepped further into the cove. She saw eight people standing in a circle around a blazing fire. They were dressed in flowing red robes, belted with gilded tassels. Hoods draped across their heads and their faces were marked with blood-red streaks. Autumn felt her insides churn when she realized the splashes of red were most likely, actual blood.

All of a sudden, one of the robed figures turned to face them. Sliding the hood down slowly, a face was finally revealed.

Autumn recognized him instantly.

It was Matt.

His lips curled into a fiendish grin. "Looks like we have company sycophants."

18

Autumn had her scythe at the ready. It felt wrong to be pointing weapons at human beings, but Nathaniel was right: they needed to be prepared.

"You know these people Matthew?" A girl spoke grimly. Sliding down her hood, Autumn saw she had a flowing golden mane and icy blue eyes.

"Not well," he said offhandedly. "But I have seen them around."

"They need to leave *now*," hissed another robbed girl. "They are impeding us. We need to finish the ritual."

Matt nodded. "I understand. Time is of the essence."

He turned back to Autumn and the others, his expression taciturn.

"Unless you want to be sacrificed, go and don't return. This isn't your concern."

"Actually, it is," Rick said firmly. "We aren't going anywhere."

"We came here to help you," Autumn said.

The blonde girl looked at them with distrust. "That is a little hard to believe when you have weapons pointed at us."

"We aren't going to use them," Autumn began.

"*Unless* you give us trouble," Nathaniel added, his tone hard.

"Matt." A tall lanky boy with dark hair stepped forward. "Enough with the niceties. We must finish the ritual."

Matt scowled at Autumn and the others. He was clearly growing impatient but he didn't move towards them or try to start a fight. Instead, he just smiled, a maniacal, hideous smile that made Autumn quiver.

"If you won't leave, so be it. When we summon her, she will come and devour you all whole like the pathetic fodder you are."

He pulled his hood back up and followed the others back into the circle.

"Son of a bitch," Mandy muttered and she launched herself at the closet person, the blonde, gripping the needle in one hand and her gun in the other.

The girl shrieked as Mandy stuck the needle into her arm, the tip piercing easily through the flimsy fabric of the robe.

The girl stumbled back, gripping her arm in pain.

"What did you do you little bitch!" she screeched.

"I tranquilized you," Mandy said bitterly. "You guys are getting our help, whether you like it or not."

Rick had given them all portions of the magic dust in small satchels. Mandy pulled her bag out and sprinkled the dust onto the girl, who lay on the cave floor, her eyes looking heavy.

She coughed as the dust overwhelmed her senses.

"What is that stuff?"

"Get away from her!" Matt was coming towards Mandy. But it was too late. The girl's eyes fluttered open one last time, then slowly closed and she fell into a peaceful sedated sleep.

As Matt edged closer to Mandy, Nathaniel pointed his shotgun at him, cocking it.

"Back off dude. It's over. You guys will take the antidote willingly."

"Antidote?" Matt trembled with rage. "For what?"

"We are pretty sure you are all possessed by the darkness that once resided here," Eric explained.

"That isn't possible!" One of the hooded girls piped in. "We are reviving the queen of our volition."

"You *think* you are," Eric corrected her. "But really, she has you doing her bidding. All of you must have had contact with these caves before we cleansed them. It is the only way to explain the possessions."

Matt looked at Eric, his brow furrowed in confusion.

"You are the band of so-called *heroes* that purified this place and slayed the queen Bianca and her horde?" he asked bitterly. "No wonder you came back to encumber us."

"Regardless of why you *think* we are here, you have no choice now," Rick said soberly.

"We still outnumber you!" Matt shot back.

Rick chuckled lightly.

"You may have numbers Matt but *we* have weapons."

* * *

Realizing they had no other choice, the group of misguided teenagers allowed Autumn and the others to sprinkle them with the magical dust. The blonde would remain sedated for the rest of the night. The others were instantly relieved of their possession. When Autumn spoke to Matt, he explained his mission. He and the others were to gather blood for a ritual to revive Bianca and in turn reawaken the caves festering darkness. He said he and his friends had entered the cave as a dare six months ago. Though they didn't delve too deep into the caves they were immediately bombarded by a strange thick mist. The mist itself seemed harmless enough. They hadn't become ill or poisoned so Matt and the others thought nothing of it.

Then the dark thoughts began.

"We all became consumed by the need to revive Bianca," he said grimly. "We gathered blood. We never killed anyone. Just took enough from each person to complete the ritual. With eight of us gathering, it didn't take long."

"I loved her. Allison, I mean. I didn't want to hurt her. I just couldn't help myself. The ritual, Bianca, it was all that mattered."

Autumn could see the sorrow and remorse in his eyes. It made the weariness of his face, the bags under his eyes, his sallowness, more noticeable.

"I saw her at graduation," Autumn said quietly.

"How is she?"

"She is doing better. She was with her family. She seemed happy."

He smiled, a huge grin that touched the corners of his eyes.

"I'm glad to hear it. She deserves to be happy."

* * *

"They did it. Incredible."

The girl couldn't believe a group of teenagers had managed to cure the possessed. It was remarkable, really.

"I'm hardly surprised," the man said as he clicked away on the keys of his high-tech laptop. "Did you tell Blaze?"

"Already heard." Blaze appeared suddenly through the nestling of trees. "Edmond was right all along about them."

The girl sat against a tree, staring at the sky. The full moon glowed like a beacon and the stars were like sparkling diamonds interwoven throughout the blanket of black.

"*You* knew he was *the one*," she said, her eyes still fixed on the heavens. "Edmond had visions yes, but it was your instincts Blaze that got us this far. Give yourself credit, when it's due."

"Thank you Raven but it was Edmond's prophecies that led me to him and the others."

Blaze was modest. Despite being a leader, he knew his strengths and weaknesses quite well. He also recognized that without his team, he was just one man.

Without them, he didn't stand a chance nor did the prophecy.

"Tracer, where is Night Owl at? He was supposed to be here tonight." Blaze spoke to the young man typing away on his laptop.

"He was here," Tracer said looking up from the screen. "He saw dinner and went to chase it."

"He's hunting again?" Blaze asked in disbelief.

"Night Owl loves the thrill of the chase," Tracer said, smirking. "About as much as you love your guns Sir."

Blaze shook his head, slightly amused. "What is it this time?"

"A rabbit."

"Can't he just eat hamburgers like the rest of us?"

"Not much of a chase getting those."

"I'm impressed by them," Raven added. "They went into that cave and did what had to be done. After what they've been through, it couldn't have been easy going back there."

"Nothing the comfort of a gun in their hands couldn't fix," Blaze said, patting his holster proudly.

Tracer, who was back to his typing, looked up again.

"I beg to differ. They are still learning how to shoot properly."

"Meaning?" Blaze pressed him.

"Meaning I feel more comfort when they aren't wielding loaded guns around civilians."

Blaze looked thoughtful. "They have come a long way and proven to us what they are capable of."

"And yet we still leave them in the dark."

Blaze was about to reply to Tracer's remark but the sound of approaching footsteps made him look out into the forest. He watched as light weaved through the pitch black, growing brighter as it got closer. A figure stepped out from the trees.

"Hello all."

Night Owl stood there, lantern in hand, looking ragged and out of breath.

"Enjoy your dinner?" Blaze said, unable to resist the opportunity to rib his comrade.

Night Owl rubbed his belly dramatically. "I did indeed, but it was quite the chase. That rabbit was quick!"

"Or you are just getting old," Tracer teased.

"We are all getting old," Night Owl said plainly. He turned to Blaze, his face grim. "How did they do?"

Blaze took a seat beside Raven against the huge evergreen tree.

"They cleansed them. It wasn't much of a fight either. I was quite impressed. I admit I was a little worried they might need to recruit those giant wolves again."

"Not me," Night Owl said, pulling his shabby baseball cap off and smoothing his hair. "They do need help here and there but they're strong. They have some combat training."

"According to my records, research and analysis," Tracer began.

"You mean your *hacking*," Raven corrected him as she stood up, dusting the dirt off her jeans.

Tracer ignored her. "Eric King has been honing his craft for years. Rick Jacobs knows martial arts. Ditto for the little spitfire."

"Mandy Jensen," Blaze said.

Tracer nodded. "Nathanial Abrams was gun trained from a rather young age. His father wanted him to be able to defend himself *and* hunt food. He is actually survival trained."

"That only leaves the other girl," Raven said. "Autumn Kingston."

Tracer smirked. "Not my type but even I can appreciate how beautiful she is."

Raven crossed her arms over her chest, looking irritated.

"It doesn't matter how *beautiful* she is Tracer. That won't help her in a fight!"

"She could be the bait!" Tracer joked.

"Of course the woman is the bait," Raven growled.

"She has been training adamantly with her friends. She is improving."

"I never questioned her tenacity," Raven said sharply. "I just hope she can keep up. If anything were to happen to her, we would be up shits creek…" she trailed off.

"We can't be sure she is the one," Blaze interjected.

"Or that she *isn't*," Night Owl added pointedly. "I have seen them together Blaze. They have the spark."

"A spark and an inferno are two different things Night Owl," Blaze said, looking up at the star-filled sky. "But you can't have one without the other."

Suddenly, beyond the sound of crickets chirping and owls hooting, a bloodcurdling scream escaped into the night. Blaze looked at the others, his loyal team. He didn't need words. They were already in tactical mode.

Raven reached into her bag, pulling out her quiver and bow. Night Owl had his rifle and Tracer had his staff. Blaze drew out his lucky gun from his holster. He called it *bullseye* because it never missed a target.

They had no light, besides the stars and moon, to guide them as they moved through the trees and brambles, as quietly as possible. They didn't want to alert whoever was out there that they were coming. The screams continued, getting louder and more urgent.

It didn't take them long to find the source.

Not far from them, in the clearing, was a body. Crumpled on the ground, wailing, the body seemed to shiver, despite the humidity.

Blaze looked around, his senses keen, searching for anything out of place. Finding nothing out of the ordinary, he motioned for the others to follow.

As they moved in closer, they realized it was a boy. His clothes were tattered and filthy and he smelt of sweat and fear.

His screams stopped temporarily and he looked up at them tentatively.

Blaze knelt over the boy, being careful not to startle him.

"We are here to help you," he said gently. "Are you alright?"

The boy said nothing, just shook his head. *No.*

"Tracer, get your kit and check him over," Blaze instructed. "Raven, do you have any water in your bag?"

"Yes Sir," Raven said as she began rummaging through her backpack. She found the bottle and unscrewed the cap as Blaze and Tracer helped the boy sit up. She handed him the water.

"Can you hold it? Do you need help?" She asked. The boy said nothing and grabbed the bottle. He drank the water, guzzling it eagerly until the bottle was empty.

Using a flashlight to see in the darkness, Tracer quickly looked the boy over.

"He has some cuts and bruising, but nothing life threatening," Tracer said. "We should take him back to the medical centre for a full examination though."

Blaze looked at the boy sympathetically. Though he was silent, his eyes told a story. The tale of a frightened boy who was abandoned in the woods, discarded after going through something that was obviously horrific.

"We are going to help you," Blaze said, his tone even and calm "But first, can you tell us your name?"

The boy looked away, his expression hesitant. He wasn't sure he could trust them. Blaze knew that much. He didn't push the issue, letting the silence stretch on for minutes before the boy finally answered.

"My name is Andy. Andy Carson."

19

"Can I get a medium latte with milk and a mocha shot?"

The lady at the counter, dressed in a floral sundress and oversized sunglasses, looked at Autumn impatiently.

"Of course." Autumn smiled, punching the order into the register. She had been smiling so much today, her face was starting to ache. "That will be 5.50."

The lady furrowed her brow in confusion. "5.50?"

Autumn smiled again. "Yes."

"For a medium latte?

"Yes."

The lady tapped her fingers on the counter, her lips pursed in agitation.

"*That* is just ridiculous. I could make my latte at home for less!"

Why don't you then? Autumn wanted to scream, but she didn't.

Besides, she wasn't surprised by her reaction. She had been working at the coffee shop in the bookstore for two weeks and numerous patrons felt the need to complain about the beverage prices.

The lady continued to tap her fingers, clearly expecting Autumn to fix this expensive injustice.

Autumn looked behind her. Her barista was busy making the pervious order for a man who patiently awaited his coffee.

She was on her own.

"I'm sorry but I can't change the price," Autumn said diplomatically. "I will gladly void the order if you wish."

The lady pushed her giant sunglasses atop her head, rolling her eyes.

"I never asked *you* to change the price or void anything but *this* is outrageous."

Autumn's blood began to boil. She was getting nowhere with this irrational woman.

"Would you like to order something else? Perhaps a regular coffee?"

"I don't want a regular coffee!" She was shouting now. Other customers looked up from their conversations and novels to watch this irate stranger having a total meltdown.

"I want a *not* overpriced medium latte with milk and a mocha shot!"

Autumn's co-worker, Gina, looked over at her, concerned. "Aut, do you need help?"

She shook her head. "I'm good Gina."

She didn't want to appear useless. She had been here two weeks now. She had to deal with ridiculous customers on her own. This wouldn't be the first or last time she was faced with an angry individual.

"If you want your original drink, that will be 5.50," Autumn said firmly. She could see beyond the annoyed woman, a huge line was forming. They were getting backed up in the middle of the afternoon because of her.

The lady snorted in disbelief and opened her mouth to speak but a voice cut her off.

"Look lady, the girl can't adjust the prices for you. She only works here. So either pay the poor girl, who in my opinion, has been infinitely patient considering your rudeness, or move on so the rest of us can pay for our *overpriced* drinks."

Autumn froze up, her heart caught in her throat. She knew that voice.

It was her former guidance counselor Ryan Garrison.

He met Autumn's gaze for a second and winked before turning his attention back to the woman. She said nothing, but glared at Ryan before heading towards the door while muttering something about *the world going crazy.*

Ryan approached the counter, his smile warm and familiar. Today he was dressed in jeans and crisp white t-shirt. His dark hair was unkempt and he sported some serious five o'clock shadow, but he still looked handsome enough to make Autumn's stomach flutter.

"Good morning Ms. Kingston," he said. "Excuse me. I mean, *Autumn.* You aren't a student anymore."

Autumn's cheeks burned. "Hey Mr. Garrison."

"Ah ah ah," he scolded her teasingly. "Call me Ryan."

"Alright Ryan," she said unsurely. "What can I get you?"

Ryan pulled out his wallet. "A large coffee, black."

Autumn punched the order into the register and started on his drink.

"Thanks for what you said to that woman," she said, grabbing an empty cup and pouring the coffee into it. "She was being completely irrational."

"No problem. I am happy to help," he said casually. "She was a real piece of work."

Ryan and Autumn continued their conversation while Autumn finished his order. He asked how she liked her job, how Rick and the others were doing and other general chitchat.

She was putting his money into the register when Gina came over, her eyes fixed on Ryan's handsome face.

"Autumn, you never told me your boyfriend was older and so handsome," Gina said, placing a hand on her hip.

Autumn *never* discussed her personal life in detail at work. Rick, her friends, her family, she kept all those things to herself. This left all her coworkers clueless when it came to her love life.

"Gina, this is Ryan Garrison, my high school *guidance counselor*."

Ryan nodded at her politely. "Hello there."

Gina's face brightened at the news that Ryan *wasn't* Autumn's boyfriend. She reached over the counter and jutted her hand out towards him.

"I'm Gina Robins. Nice to meet you."

Ryan shook her hand. "Likewise."

He turned back to Autumn. "I'm meeting someone in the bookstore so I should be going."

Autumn handed him his coffee, unsure of what else to say. She had never felt this uncomfortable around Ryan in the past. Then again, they had always been guidance counselor and student, until now.

"Thanks again for what you said to that lady."

"Anytime." His eyes locked onto hers. "I'll be seeing you."

He turned to Gina. "Nice meeting you Gina."

She grinned, her smile so wide it was almost unnatural. "You too Ryan!"

Autumn watched as he sauntered past the coffee shop tables, through the attached bookstore and out of sight.

"Did you hear that?" Gina grabbed Autumn's forearm. "He remembered my name!"

Autumn forced a smile. Being in retail was great practice for feigning smiles. She didn't have the heart to tell Gina that Ryan had a girlfriend. A beautiful one, at that.

Instead, she said nothing and got ready to serve the next customer.

* * *

Autumn roamed around the bookstore on her break, taking in all the new novels. She told herself she wasn't searching for Ryan, to spy on him or otherwise, but even she knew better. She wondered *who* he was meeting, if it was his girlfriend, the leggy beauty or someone else. Mandy and her were still trying to dig up information on him. So she shouldn't feel *guilty* she wanted to know right?

A text message alert jolted her from her thoughts. She pulled out her cell. It was from Mandy.

Just saw the news. They found Andy Carson.

Autumn and the others were convinced, whoever was after Rick, also took Andy. Autumn texted back: *Is he alive?*

Yes. He said a group of people dropped him off at his house after nursing him back to health. He has no idea who they were.

Is there anything else? Anything we can use to figure out who's after Rick?

Mandy didn't answer right away and Autumn waited, absently flipping through a book. A few minutes later she got another message.

Nope. He doesn't remember anything. Just camping with his friends. Everything after that is blank. I texted Eric about it. He thinks his memory was wiped.

Autumn's stomach flipped unpleasantly. They were back at square one. The spying on Ryan, the cryptic blogger, and now Andy; they had no leads and the danger Ryan had spoken of was slowly stalking them. They were rudderless and helpless.

She felt panic choking her, threatening to take over, when a voice called her name, pulling her back from the brink.

She looked up and saw Stuart approaching. She blinked her eyes, unsure if she was seeing correctly.

Stuart was usually unkempt, filthy and dressed in ragged clothes. Now he stood before her in a tailored blazer, a dress shirt, and crisp slacks. His sandy brown hair was neatly combed, his face clean shaven.

"Stuart? Is that you?" she asked, unable to hide her astonishment.

He bowed ceremoniously, a huge grin on his face. "I clean up alright huh?"

"Are you kidding? I barely recognized you!" Autumn admitted. "Do you always dress up to go shopping for books?"

"Actually, I have a job interview here," he said, throwing his shoulders back with pride.

"Really? I work at the coffee shop next door," Autumn said excitedly. "We will be neighbours Stuart!"

Stuart beamed, the corners of his eyes crinkling. "Well isn't that serendipitous."

Autumn's heart swelled with happiness. Stuart was always good-natured and it was nice to see him having a run of good fortune. He deserved it.

"I shouldn't keep you," she said, reaching out to touch his shoulder. "Good luck with your interview."

"Thanks sweetheart." Stuart began fussing with his shirt. "They won't hire a guy who can't button his own shirt properly."

As Stuart adjusted his shirt, it shifted and as it did Autumn saw it, clear as a day, on his chest.

It was a tattoo.

A black tribal design, with intricate swirls and lines.

Her heart stopped for a second, her mouth ajar.

She had seen that tattoo before, on someone else's chest, not long ago.

Stuart had the *exact* same tattoo as Ryan Garrison.

20

Sitting in Eric's massive library, Autumn was jotting down notes in a blue spiral notebook. Her and Rick, Mandy and Nathaniel and Eric were sitting around a crackling fire, trying to piece together the puzzle that haunted them all.

Who was after Rick and what exactly was the danger Ryan had warned Autumn of?

On a large corkboard stationed in front of them, were the clues.

The partially torn photo of Ryan and their elusive saviour with the jet black hair. A detailed drawing Autumn sketched of the tattoo Ryan and Stuart shared. A clipping from the newspaper discussing the five missing Whitan High students. The front page of the *Whitan Weekly* with a story on Andy Carson's return. And lastly, a print out of the blog entry implicating DSI.

Autumn looked down at her notebook, reading her musings so far.

1. Dangerous people are after Rick and they are most likely linked to the abduction of Andy Carson
2. The same people that took Andy likely infiltrated Whitan High and snatched the five students
3. Stuart is hiding <u>something</u> involving Ryan, the shared tattoo is proof but of what?
4. The mysterious blogger seems to think DSI is involved with <u>everything</u>
5. The identity of the missing person in the torn photo; could it be Stuart?

Autumn sighed, burying her head in her hands. All she saw was more questions not answers.

Eric was looking through a book of ancient symbols, trying to decipher the tattoo. He was so engrossed he barely heard the knocking on the library door.

"Yes?" he said, his eyes not leaving the pages.

"It is me Mister Eric."

It was Simon, Eric's butler.

"Come in Simon."

Simon stepped in, carrying a large silver tray filled to the brim with appetizers. Dressed in an impeccably pressed tuxedo, with his silver fox hair combed flawlessly, he looked rather dapper. Simon regarded them all with a warm smile and everyone exchanged greetings.

"I have the refreshments you requested Mister Eric."

Eric looked up from his reading.

"Thank you kindly Simon. Can you leave the tray on the coffee table please?"

"Of course," he said, bowing slightly. After he had put the tray down, he looked to Eric expectantly.

"Will you be needing anything else Mister Eric?"

"The minibar is stocked with beverages?"

"Of course. Mrs. Anderson took care of it this morning."

"That will be all then," Eric said graciously. "Enjoy your night Simon."

Simon smiled pleasantly and turned to go but before he reached the door he froze.

"Oh curses! I nearly forgot."

Eric raised his eyebrows inquiringly. "Yes Simon?"

"Ms. Arabella said she will be stopping by. She thinks she might have something to aid you all in your endeavour."

Eric nodded. "Wonderful. Please send her this way when she arrives."

When Simon had gone, Rick made a mad dash for the snack tray, his eyes wide with anticipation.

"Hallelujah food!" he said, as the book he was thumbing through got tossed haphazardly onto the couch.

"Abandoning the research already?" Eric asked, not sounding the least bit surprised.

"Dude I can't concentrate on an empty stomach and my tank is empty," Rick said as he began piling food onto a plate.

Nathaniel piped in, "You are *always* hungry dude."

"Which explains his attention span," Mandy mused as she grabbed a plate for herself.

Eric sighed and slammed his book shut. His brow knitted with frustration, he looked at Autumn and said, "Are you sure this sketch of the tattoo is accurate?"

Autumn looked up from her notebook.

"Every detail Eric. You should know by now. I don't forget anything."

Autumn had a remarkable memory. Faces, names, birthdays, her mind retained it all. Her mother and father were convinced she had an eidetic memory.

"These books belonged to my parents," Eric said. "They have symbols in them dating back centuries and there is nothing that matches what you saw on Stuart and Garrison."

Between mouthfuls of cheese Rick added, "I have known Aut my entire life and I can tell you her mind is a vault."

Eric stood up, went to the shelf and began hunting through the mass of occult books.

"I had a book, a really old one, maybe it might be in there. The only problem is the language is ancient so it needs to be translated."

Mandy, who was sitting on the couch with Nathaniel, dived into her plate of snacks and said,

"So are we still thinking Stuart is the missing person in the photo with Ryan?"

"I am just guessing," Autumn admitted.

"They are in cahoots!" Nathaniel erupted. He grinned. "I have *always* wanted to say that."

"I can't believe Ryan showed up at your work Autumn," Mandy said, stabbing at a piece of fruit with her fork. "He misses you."

Rick's face inflamed with anger. "Geezerson *has* a girlfriend Jensen."

"And she is gorgeous, might I add," Autumn pointed out.

Eric's frustrated sigh cut through the conversation.

"I don't understand," he said as he continued riffling through the books. "This book was sitting on my shelf the last time I saw it."

Without warning, the library doors flew open and Arabella King strutted in, carrying a stack of books. Dressed in a leather dress, with her auburn ringlets framing her heart-shaped face, she smiled a toothy grin.

"Evening ragtag band of misfits," she said as she sauntered towards her brother.

"I believe I may have the book you are so adamantly searching for Eric. I borrowed some books when I was here last."

"Without telling me?" Eric's eyes narrowed.

"The books are ours to share brother dear," she said, placing them on the wooden table with a thud. "I didn't think you would care. Most of these books had quite a thick layer of dust on them. So either you aren't reading them or Mrs. Anderson isn't doing her job."

Eric groaned with exasperation and began looking through the book pile. Arabella glanced at the corkboard in front of her. She tapped her black leather boot against the floor rhythmically, taking all the information in.

"So you guys are trying to figure out what the tattoo means?" she said. "That's why you're all in here reading through ancient texts and wasting a beautiful summer evening."

Nathaniel threw his hands into the air. "That is *exactly* what I said!"

"We have been hunting for hours now to no avail," Eric said bitterly.

"I am well aware. Simon contacted me saying you were all holed up in here. He thought I may be able to help you with your dilemma." Arabella grinned wickedly.

Eric stared at her expectantly. "So can you help?"

Autumn's heart swelled with hope. If Arabella *could* help them, it would make a world of difference. The dead-end they were facing now was maddening and demoralizing.

"As a matter of fact I can," Arabella said plainly. "The books have nothing on the symbol that is the tattoo. None of the books do."

Arabella went over to a small cabinet located in the back of the room.

She turned to Eric. "Do you still lock it Eric?"

Eric rolled his eyes. "Does it matter Ara?"

Arabella grinned. "You know me too well little brother."

She raised her hand and waved it with flourish and the locked cabinet became unlatched and popped open, revealing an array of magical items.

"Why use a key when you can do *that*," Mandy said, looking envious.

Arabella grinned and began rummaging through the items, grabbing various assortments of candles bottles and herbs.

"That symbol is a combination of more than one component. It is quite unique, not easy to decipher, and I would bet my bottom dollar that is the intention."

"Are you saying our former *guidance counselor* is hiding something?" Rick asked wryly.

"I would say so and if this spell goes off without a hitch, we may know exactly what that is."

Arabella began placing all the different magical supplies on the coffee table. Eric put the rest of the books away as she set everything up meticulously. She lit numerous candles, poured various liquids into a scrying bowl and when everything was in its rightful place, she knelt in front of the table.

"Now does anyone have anything of Ryan's with them?"

"We have the picture," Nathaniel said, pointing to the corkboard.

Mandy shook her head and said, "We don't know if it came from Ryan sweetie."

Autumn thought about it. Had Ryan given her anything recently? Suddenly she remembered and her eyes lit up with excitement.

"I have something," she said and reached into her purse.

Rick gave her a look of disapproval. "What do you have of his?"

Autumn began searching through her purse until saw it, tucked neatly inside her wallet.

Ryan's business card.

"Found it!" she said, handing it to Arabella. Rick intercepted the card, his eyes narrowing as he examined it.

"When did he give you this Aut? And why does it have his cell number on it?"

Autumn felt guilt stabbing her insides. She hadn't told Rick about the card because she knew he would overreact. Now it looked like she was hiding something from him when she really wasn't.

"Rick, I thought you would be upset," Autumn began.

"Well you thought right Autumn!" Rick said sharply.

Autumn glared at Rick. She felt like she was being attacked and she didn't like it. There was nothing going on between her and Ryan and she had reiterated that to Rick about a thousand times.

"He was only trying to help *you!*" Autumn snapped. "He was worried about you being in danger."

"So he gave *you* his cell phone number not me?" Rick shot back. "How stupid does he think I am?"

Eric, always the peacekeeper, cleared his throat pointedly.

"I know we are about due for another lovers spat but if we want answers *tonight* you might want to let my sister do her thing."

Autumn and Rick glowered at each other, neither wavering.

Finally, Rick handed the card to Arabella, looking defeated.

"Go for it," he muttered, sulkily going back to his plate of food.

"So will the card suffice Ara?" Eric asked, looking relieved. "I know it's all about the strength of the items aura."

"I think we should be fine," Arabella said. "Can you distribute the candles Eric?"

"On it." Eric grabbed four votive candles, lighting each as he handed them out to his friends.

"I will use your energy to help guide me," Arabella said, looking from face to face. "You all know Ryan and any memories you have of him will strengthen the aura for the spell."

"Are you using the scrying bowl?" Nathaniel asked.

Arabella smirked in response.

Eric said, "She doesn't need it. Arabella is strong." He paused dramatically. "You'll see."

Arabella snapped her fingers with flourish and the lights in the library went out. The table, the couches and the countless books, were bathed in the warm glow of candlelight.

Everyone gathered around Arabella, burning candles in hand, watching her with a mix of curiosity and fascination. Gently she placed the business card into the bowl of liquids she had mixed together. Chanting in Latin, she closed her eyes and a dark haze of smoke began rising from the water. She took her candle and placed it against the card, igniting it with ease. It burnt quickly and efficiently, the smoke billowing even higher.

Rick watched the paper burn into nothing, a smug smile on his face. "I like this already."

When the flames had died out, Arabella poured another potion into the bowl. All the liquids inside began to congeal and harden, morphing into a wax-like substance.

Eric watched his sister, captivated, as she took her finger and began drawing the tattoo symbol into the wax.

She spoke in Latin again and Eric translated, "She is asking the magics to help decode the symbol."

Suddenly, Arabella's eyes flew open. Her iris's had disappeared, her eyes taking on a milky quality.

"A blood oath," she began, her words deliberate and pronounced. "A secret society."

Autumn watched Arabella, awestricken, her mouth agape. No one said anything. The library was silent as Arabella pressed on.

"I can see others with the same symbol on them. They were chosen by the gods of the wild to protect the humans and others like them. They wear this tattoo to represent their allegiance. They take the blood oath and they are branded for life."

Autumn silently wished to see everything, hell *anything*, Arabella was seeing. Like Arabella was suddenly telepathic, she waved her hand and said,

"I implore you, spirits of knowledge and vision, project onto them what my mind's eye can see."

Autumn watched as her candled flickered and snuffed out. Then the visions came.

It was dusk. The sun set in a gorgeous forest. Lush evergreens shrouded a group of people, none of whom Autumn recognized. Sitting on logs and boulders, a burning fire making up the centrepiece, they looked at him. Their eyes filled with pure devoutness and respect. Ryan Garrison appeared. He was the one they were watching so adamantly. He opened his mouth to speak and Autumn's heart clenched inside her chest. His lips moved, but she heard nothing.

The images began to fade until they vanished completely. Rick, Nathaniel, Mandy, Eric and Arabella gradually came back into focus. Autumn could tell by the expressions they wore, they had all seen everything Arabella had.

"I couldn't hear anything." Mandy spoke first, her face puckered in frustration.

Arabella's eyes were back to their stunning violet color.

"They must have wards up," she said sullenly. "To prevent outsiders from prying."

"So we are basically screwed?" Nathaniel muttered. "I guess a silent movie is better than nothing."

"It was more than just the missing sound. The wards were pushing me, fighting against my magics and trying to block my sight. That is why the vision ended so abruptly. But we are *not* down and out yet."

Arabella's face was set with determination. She reached for another vial and poured it into the scrying bowl. Next she added various herbs and once everything was settled inside the bowl, she closed her eyes. She began another rhythmic chant, her voice filled with ferocity and resolve.

"Arabella. Take it easy." Eric's tone was warning.

But she disregarded him and went on chanting, her concentration unwavering.

Autumn, who was still clutching her snuffed out candle, said to Eric,

"What is it?"

Eric sighed, rubbing his temples. It was moments like this, when he was perturbed, that he looked much older than his seventeen years. The youthfulness of his face disappeared and Autumn could actually see how fast Eric had to grow up and how hard life without his parents must have been for him.

"I admit my magical skills aren't as honed as Arabella's," he said. "But if something magical wants to keep you out, like wards for instance, you are best to abide it. There can be consequences. Magic is all about respecting rules, balance and limits. It keeps sorcerers from becoming too powerful."

Eric went on. "I have heard stories of sorcerers that became power hungry. Megalomaniacs. The more the magic took them over, the less human they became. They had to give up pieces of themselves, their pasts, their souls, in trade for the power they chased so adamantly. In the end, their thirst was unquenchable and their hunger insatiable."

Autumn felt chills trace down her spine.

"What can they do?" she asked.

"The better question is what *can't* they do."

The candles began flickering wildly, capturing Autumn's attention. She could feel the tension in the room building, yearning for its crescendo. Eric watched Arabella his face twisted with worry.

She continued her chant, the Latin words falling from her lips in a steady and rhythmic pattern. An unexpected gust of air whooshed throughout the room and she stopped, frozen in a place like a statuette.

Her eyes rolled back into her head, the milky quality returning to them.

Eric's face went ashen. "Arabella!"

Her head turned to look at him, but her face was a blank slate.

"Silence boy! Your sister is not home."

Autumn's skin prickled. This couldn't be good.

"Whoever you are, get the hell out of my sister!" Eric demanded.

Arabella's lips curved into a wicked smile. "Now now. No need to get testy. I do not intend to harm her. However, she is the one that interfered with *us*."

"Who are you?" Eric asked curtly. "You owe us that much."

"I owe you nothing," Arabella said sharply. "But if you must know, my name is Raina. Like your meddlesome sister, I am a sorceress. I have been chosen to protect the people you were using magics to spy on."

"We meant no harm," Eric said, his voice fraught with worry.

Arabella nodded slowly. "He knows you were watching. Anyone else would be dead," she said, smirking. "But you all entertain him so."

"Who is *he?*" Eric snapped, getting impatient.

"Don't play dumb boy. It doesn't suit you. You know who *he* is and he will give you answers in due time. Your patience will pay off." She went on. "But you must respect the rules of magic and the wards that keep you at bay."

Against her better judgement, Autumn moved towards Arabella.

"Aut what are you doing? Don't get close to her!" Rick shouted but Autumn ignored him.

"Please," she pleaded, her eyes meeting Arabella's dead ones. "I need answers. There are people trying to harm Rick and Ryan Garrison knows who."

Arabella said nothing. Instead, she stood up and moved towards Rick, her movements graceful and almost catlike.

Autumn's heart leapt into her throat. What had she done? Was this witch inhabiting Arabella's body going to hurt Rick? Relief flooded through her as Arabella took Rick's face gently into her hands.

"What are you doing?" He flinched, trying to pull away.

"You are Rick right?"

"I am."

Arabella studied him, her eyes tracing over every inch of him. Rick tensed up, his body rigid as her hands moved across his face to his chest.

"Relax boy. I am an ancient and worldly witch. I have no interest in taking you as a lover."

"Because *that*'s my biggest concern right now," Rick said sarcastically.

Her hands rested on his chest, directly upon his heart. She closed her eyes, her brow furrowed in concentration. Finally, she removed her hands from Rick and her eyes fluttered open. She looked at Autumn.

"You need not worry about him. He is resilient and skilled. His destiny precedes him. Also, he has wise and cunning allies looking out for him."

"The wolf men?" Nathaniel piped in and Mandy nudged him sharply in the ribs.

"Ow!"

"Don't interrupt."

Arabella crossed her arms, her white eyes focused on Mandy.

"The boy is thirsty for knowledge, yet you wallop him unkindly. Knowledge is power. Ignorance is weakness."

Nathaniel pumped his fist in the air. "In your face Mandy! Old witchy poo is on my side!"

Suddenly Nathaniel leapt from his seat like he had been prodded.

"OUCH!"

He looked at Arabella, eyes narrowed.

"Did you just *zap* me?"

Arabella frowned. "Yes. Do not call me *old*."

She looked back at Rick and said,

"The wolves are sage but you don't need to look far when it comes to allies. All your friends have strong auras and brave hearts. They may not be at the apex of their powers *yet* but eventually they will become forces to be reckoned with."

"Let's see you zap me then lady," Nathaniel muttered under his breath.

Arabella smiled at Rick. "You are safe. Wherever you go, whatever troubles you endure, rest assured you are protected by many. You must live to fulfil your destiny."

"My destiny?" Rick's brows knitted with confusion. "What do you mean?"

Arabella wagged her finger at him. "Ah ah ah. Sorry but that isn't my secret to tell. "It was quite an honor to meet you all. You're just as entertaining as he says."

She looked at Eric and said,

"I shall return your lovely sister to you. But be fair warned that next time you try meddling with my magics, I may not be as accommodating."

Eric said nothing. They all watched as Arabella closed her eyes and another strong gust of wind swept through the room. Arabella's hair whipped around her violently and silver light omitted from her form. The candles flickered wildly, threatening to extinguish and sink them into complete darkness. The winds stopped abruptly and Arabella stood there, violet eyes staring back at them. She opened her mouth, words trying to escape, but she only let out a feeble croak before falling to the floor with a piercing thud.

21

"Ara!" Eric hovered over his sister, his face a sheet of white. "Wake up!"

"Should I call 911?" Autumn offered but Eric just shook his head.

"She is breathing. She will be fine," Eric said weakly. "She is out cold. Raina taking over her body was probably exhausting for her. I warned her that dabbling in powerful magics could be dangerous."

"Apparently stubbornness runs in the family," Autumn said lightly.

Eric looked up at her, a slight smile on his face. "I've heard it's passed down through the generations."

Eric and Rick carefully lifted Arabella onto the couch. Eric covered her up with a blanket and sat down in the chair across from her. His face was twisted with worry, his dark eyes weary.

Autumn volunteered to continue researching, though she was certain they had hit another dead end. Raina had provided them with some answers but nothing concrete. They still had no idea *who* was after Rick, what DSI was or how anything, including Ryan and Stuart, fit into the equation.

The uncertainty of it all made Autumn's stomach knot up so she pulled a book from the shelf, hoping to distract herself. She didn't know how long she had been reading when the words in front of her began to blur and bleed together. She closed her eyes, for only a split second but her exhaustion overcame her, pulling her into a deep sleep.

* * *

Autumn awoke with a start.

Her heart was pounding, thudding so hard she thought her chest might explode. She could feel sweat tricking down her neck and warmth cocooning her. It took her eyes a minute to adjust to the dim lighting from the lantern beside her. She rubbed her eyes wearily before looking around.

She was in a sleeping bag, in the middle of the woods. A fire burned in front of her and she inhaled deeply, the smell of smoke and pine overpowering her nostrils. The embers were still blazing fiercely and she was overheating. A pool of sweat was forming on her lower back as she wiggled her way out of the sleeping bag, standing up to cool off.

Why am I here? The question danced inside her head, beckoning for an answer.

She snatched the lantern and began walking. Where to she had no idea.

She was suddenly aware of what she was wearing. A white lace nightgown, her long dark hair flowed behind her, her skin cooling instantly in the frigid night air.

Where is Rick? Did Arabella wake up yet? She didn't see anyone else. Was she alone, in the woods, camping in the middle of the night? The thought seemed absurd and she chuckled. Her laughter echoed vivaciously around her.

She trekked along, her skin prickling with cold and quickly becoming numb. Autumn didn't mind. The crunch of leaves startled her and she jumped. She caught movement in the corner of her eye. She held her lantern up, cutting through the darkness to see a figure standing against a tree.

Maybe they have the answer. Maybe they know why I am here.

Slowly and cautiously she moved towards the figure. When she got closer she realized who it was.

Her breath hitched and she couldn't move.

Leaning against the tree, eating a shiny red apple was Ryan. He looked up at her, unruffled by her sudden arrival. He was shirtless, his skin golden, muscles taut and defined. She took a deep breath, trying to steady herself. Her eyes fixated on the tattoo on his chest.

"Mr. Garrison?" She finally found words.

He bit into the apple, crunching as he chewed.

"It's Ryan remember? I am not your guidance consoler anymore."

"Sorry," she whispered. "I am having a hard time seeing you as anyone but my guidance counselor."

"Funny that," Ryan said. "I am having a hard time seeing you as a former student."

He moved towards her, a coy smile on his face. Her heart raced as he stepped close to her, so close she could feel his warm breath on her skin.

He touched her arm, gently trailing his warm fingers across her skin. They moved gradually along her shoulders then her neck before ending at her face. He cupped her cheeks in his hands, his dark eyes burning into hers.

"You are ice cold," he said.

"Never mind that," she said softly. She was trying so hard to focus but his touch was so distracting.

"Do you know why I am here?"

"Sweetheart, you are asking me?" Ryan asked. "*You* wanted to meet me here."

Autumn's emerald eyes were wide with shock.

She said, "Excuse me?"

"Let's go somewhere more private."

Ryan grabbed Autumn's hand and began guiding her through the maze of trees and brambles with ease and grace. She was aware of his hand clutching hers tightly and even more aware of how treacherous it was. Still, her instincts urged her not to let go and she willfully obeyed.

They pressed on together, quickly weaving through the entanglements of branches and leaves. Autumn felt light as a feather, her feet barely touching the ground as she moved. The journey was all consuming and her senses were in overdrive, taking everything in.

"Here we are," Ryan announced. They came to an abrupt halt, finally at their destination.

Autumn was breathless.

They were standing on a bluff that overlooked the ocean. The sun was cresting lazily in the horizon and the water was unlike any lake or river Autumn had ever seen. The water was crystal clear and so cerulean, it was almost hypnotic. It shimmered and rippled in the distance, the waves crashing gently against the rock face.

They sat down on the edge of the bluff, Autumn easing herself cautiously into a seated position. Her legs dangled over the edge and she automatically pulled them back for fear of falling. Ryan looked at her and chuckled.

Autumn shot him a dirty look. "What the hell is so funny about possibly falling to my death?"

"You can't die," he said simply. "Or have you not figured it out yet?"

Autumn looked at him, baffled. "Figured what out yet?"

"This isn't real," he said as he outstretched his legs. "You are dreaming."

Ryan kicked his legs back and forth, gazing out at the endless sea.

"You look stunned."

"I am," she said. "Stop kicking. Dream or no dream, you are making me nervous."

Ryan smirked at her and said, "Dream you is pretty feisty." He paused. "So why did you bring me here?"

Autumn looked at him, eyes narrowed. "Really? Are you still on that?"

"Autumn, I am telling you the truth. I can only enter your dreams if you let me. You wanted me here."

Autumn thought about it. It rang true, if only due to her subconscious. After all, they had been trying to figure out what Ryan and Stuart were hiding. Maybe this was her way of piecing it all together.

"Maybe this is what I wanted," she said finally. "But I already know you won't tell me anything I want to know."

Ryan looked at her, eyebrows knitted with confusion. "And why is that?"

"Because you aren't *actually* here and my mind holds the same information as when I'm awake."

"True but the sleeping mind can piece together parts of a puzzle that the wakeful mind cannot," Ryan said. "Your dreams can also reveal repressed feelings."

Autumn looked at Ryan and their eyes met once more. The lingering stare made her insides flutter and she tried to look away, but couldn't. He was so beautiful. His extremely symmetrical face, his crooked smile, his chiseled body. She grunted in exasperation, putting her head in her hands.

"There is nothing I'm repressing!" she said curtly. "Also, put on a shirt!"

"Your friend Mandy seems to think we have a spark," Ryan said, stretching his arms above his head with flourish. "Rick seems a teensy bit jealous too."

She bristled and said, "We aren't here to discuss my feelings towards you."

"So there are feelings to discuss?"

She ignored his prodding. "I want to know the truth... about you."

"Nice deflection," Ryan said. "You already know the truth about me. I am your former guidance counselor. And I am ridiculously handsome."

He winked at her and she rolled her eyes.

"Yes I know surface Ryan," Autumn said, frustrated. "Everyone knows him."

"Not everyone but that is how it works sweetheart. All you ever know about anyone is what they permit you to."

Autumn looked at him and said, "What do you want me to know about you?"

"Everything," he murmured. "And you will, in due time. You are hurtling towards the answers but the more you chase them, the further away they get." He paused. "Watched pot and all."

"I don't have time to wait," Autumn said. "Rick is in danger I can feel it."

Ryan's eyes softened. It was like he finally understood the message she was trying to get across: her love for Rick was strong and their bond was unbreakable.

She would do anything for him.

Even die for him.

"You don't need to worry about him Autumn. He is more capable than you know. Sometimes only when you're put to the test can you realize your true potential."

"Rick is everything I want him to be *now*," Autumn said, arms folded across her chest.

"He is thoughtful, selfless and loving."

Ryan smiled indulgently and said, "But he can be so much more. He needs to go through the trials set ahead for him, for him to be the man he was destined to be. If he doesn't, he will be a husk of the man he was meant to become."

Autumn opened her mouth to respond when the image came, tearing through her mind.

Rick on the battlefield, eyes ablaze, lips smirking, while wielding *his* sword tightly in his hands. Shadowed figures flanked him, and behind him, poised and ready for battle, was a full-fledged army. Faceless figures, prepared to strike when the time was right.

Ryan's hand touching hers brought her back.

"I need to go lovely. Duty calls," he said, pulling her up from the bluff.

"I saw Rick," she murmured. "He was about to fight."

Ryan took one last look at the ocean. "He looked happy didn't he?"

Autumn followed his gaze, taking in the beautiful blue with him. "He did."

She frowned and said, "In the vision I wasn't there with him."

"You will *always* be with him. Without you, Rick is rudderless. You are his compass."

Still holding his hand, Autumn looked at Ryan. "This man he becomes... Am I a part of his great destiny?"

Ryan looked back at her, squeezing her hand reassuringly.

"You aren't just *a* part of it Autumn. You are the most integral part. But I have already said too much. The powers that be won't like it but what can I say? I was coerced by your beauty."

Her cheeks flamed with embarrassment but she couldn't stop now. She had to know more, she needed answers.

"Tell me what happens now," she pressed. Her voice had an edge of desperation she reviled.

Ryan relinquished her hand and began walking towards the cliff edge. He looked over his shoulder at Autumn, a wicked grin on his handsome face.

"Now *I* jump and *you* wake up."

Autumn watched, fascinated and terrified all at once, as Ryan flung his body over the cliff and took a smooth swan dive. She heard the crash, loud and clear, as his body made contact with the water.

22

Autumn jolted awake. Her heart was pounding in her chest and sweat clung to every inch of her body. She brushed away the hair that was matted against her face and neck. Her eyes still adjusting, she looked around. Dawn streamed through the window, indicating she had indeed fallen asleep.

The room was familiar and unfamiliar all at once. The beautiful tapestries, the Persian rug, the huge bed with four iron posts, the dark and morose paintings on the wall. She was in Eric's house; that much she knew.

She wanted to get up. Go find Rick and the others but exhaustion washed over her. The dream she had just had forced itself to the forefront of her mind. It had felt so real, so visceral, like her and Ryan really had spent the night together. Her body prickled at the thought, her gut clenched with guilt. She laid back down, her body relaxing against the soft sheets and plush mattress.

I will just rest my eyes, she thought. A minute later, she had fallen back asleep.

* * *

"Rise and shine beautiful girl."

Autumn felt fingers gently tracing along her cheek. Her eyes fluttered open to see Rick lying beside her. He beamed at her, his ice blue eyes lighting up.

"Good afternoon sleepy head."

"Afternoon?" Autumn frowned. She had been asleep that long? "How did I end up in here?"

He kissed her on the forehead gently. "You zonked out so instead of letting you sleep on a stack of very uncomfortable books, I carried you up here to rest."

"What about you?"

"I helped everyone research for a couple more hours then I went to sleep. You must have been exhausted. You hardly stirred when I got into bed with you."

Abrupt banging on the door startled them both.

Autumn took a quick moment to sit up before calling out, "Come in."

The door flew open to reveal Nathaniel wearing a big dumb grin on his freckled face.

"Morning love birds, sorry to interrupt."

"No you aren't," Rick grumbled. "What is it?"

"Eric sent me up. Breakfast is served," Nathaniel said. "Oh and witchy woman is awake."

"Arabella?" Autumn asked, relieved. "She is alright?"

Nathaniel shrugged and said, "She zapped me again so I'd say she's fine."

Nathaniel led Autumn and Rick out of the spare bedroom and down the long corridor. Along the hardwood flooring was a long burgundy and gold carpet that extended throughout the entirety of the hallway. The walls boasted framed art prints and paintings and at the end of the hall were two large lion statutes on either side of the door.

The door opened up to a huge landing attached to a wooden spiral staircase. It corkscrewed down onto the next floor which took them into another hallway that led them to the massive kitchen.

Mandy, Eric and Arabella were seated at the rectangular table. No one was eating and the food on the table remained untouched. A variation of eggs, bacon, fresh fruit and waffles greeted Autumn and the smell made her stomach growl with hunger.

Eric looked up from his cup of coffee, his face ragged and his eyes weary.

"So the lovers finally join us," he said nonchalantly. "Long night?"

"Of researching and reading," Rick muttered grouchily.

Autumn and Rick found their seats beside Nathaniel and Mandy.

"Autumn, I trust you slept well?" Eric went on, passing her the tea pot. "Green tea?"

"Thanks," she said, grateful for the warm comforting beverage. "And yes I slept very well."

"Glad to hear it," Eric said, looking pleased.

Autumn looked at Arabella. Her color had returned. Her cheeks looked rosy and healthy, though she was being uncharacteristically quiet.

"How are you feeling Arabella?" Autumn asked, pouring tea into her mug.

"Much better. Having a spirit possess you, especially a witch spirit, really takes its toll on the body."

"I warned you it was risky Ara," Eric admonished her. "Trying to break through wards is always a gamble. You are just lucky she wasn't a malicious sorceress."

Arabella rolled her eyes. "I had to take the chance Eric. We needed answers and playing it safe wasn't getting us anywhere."

She looked back to Autumn. "It's a shame. I don't remember anything. Raina and I were sharing a mind and memories, if only temporarily. I was hoping I might remember *something* about Ryan or the tattoo but that witch is a crafty one." She smiled ruefully. "She left no traces or remnants in my mind. She is a very powerful and talented witch. I am actually rather jealous."

"So that brings us back to square freaking one," Rick complained between mouthfuls of bacon.

"How did the research go?" Autumn asked hopefully.

"Terrible," Mandy replied. Her eyes, much like Eric's, looked tired. "We were up most of the night and still nothing."

Autumn remembered what Ryan had said in her dream.

You are hurtling towards the answers but the more you chase them, the further away they get.

She knew it wasn't really him, it was her subconscious, but still the words rang true.

This whole time she had assumed Ryan was the key to Rick's salvation but maybe he wasn't.

Maybe Autumn, Eric, Nathaniel and Mandy were enough to save Rick.

Simon entered the room, placing a large tray of various pastries, doughnuts, muffins and cookies on the table.

Autumn, grateful for the sweets, thanked him. He smiled pleasantly at her. "Enjoy my dear."

Everyone ate in silence, their minds lost in various thoughts. Autumn was just finishing a chocolate doughnut when Nathaniel spoke.

"We need a night out!" he enthused. "A break from all this Geezerson symbol stuff."

Mandy rolled her eyes. "What did you have in mind Nate? Skateboarding?"

Nathaniel shook his head. "Nope. Conrad texted me. There is a party tonight at Glendale Forest."

"The forest by the caves?" Autumn chimed in. "Wonderful."

Arabella, who seemed intrigued, asked,

"What kind of party?"

"Just a bush party. Conrad said the more the merrier!"

Arabella looked at Eric disapprovingly. "We can't go."

Eric grimaced. "Why is that?"

"Because I am still your guest and we all know parties and me don't mix. Remember the last party I attended with you?" She grinned wickedly.

"How could I forget?" Eric said, forking a piece of watermelon into his mouth. "You spent the whole evening chatting up some guy. Another girl started flirting with him and *you* used magic to singe her eyebrows off."

Arabella threw her head back and began laughing heartily. "She deserved it. I saw him first!"

Eric sighed exasperatedly while rubbing his temples.

"You guys *do* deserve a break. I however, will pass. Firstly, I need to keep researching and secondly my sister can't attend parties due to her penchant for burning people's hair off."

"Man, I feel kinda bad leaving you here with all these stinky old books," Rick said, his mouthful of bacon.

Eric waved his hand in protest. "Don't worry about me. Go and enjoy the night. Be normal, act like teenagers."

"But you'll need help," Autumn began but Eric cut her off.

"You are going to the party Autumn Kingston," he said sternly. "End of story."

* * *

Four rowdy guys dressed in letterman jackets surrounded a beer keg. Red cups in hand they hollered then began to guzzle. Autumn watched as Ben Mills stumbled over to the keg, eyes hooded, looking wasted. He poured himself a drink and downed it as the other guys cheered him on.

Autumn crinkled her nose in disgust as Rick put his arm around her.

"There's someone I hoped I'd never see again."

Autumn frowned. "No such luck. He comes into my work daily for coffee."

Glendale Forest was packed to the brim with people and dancing, drinking and other general debauchery was on tap for the night. Music thumped from a booming sound system, a fire burned sending smoke billowing into the night sky. Autumn scanned the throngs of people for Mandy and Nathaniel to no avail.

"They went looking for Conrad. They will be back," Rick assured her. "Just relax sweetie."

He kissed her neck gently, making his way up her to her lips in haste. She kissed him back, falling into his familiar and comforting embrace.

"Get a room Jacobs!" Ben called out, his words barely decipherable through his slurring.

"Ignore him," Autumn instructed when she felt Rick's muscles tensing up.

She turned to Ben, glaring at him.

"Maybe if *you* had a girl to kiss you wouldn't be so interested in us."

"You just told *me* to ignore him," Rick said in disbelief.

"He is so aggravating I couldn't help it," Autumn grumbled.

Ben made his way over to them, his friends in tow.

He looked at Rick and said bitterly, "Getting a girl to fight your battles for you Jacobs?" Ben said. "Pathetic."

"You're calling me pathetic?" Rick shot back. "High school is over now Ben. You can take off the varsity jacket!"

"You have a big mouth Jacobs. You and *her*," he gestured to Autumn.

"I heard Candice dumped you Ben," Autumn spat. "Not the brightest girl but *that* was a smart move."

Ben's face went from smug to livid in seconds. Obviously Autumn had hit a nerve. His hands balled into fists as he stared Autumn down menacingly.

"You're a real bitch you know that Kingston?"

"Back off!" Rick was standing between Ben and Autumn now. His body language indicated he was ready to throw down.

"Now quit talking shit and fight me like a man Mills!"

"Gladly!" Ben replied and he and his goons began closing in on Autumn and Rick.

"What the hell is going on?"

Autumn turned to see Mandy, Nathaniel, and Conrad approaching. Conrad had brought his friends along and it occurred to Autumn she had never met them. Seeing them now, she understood exactly what Nathaniel meant when he had described his brothers buddies as *scary*. Their posture, body language and the distinct gleam of menacing in their eyes sent cold chills down her spine.

Ben must've felt the same, because he slowly stepped away from Autumn and Rick, his hands in the air like he was ready to surrender.

"Everything is cool man. We were just talking."

"Funny, it didn't look like friendly chitchat to me," Conrad said. "So how about you and your gang of weasels get lost."

Ben opened his mouth to argue but Conrad cut him off, barking, *"Now!"*

Autumn watched with delight as Ben and his minions scampered off looking shamefaced.

"Thanks for that." She smiled at Conrad gratefully.

Rick crossed his arms over his chest defiantly.

"I would've kicked Mills' ass if *you* hadn't shown up Conrad," he grumbled.

Conrad shrugged. "Sorry. I was just trying to keep the peace Rick."

"By putting the fear of God into those guys," Mandy said, smirking.

She reached out and grabbed Autumn's arm. "Boys, Autumn and I are going to grab drinks and some much needed girl talk. Try not to kill anyone."

* * *

"Are you drunk yet?" Mandy asked.

Autumn sipped the rum and cola, her eyes traced over the stars in the sky. Nestled inside the pitch black, they gleamed like beacons in the night.

"Buzzed," she said, turning to Mandy, a silly grin on her face.

The two girls sat, side by side, in vibrant yellow and orange lawn chairs. They had managed to find a mostly secluded spot tucked under a bunch of evergreens. In the distance, mirth and music resonated through the crisp night air.

They didn't discuss Ryan Garrison, the tattoo or DSI. In fact, they didn't talk much at all. They drank, looked up at the stars and enjoyed the peace and ease of being together.

Autumn rarely felt comfortable with silence. To her it always symbolized awkwardness. But she knew if she could sit with someone in complete and utter quiet it was a sign. She was comfortable with that person and relaxed around them.

She had felt it before, with Rick, Audrina, and her best friend Kristin. Now with Mandy. It spoke volumes about their friendship and how close they had become that the silence between them didn't make Autumn feel awkward in the least.

The silence broke suddenly when Mandy said, "I love him you know."

Autumn turned to look at her, hardly surprised. "Nate?"

She nodded slowly, a goofy grin forming on her face. "I never thought I would. I figured we would date, drive each other nuts and go our separate ways after graduation. But now, when I imagine my future the only thing I am sure of is him."

"It sneaks up on you doesn't it?" Autumn murmured.

"It does."

The sudden rush of footsteps running towards them jolted the girls from their conversation.

Seconds later Nathaniel appeared in the clearing, panting with effort, his face white as a ghost.

Autumn's body tensed and her stomach dipped unpleasantly. She stood up.

"What is it?" Mandy asked plainly.

"We were by the pond talking. I told Rick I would go get us some drinks and when I came back he was gone."

23

Autumn's blood ran cold.

"What do you mean he's gone?" she asked. "Did you try calling him?"

She pulled out her cell phone frantically and began dialing when Nathaniel spoke. "Don't bother."

He put out his hand which held Rick's cell phone.

Autumn looked at Mandy. Her expression was unreadable.

"We need to go back to the pond. See if we can find any clues," Autumn said finally.

Nathaniel nodded. "Conrad is checking around, asking if anyone might have seen him."

* * *

They arrived at the pond and began their search. It was dark and Autumn used her phone to light up the areas that weren't already highlighted by the moonlight. She was searching for something, *anything* that might show her where Rick was. She was examining the pond itself when she heard commotion not far from where she stood.

Autumn looked at Mandy and Nathaniel. Their expressions indicated they had heard something too. She motioned for them to follow her, and began running as fast as she could. Weaving through the masses of trees, branches and undergrowth, Autumn was thankful she had been training so much. Her endurance was unbelievable and she could hardly feel any fatigue as she raced along. She was barely winded when she stopped dead in the clearing. Her heart however, caught in her throat.

In the middle of the field was Rick. He was beaten, bloody and unconscious, his eyes blindfolded, his mouth gagged. Surrounding him were a dozen men in black combat attire. All of them had guns and all of those guns were pointed at Autumn and the others.

Nathaniel and Mandy slowed to a halt beside her.

"Holy shit," Nathaniel muttered.

One of the soldiers spoke into a headset. "We got company Commander."

Autumn stared at Rick, unable to correlate the beaten form with the man she loved and had just been with only an hour ago.

Compelled, she started moving towards him only to be grabbed. She looked over her shoulder and saw Mandy holding her arm.

"They have guns," she said plainly. "You can't."

The words failed to register and Autumn yanked her arm from Mandy's grasp.

A sudden violent hatred began bubbling up inside her. She looked at the soldiers, her eyes facing down cruel dead eyes and barrels of guns.

"Let him go." Her voice came out eerily calm. It sounded completely opposite of the bedlam and rage that swirled throughout her.

"Impossible." A voice spoke as a man stepped out of the shadows.

His lips spread into a haughty smile as he took Autumn and the others in.

"You see, we have been searching for Mr. Jacobs here for quite some time. We would've had him by now if our plan to retrieve him at your school that fateful day hadn't been foiled."

Autumn's mind flashed back to the news report after the attack on Whitan High.

The men were masked, prepared and announced they were looking for someone, though they didn't specify who.

Only that whoever it was wasn't there.

It was Rick. They *had* been after Rick. Her instincts, and Ryan's, had been right all along.

"What do you want with him?" Her voice was a low growl.

His eyes were stone-cold. "For me to know and you to never find out." He reached into his holster and pulled out a pistol.

He pointed it at Autumn, hands steady, face vacant.

"Looks like the end of the line for you sweetheart."

Autumn stepped back, trying to put distance between her and the crazed gunman. She was quick but she couldn't outrun a bullet. She had resigned herself to a grisly death when a large body darted in front of her.

"Picking on teenagers Commander Fleming? That is pretty low even for you."

Autumn knew the voice immediately.

Her white knight was none other than Stuart.

"Get the boy out of here!" Commander Fleming barked at his underlings. "Now!"

"Yes Commander Sir," The soldier replied, retrieving Rick's body.

Panic rose inside Autumn. They were going to take Rick. She tried to run after them but it was too late. A large van appeared and Rick was loaded into the back of it before she could reach him. The other soldiers stood by, guns at the ready, creating a blockade.

"Don't even think about chasing him." Stuart said, like he'd read her mind. "We will get him later. Right now, you and your friends step back. Things are about to get ugly."

"Go!" Commander Fleming growled. "All of you! Leave this idiot to me." He gestured to Stuart.

The soldiers didn't hesitate. They followed their orders in haste and piled into the van. The engine revved noisily as the vehicle sped off into night.

Autumn stood beside Mandy and Nathaniel, shivering despite the night's warmth.

Mandy and Nathaniel wore grim expressions. Both were thinking the exact same thing Autumn was.

Rick was gone.

Long gone.

Autumn felt Mandy's hand on her shoulder. "We will find Rick," she said comfortingly. "We will bring him home."

Autumn said nothing. She just watched as Stuart and Commander Fleming circled one another, sizing each other up.

Stuart had pulled out a large hunting knife to which Commander Fleming snorted in disbelief.

"You brought a knife to a gun fight! You think you stand a chance against me?"

"I *know* I do." Stuart paused for effect. "But someone else wants a piece of you more than I do buddy."

He stepped out of the shadows then. Broad and looming, his eyes burned like pits of fire.

Ryan Garrison was standing next to Stuart.

"You just had to make the dramatic entrance didn't you Ry?" Stuart joked as he joined Autumn and the others on the sidelines.

"Always," Ryan said with a wink before he turned back to glower at Commander Fleming.

"Are you ready Commander?"

The Commander said nothing. He just smiled sinisterly, pointed his pistol and began unloading rounds into Ryan's chest. The sound of the gunshots was like fireworks exploding in the dead of the night. A shrill scream of terror erupted from Autumn's throat.

She closed her eyes, unable to watch anymore. She felt disoriented and her heart pounded steadily in her ears. She was going to pass out if she didn't calm down. She inhaled deeply and exhaled slowly.

Ryan is dead.

Rick is gone.

It was only a matter of time now before Stuart was killed then Mandy, Nathaniel and her.

"No freaking way," Nathaniel said in disbelief.

Autumn opened her eyes and couldn't believe what she was seeing.

Ryan was still alive and he was convulsing.

His body rapt with tremors as his muscles tensed and stretched. Autumn could hear bones snapping and cracking as his form altered. Sharp claws sprouted from his hands and his jaw dislodged and reformed creating a vicious deadly maw filled with razor sharp teeth.

He was transforming and when it was over, Ryan Garrison was no longer. He was replaced by a figure Autumn recognized instantly.

Her saviour from the caves, the reason she still lived and breathed.

Ryan was the towering grey wolf.

A paradox to its uncanny beauty, the wolf growled menacingly as the bullet wounds in its body closed and healed like magic.

Autumn had no words. Instead, she blinked, willing herself to wake up but when she opened her eyes, the wolf was still there.

"Your eyes don't deceive you." Stuart's voice came from beside her now. "He's real."

"He is," She paused, looking for words. "A wolf."

"A werewolf," he corrected her.

"He is huge."

"And pissed. Aren't you glad he's on our side?"

She nodded in agreement, still mesmerized by the wolf.

"I just can't believe that wolf is Ryan."

"That's because it really isn't," Stuart said.

Autumn was confused by his statement. That was until she watched Wolf Ryan in action. He growled at Commander Fleming who reached into his holster pulling out another gun. Stuart sniffed the air then cringed.

"Silver bullets."

Commander Fleming gave a crooked grin and unloaded on the grey wolf.

The wolf, despite its enormous size, moved with grace and speed, dodging and weaving to avoid the bullets. It sprung into the air, hackles raised and landed mere inches from the commander. The wolf let out a howl that reverberated in the still night. Commander Fleming's face went ashen as the realization sunk in that his bullets had missed. He pointed the gun at the wolf again, hands trembling. The wolf lunged at him and he opened his mouth to scream but he didn't get the chance.

Wolf Ryan began tearing into Commander Fleming, ripping him to shreds with his deadly claws. The wolf showed him no mercy as he tore into his neck, not letting go until his body was unmoving and his eyes lifeless.

The blood, there was so much of it.

Autumn closed her eyes, knowing if she didn't, she would vomit.

When she opened her eyes Mandy and Nathaniel were standing there, their expressions a mix of fascination and wonder.

Autumn watched Ryan. He morphed back into a human and stood naked, his back to her.

She took him in, every inch of him. His long, lean physique and his taut, defined muscles. She felt her cheeks burning and quickly averted her eyes.

Stuart noticed her chagrin and grinned impishly.

"Ry, it isn't just the guys tonight. Maybe you want to grab some clothes?"

Ryan turned to look over his shoulder, smiling.

"Sorry about that," he apologized before darting off into the clusters of trees.

"No apology necessary," Mandy said, her eyes gleaming with appreciation.

Minutes later, Ryan returned. He appeared to have improvised clothing as he held a chunk of bush over his private parts.

"I seriously hope you get poison ivy," Nathaniel grumbled, his face twisted in disgust.

"Sorry. I wasn't planning on shifting tonight. Usually I bring extra clothes."

Mandy stared at Ryan's chiseled body in complete awe.

Nathaniel rolled his eyes at his lustful girlfriend. "Your mouth is hanging open Mand."

She replied, unfazed, "I am entirely aware."

Stuart chuckled lightly and looked at Ryan. "Your clothes are by the forest entrance. I figured you might need them."

"You are a lifesaver Stu!" Ryan said gratefully, taking off into the forest with haste.

"Or the bane of my existence," Mandy muttered as she watched Ryan's form fade into the distance.

Autumn heard the conversations going on around her but it was like she wasn't really listening. Her mind was trying to piece the night's events together but her brain was becoming inundated with information. Rick was taken. Ryan was a werewolf.

Now what?

Did they go find Rick? Where would they look? Who took him?

"Autumn," Mandy's voice cut through her thoughts. "Are you alright?"

"She's had a hard night." Stuart's voice seemed distant. "She needs sleep. You all do."

Had she gone catatonic or something? She stared at Mandy blankly, trying to form words but they wouldn't come. Her world was slowly closing in on her and her vision became hazy.

It was all too much. Everything was too much.

Her body went limp and the last thing she heard was someone yelling *catch her* and then the feeling of strong arms encircling her.

24

Autumn awoke with a jolt.

Her eyes open, she looked around.

The bed she was in wasn't hers.

The walls surrounding her were painted a demure and muted taupe color.

The bed was enormous; the vintage nightstands had only lamps resting on them.

In the back of her mind a dreadful and nagging thought was pushing its way to the forefront.

Rick was gone. She had no idea who had abducted him or better yet why.

Thinking on it made her stomach churn and she stood up abruptly, feeling bile rise in her throat. She stood trembling, sweat rolling off her brow, trying to fight the urge to retch. A moment passed and it subsided.

She took a deep breath, smoothed her hair back and headed out through the white wooden door. She was greeted by a long, wide hallway. All the doors along the hall were closed. She saw a staircase at the end and began walking cautiously across the plush tan carpeting. As soon as she reached the top of the stairs she smelt cooking. Bacon specifically. Despite wanting to vomit only moments ago, her stomach growled in hunger. She headed down the stairs, through a foyer and towards the delectable aroma. When she reached the kitchen she saw him there, cooking atop a glass top stove.

Ryan looked up from the frying pan, smiling at her.

"Good morning."

"Morning," she said. "Where am I?"

Ryan flipped the bacon over. "My house."

"What am I doing here?"

"Last night you passed out. Understandable considering the circumstances."

"And you brought me here?"

"Apparently Rick's parents are gone to visit family in Florida. Mandy thought it best you weren't left alone."

Autumn couldn't contain her smile. "Oh did she?"

Ryan pulled a carton of eggs from the fridge.

"You are definitely much safer with me around. Though I think those men got what they wanted last night. I doubt they would come back for you."

He gestured to some chairs surrounding a huge, oblong wooden table.

"Have a seat. It won't be much longer. How do you like your eggs?"

"Surprise me." Autumn sat down. "Who took Rick?"

Ryan considered her question for a moment then said, "DSI."

He brought a pot of tea to the table along with sugar and milk. A mug sat in front of her, waiting to be filled.

"Unless you want coffee?"

"Tea is fine."

"I vaguely remember you saying you aren't a coffee girl."

Autumn had several questions last night but now all she could think about was how ravenous she was. Ryan finished cooking and placed a plate of eggs, bacon and toast in front of her. Autumn tucked in without restraint.

"I know you probably have quite a few questions you want to ask me," Ryan said as he sat down across from her.

"I do," she agreed. "First and foremost, I want to know where Rick is."

"Rick is being held at a DSI facility. Unfortunately, we are still tracking down its location."

"We?" Autumn asked between bites.

"My pack. Stuart, Vincent, Garrett, and Malaya."

Autumn looked up at Ryan, unable to hide the betrayal behind her green eyes.

"I know what you are thinking," he said quietly.

"So werewolves can read minds too?" she said flatly.

"No," Ryan said. "I didn't tell you I knew Stuart."

"Really, you don't owe me anything," Autumn admitted. "I just wish you guys had trusted me." She paused. "I mean, you *can* trust me."

"I know," Ryan said, before taking a swig of tea. "I never doubted your loyalty Autumn. I was concerned. Telling you and Rick the truth could've put you both in even more danger."

She couldn't argue his logic was sound so she said, "Fair enough. What's the plan?"

"As we speak Garrett is working on tracking Rick." Ryan paused. "He dropped his phone so GPS isn't an option."

"I also instructed Mandy and Nathaniel to inform your friend Eric of the events of last night. We are going to need him on board when we finally liberate Rick."

Autumn continued eating while listening intently to Ryan. He had arranged a meeting with him and his pack to become better acquainted with Autumn and the others. They also needed to come up with a strategy, even if Garret's investigation came up empty.

Another thought came to her, a nagging question she had to know the answer to. She looked at Ryan and said, "That night at the caves when we did the cleansing ritual, you saved us."

"*We* came to aid you all," he corrected her. "But *I* saved *you* specifically if memory serves."

He was right. She remembered the grey wolf holding her safe and steady in its strong arms, all the while she never knew it was Ryan behind the fur.

"Was your pack there too?"

"Of course," he said, finishing his tea with a gulp. "Everyone except Malaya. She hadn't joined us yet."

"And Stuart is part of your pack?"

Ryan smirked. "The chocolate colored wolf with the affinity for using his claws? That's Stu."

Autumn finished eating and felt a wave of unbridled exhaustion flood over her. She buried her head in her hands.

How could this happen? How did she end up at Ryan Garrison's house, discussing how to get Rick back from DSI over bacon and eggs?

She pictured Rick, unconscious and beaten, tossed haphazardly in a cell, unware that when he woke he would be a prisoner. Her heart filled with sorrow and her eyes prickled with impending tears. She tried her best to hold them back, but the tears were relentless. They began flowing freely and her body heaved with sobs. Ryan rushed over to her.

"Don't cry Aututmn. We will find Rick. Garret is our best tracker." He ran his hands through her hair soothingly.

Autumn had no words. She rested her head on Ryan's broad chest and let him comfort her. Her tears were an endless stream, her guilt and fear unyielding. Eventually, exhaustion caught up with her and she closed her eyes and let it steal her away.

Autumn awoke on a huge plush beige couch. Covered up with a blanket, she could see Ryan pacing back and forth in the kitchen. He was talking on his cell phone and she picked up some of the conversation.

She's exhausted and asleep. The Jacobs are away visiting family thankfully. We are hoping to have him back as soon as possible. The pack is convening here in an hour.

Autumn sat up. She couldn't keep sleeping. It wasn't helping. She was supposed to be helpful. In a crisis, she was proving to be useless. Rick needed her. Even if she couldn't do anything until Garret tracked him down, she had to remain vigilant.

"Hello there sleepy head." Ryan's voice was a welcome distraction from her thoughts.

Autumn looked at him, a genuine smile on her face. She appreciated him taking care of her.

He handed her a bottle of water.

"I thought you might be thirsty."

"I am. Thank you." She took the bottle gratefully and began drinking.

Ryan said down beside her. "How are you feeling?"

"As good as can be expected," she admitted.

Sitting next to him, she was suddenly aware of her ragged appearance. Her messy hair, smeared makeup and sweaty skin. She was in desperate need of a shower.

"Would you mind if I used your shower?" she asked.

Ryan didn't seem bothered by her request. "By all means. I had Malaya bring by some clothes while you were resting. Hopefully they fit. I had to guess your size."

Autumn flushed at the thought of Ryan guessing her size.

"I appreciate it. All of this actually," she said meaningfully.

He smiled at her. "My home is your home. The clothes are on the bed in the room you spent the night in. There's also an attached bathroom. It's yours."

* * *

An hour later, Autumn was done showering and getting dressed. The clothes, jeans and a basic red tank top, fit perfectly. Ryan had even left her a brand new toothbrush and toothpaste in the bathroom. Grateful, she brushed her teeth and combed through her wet tangled hair before heading downstairs. As she walked towards the kitchen, she was greeted by the sound of people chatting with Ryan. As soon as she came into the room the conversation stopped.

Ryan stood by the kitchen counter talking to two people. Autumn recognized them both instantly. The man with the black hair from the picture and the beautiful woman she had seen Ryan with.

His girlfriend, she had suspected.

Both of them looked at Autumn appraisingly.

Ryan smiled. "Please join us Autumn, don't be shy. We were just talking about you."

She looked around the room at the grave faces staring back at her. "I noticed."

"I am Malaya." The woman spoke first. She reached out, shaking Autumn's hand cordially. Up close she was even more stunning than Autumn had imagined. With huge doe-like chocolate eyes and olive skin that was flawless upon inspection, it was enough to make any girl feel inadequate.

The man was rugged looking, with a worn face that indicated he'd weathered many storms. He had attacked the agents at the school that fateful day, allowing them to escape.

"I'm Vincent," he spoke gruffly.

"Vincent is my second in command," Ryan began.

Vincent snorted, his arms crossed. "You just *had* to add that in didn't you Alpha dog?"

Ryan chuckled lightly. "Every chance I get."

Autumn would've thought it was a dig, but their rapport seemed quite relaxed, like old friends teasing each other for kicks.

"Now that everything is out on the table, let's get to business," Ryan said. "The others should arrive soon and we can commence. Follow me into the study."

As they headed towards the study, Autumn was preoccupied. She thought about Rick and the devastation and fear felt fresh, as if she was realizing he was gone all over again.

"He will survive this Autumn." It was Malaya speaking. Autumn looked at her, surprised.

Malaya smiled reassuringly. "He is strong-willed. He will survive, if only to spite those who captured him."

Autumn smiled in spite of herself. Rick was definitely stalwart when he wanted to be, perhaps even vindictive.

"How did you know I was thinking about him?"

"I am excellent at reading body language," Malaya admitted. "Ryan also says I am very empathic."

"You are," Autumn agreed. "And thank you for the concern. Ryan is very lucky to have you."

Vincent turned to look at Autumn, bemused.

"What do you mean by that?"

Autumn shrugged. "Ryan is lucky to be dating someone so considerate."

Vincent snickered. "Sweetheart, you got it all wrong."

Autumn looked at him, stunned. She had seen Malaya and Ryan *together* hadn't she?

Unless it wasn't actually a date.

After all, Stuart had shown up halfway through the night.

"You look surprised by this?" Vincent went on. "Trust me. Two werewolves dating is seriously frowned upon in our society."

Autumn was fascinated by this information. "Why is that?"

Vincent smirked. "Let's just say wicked things happen when werewolves make the beast with two backs."

Autumn started to press Vincent on what exactly *wicked things* entailed, but she was interrupted by the sound of door opening. Ryan escorted them through two huge double doors into a study. It wasn't half the size of Eric's library of course, but it was definitely spacious.

Unlike Eric's library that boasted shelf upon shelf of books and walls adorned with tapestries and antique artwork, Ryan's study was quite minimalist. The only thing that caught Autumn's eye was the single painting that hung above the wood burning fireplace.

She walked towards it, as though it was calling out to her. The painting was immeasurably beautiful and she stared at it, utterly enraptured.

The painting depicted a werewolf with stunning golden fur perched beside a woman. The woman was elegant and breathtaking, with alabaster skin and cascades of dark hair. The wolf rested its large head in the girl's lap, its eyes filled with a boundless love. Looking closer, Autumn noticed the woman was cradling a baby, swaddled in blankets, in her arms. Behind the trio, the heavens were colored sapphire, and the stars glimmered like thousands of tiny diamonds.

Autumn tried, but she just couldn't pull herself away from the painting.

"Beautiful isn't it?" Ryan was standing beside her, his eyes on the portrait.

She nodded slowly. "It's breathtaking."

She stood, rooted to the ground, wondering why the painting resonated with her so greatly. She had no explanation. She just couldn't tear her eyes away from it.

"Who painted this?" she asked suddenly but when she looked to Ryan for an answer, he was gone.

25

The door to the study opened, pulling Autumn from her reverie and her attention from the painting. Eric, Mandy and Nathaniel came in, followed closely by Stuart and the man she assumed was Garret. Autumn could hardly contain her joy as she rushed towards her friends. Eric seized her, pulling her into a hug.

"I am so happy to see you," he spoke into her hair. "I should've come to the party. I should've been there for you."

"Don't even think that way," Autumn admonished him. "You stayed home with Arabella. You did the right thing."

Eric sighed and held her tighter.

"We are going to get him back."

"So I keep hearing."

"Eric you have hogged her long enough!" Mandy barked. "Move!"

Eric pulled back, rolling his eyes. He smiled at Autumn, gave her a kiss on the forehead and let Mandy step in. She looked at Autumn appraisingly.

"I won't bother ask you how you are doing because I already know," she began.

"I am surprisingly numb," Autumn admitted, biting back tears. Mandy hugged her.

"You are in shock. We all are. The only thing keeping me going is imagining all the nasty ways I will hurt the people that took Rick."

"Eric is right. We *will* get him back Aut. We just need a plan, some weapons and we are good to go."

Autumn felt the tears escaping and desperate words followed.

"I failed him. I feel like I could've done more."

"We all feel that way but it isn't true," Mandy said reassuringly. "Against an army of DSI soldiers, without any weapons, we would've ended up dead."

"I feel the same way," Nathaniel spoke up suddenly. "I just stood there while they took him. I am his best friend and I did *nothing.*"

"Nathaniel, we have been through this," Mandy said quietly. "No one is to blame for this, except DSI."

"Enough!" Eric said, his tone resolute. "Enough discussions of the past. We need to focus on the future and what we can do to help Rick now."

"The perfect segue," Ryan said. "Thank you for that Eric."

"You guys need to stop blaming yourself for Rick being taken," Stuart chimed in. "DSI had this abduction planned long ago. When they didn't get him at the school assembly that day, they were even more determined to snatch him. If you guys had gotten in the way, you were just collateral damage. They wouldn't have thought twice before killing any of you."

Autumn felt a question nagging at her, niggling at her brain, begging to be asked. Part of her was scared of the answer yet she couldn't ignore it any longer.

"Why do they want Rick?"

The whole wolf pack, Malaya, Stuart, Vincent, Garret and Ryan, looked at one another, exchanging glances and unspoken words.

Autumn put her hands on her hips, unwavering.

"What do you guys know?"

The packs eyes shifted to their esteemed leader. Ryan rubbed between his eyes, looking exasperated.

"Why are you guys looking at me?"

"You are the Alpha. You can tell her." Garret spoke for the first time, a sly grin on his impish face.

Ryan sighed, clearly unable to argue Garret's sound logic. "Fine." He turned to Autumn and the others.

"You all might want to sit down."

After everyone had taken their seats, Ryan sighed deeply and clasped his hands together.

"Before I get into other things, I want to inform everyone that Garret hasn't had any luck figuring out Rick's exact location."

Autumn felt like she had been kicked in the stomach. She should've known finding Rick wouldn't be easy but she had let that tiny shred of hope into her heart. Now it was breaking all over again.

Ryan caught her grave expression and added quickly, "That doesn't mean we *won't* find him because we *will*. It just might take some time."

"I might be able to help with that," Eric offered. "Perhaps Arabella and I can try a locator spell? They aren't foolproof but sometimes they work."

Ryan smiled gratefully. "I appreciate the offer Eric but we are operating under the assumption that the DUI facility is heavily warded with magics. This leads me to my next point. DUI have a sorceress working for them."

"Which isn't a huge ordeal because so do we," Vincent chimed in, a sinister grin on his face. "And our witch is far superior."

Eric's eyes lit up. "Really? I would love to meet her."

"You already have," Ryan said.

Eric looked confused for a moment then realization flashed across his face.

"The witch that took on Bianca in the caves?"

Ryan nodded. "Her name is Raina."

Eric looked pleasantly surprised by the tidings. He had been hoping to find the mysterious sorceress that had helped them all that fateful night, but had no actual leads.

"Raina has already begun a locator spell of her own. She is extremely powerful so we are hoping she might be able to bypass the wards that cloak DUI's location."

Ryan looked at Autumn. "How long are Rick's parents away?"

"Two weeks," Autumn replied.

Ryan looked thoughtful. "Perfect. Rick should be home safe and sound before they return. Until then, Autumn, Mandy, Nathaniel and Eric, you guys will begin training. Since we are going up against armed men, we *will* be teaching you how to operate various weapons, including firearms."

"I already know how to shoot a gun," Nathaniel piped in arrogantly.

Vincent snorted. "But can you actually hit a target boy?"

Nathaniel opened his mouth to speak, but quickly shut it after Mandy nudged him sharply in the ribs.

"We can all use the extra training," she said. "Especially those of us who never use guns."

"So it is settled," Ryan continued. "Autumn, Nathaniel and Mandy will train with the pack and Eric with our gifted witch Raina."

Eric looked pleased. "I would be honored. Though I am quite the warlock already."

Vincent rolled his eyes. "So are you all this arrogant?"

"It's awfully familiar isn't it Vincent?" Stuart added with a grin.

Ryan cleared his throat.

"Training begins tomorrow at 10 a.m. sharp. Are there any questions?"

"You still haven't answered *my* question," Autumn said, standing up. "Why did they take Rick?"

Ryan was silent for a moment as he quite obviously weighed his words. Everyone else was silent, their eyes fixed on him, awaiting his response.

"There is no easy way to say this so I will just say it," he began. "Rick has what we call The Potential."

Autumn didn't understand. She looked at Ryan, confused.

"The potential for what?" she asked her voice quiet.

"To change," he said, his eyes fixed on hers. "Rick is possibly one of us. He might be a werewolf."

26

Autumn had been rendered speechless.

Her mind was struggling, grasping to understand the words Ryan had just spoken. Between losing Rick and these tidings, she felt like she was on the precipice of madness. She sat back down, her legs weakening beneath the weight of her grief.

Mandy placed a hand on her friends shoulder.

"Sit Autumn and breathe," she instructed. "Ryan will explain."

Mandy turned to Ryan, eyes narrowed. "You can explain can't you?"

Ryan was watching Autumn apprehensively, like he expected her to break. He gave Mandy a grave nod.

"Of course I can. Rick was born with the wolven gene. That gene allows him to change into a werewolf. However, it's a distinct possibility his ability could stay dormant without the right stimulus."

Autumn frowned, echoing Ryan. "Stimulus?"

"Put simply, raw emotion," Ryan replied. "Most often the shift is caused by anger, though it can be any overwhelming emotion."

Suddenly, a memory came back to Autumn. She remembered Ryan stopping the fight between Rick and Ben at the mall. Was Ryan aware at that time that Rick's rage might cause him to shift? Is that why he intervened before it got ugly?

Autumn looked at Ryan, her eyes wide.

"How long have you know?"

Ryan closed his eyes, only for a moment.

He sighed deeply then said,

"Since the first day I met you both. It's the real reason I came to Whitan High to be a guidance counselor. It meant I could keep a close eye on Rick."

Autumn couldn't believe it, but it rang painfully true.

Ryan had lied all along about who he *really* was.

He had been watching Rick, watching her, watching all of them, since the beginning.

It explained everything.

His interest in Rick and in her.

What better way to involve himself in their lives and keep tabs on Rick then becoming a guidance counselor at their high school. Students are encouraged to foster trust with their guidance counselors. Ryan knew this. He needed to be on the inside track with Rick and he wanted Rick to trust him implicitly.

Ryan continued. "After the first change, there is no turning back. That person will be a werewolf for the rest of their days."

"And they will transform every full moon?" Nathaniel asked his eyes wide.

Vincent snorted loudly. "During the full moon, half moon, quarter moon. We can change whenever we want." He looked at his comrades, amused. "I thought you guys said they knew of the supernatural world."

"They know of it but they don't know everything," Stuart grumbled, his arms crossed. "Go easy on them Vincent. They are still green."

"As grass, Vincent muttered, rolling his eyes.

"So they want Rick because he might be a werewolf?" Autumn asked.

"We believe DSI are abducting kids who have the wolven gene and experimenting on them. We aren't sure what their end game is, other than possibly finding out what makes them tick."

Autumn felt her world closing in on her. She was helpless. Rick was being poked, prodded and tortured and they had no idea where he was.

Tears prickled her eyes but she forced them back. She could cry later. She had to remain focused. She would be of no use to anyone if she fell apart.

"Has anyone noticed any drastic changes in Rick's behaviour?" Garret inquired. "Is he quick to anger, moody or always looking for a fight?"

Everyone turned their gaze onto Autumn.

"Sure. Rick has been sort of moody lately," she admitted. "And somewhat more angry than usual."

"Don't forget the intense jealousy," Nathaniel added.

He looked at Ryan, a huge smirk on his face. "I think he might actually hate you Garrison."

"Nathaniel!" Mandy spat, her eyes wide with disbelief. "You seriously have no filter!"

"Or brain," Vincent muttered.

Ryan looked shocked by these tidings. "He hates me?"

"He doesn't hate you." Eric said. "He is jealous of you."

"Jealous of *him?*" Vincent said, his lips curling into a wicked grin. "But why?"

He looked around the room until his eyes stopped on Autumn. His grin deepened. "It's because of *her* isn't it?"

Eric shrugged noncommittally. "Rick isn't very fond of guys talking to Autumn."

Vincent looked at Ryan, a smug smirk on his face. Ryan shot him a look of exasperation and went about his spiel.

"The wolven gene can cause people to be short-tempered and irrational. It's nature's way of bringing out the beast. The problem is, if Rick does shift due to DSI's prodding, the situation will become much graver."

"He will be a wild, feral wolf cub that knows nothing of control. If they let him loose, he could not only kill innocent people who have the misfortune of crossing him, he could start a path of pure destruction."

* * *

Rick woke up shivering, his body drenched in a cold sweat.

The small glass cell that had contained him for what felt like days now grew smaller every day, as did the hope that someone would come rescue him from this hell.

He had the basics here. Water, a cot, a filthy toilet stained with remnants of piss and shit that didn't come from him.

Every day, like clockwork, meals were provided. Trays of disgusting slop he wouldn't deign to call food, meant to sustain him.

His biggest fear wasn't his own demise. He had come to terms with that long ago.

Instead, he worried about Autumn. What happened to her after they had beaten him unconscious? Did they harm her? Was she a prisoner here too? He called out to her but never got a response.

His phone was missing and he had no recollection of where he was or how he came to be here.

Rick's stomach rumbled loudly, announcing his hunger and just his luck, a guard came, carrying a tray of what looked like soup. He unlocked the cell door and placed the tray on the floor.

The guard, with his gun prominent in his holster like a badge of honor, fixed his gaze on Rick.

"Where is she?" Rick spoke suddenly.

The guard looked mildly surprised by Rick's sudden outburst.

His eyes narrowed. "Who the hell are you talking about?" He grumbled. "You got your nerve questioning me."

Rick sighed deeply, as the familiar feeling of helplessness washed over him. He was desperate to know Autumn was alright. And if she was safe, he was pretty certain the others were as well.

"My girlfriend. I just want to know she is okay."

The guard watched him appraisingly. "And how the hell would I know that? I don't keep tabs on your girlfriend."

"Is she here?" he pressed.

The guard laughed bitterly. "Why should I tell you shit?"

Pure anger bubbled up inside Rick, pushing away his fear and restraint. Soon rage would be all he felt. Red would be the only color he could see.

He slammed his fist against the concrete wall, feeling no pain though his hand throbbed.

"DID YOU GUYS TAKE HER OR NOT?"

The guard remained stoic, his voice mild and controlled.

"We only took you. The others are useless." He smirked. "Now shut up and eat. You have to keep your strength up. Tomorrow is going to be a big day for you."

27

"As the saying goes, today is the beginning of the rest of your lives. All of you have strengths and weaknesses and I won't sugar coat it: Enemies will capitalize on them. They will find your Achilles heel and they *will* use it to their advantage. With this training we will endeavor to limit your weaknesses therefore limiting your enemies' chances to exploit them."

It was precisely 10 in the morning and Vincent stood before Autumn, Mandy, Nathaniel and Eric, his face grave, his tone all business. The morning was crisp, the air cool and the blades of grass shimmered with dew that hadn't yet dissipated. Already dressed in their armor, they were gathered in a clearing that led towards a massive forest. The forest was far larger than anything in Whitan and though Autumn spent most of the car ride snoozing, she figured they were about an hour or so north of Whitan.

Ryan had described it as a fortress and sanctuary where werewolves came to work and play. The land was owned by Ryan and was a place where werewolves were free to be themselves. There were no houses or businesses for miles. Ryan refused to sell his land, no matter how much money he was offered. Essentially, he wanted to ensure werewolves privacy and asylum and what better way than making sure nobody was in the vicinity? The area was also shrouded with powerful magical warding and went mostly unnoticed by people because it was so far away from civilization.

Vincent continued on. "Now we shall enter the wolven sanctuary. Before you go in, you will be greeted by two guards. Bosco and Plank will do a security check. This is procedure and if you pass you will be given permission to enter the sacred grounds. Please keep in mind, outsiders are rarely welcomed here. It's not only dangerous for *us* but for humans as well. New werewolves are not able to control their abilities and can be unpredictable. I would not wish a wolf attack on my worst enemy and I am vindictive. So please, do not wander."

After Vincent was finished with his list of instructions, the group followed him through the clearing and towards the entrance of the forest. As they approached, they were greeted by two burly and intimidating men. Both stood with their bulging arms crossed over their massive chests, their faces unyielding as Autumn and the others stepped up to be checked over.

"You *could've* vouched for us you know," Nathaniel griped to Vincent as the guards began patting him down aggressively.

Vincent, who was the on the other side of the threshold, snorted loudly.

"And I might have. If I was an idiot."

He went on to explain the guards were not only searching for weapons, but they also used their powers to detect spiritual corruption.

"This place where the wolves meet is sacred ground. We cannot allow it to become tainted by evil. Malevolence is like a plague that can spread, you see. And though everyone has a dark side, it is quite different than being truly evil."

"What happens if someone is tainted?" Mandy asked. "They can't enter?"

Vincent looked at her gravely. "They must be cleansed using an age-old werewolf ritual performed by one of our clerics. Garret is one of the wolven clergy. He is our healer."

After Autumn and the others passed their inspection, they were led past the guards and through the masses of trees and wild underbrush. They trekked for about fifteen minutes before reaching their destination.

Leaning against a tree, eating a shiny red apple, stood Ryan Garrison.

"Welcome everyone," he announced, his lips curling into a knowing smile. "I trust Vincent has treated you all well so far?"

"You trusted wrong," Nathaniel grumbled as Vincent rolled his eyes.

Ryan couldn't help but chuckle. "I know many of you would like a tour of our humble grounds, but alas, the lands are vast and we have not the time to waste." He looked at Autumn who smiled back at him gratefully.

"So we will get right to training. First, I want to introduce someone who will be working with us today."

Ryan gestured as a figure materialized at his side. Dressed in a long white cloak, with eyes as blue as the ocean and long hair as white as snow, stood a woman. She was quite stunning, and when she smiled even Autumn felt goosebumps dance across her skin. She looked at them all appraisingly.

"Hello," she said. "I am Raina Ravine. It is my tremendous honour to be here aiding you all in your rescue mission."

She turned to look at Eric.

"Hello Mister King. It is nice to see you again."

Eric, not missing a beat, reached out his hand to her.

"Likewise. It's definitely nice to put a name with the face."

Ryan went on to introduce the rest of them to Raina though Autumn got the distinct impression that introductions weren't necessary. Raina had helped them in the caves and taken over Arabella's body. She knew *exactly* who they all were.

When Ryan got to Autumn, Raina's expression turned grave instantly. She took Autumn's hands into her own and looked directly into her eyes.

"What has happened to Rick is a great injustice my dear. I want to assure you his rescue is imminent. You couldn't ask for a better man to spearhead a rescue mission than Ryan or a better team to train you. I am also working on a locator spell. DSI have covered their tracks quite thoroughly but I am confident my magics will prevail in the end."

Autumn felt her wounds torn anew as Raina tried her best to reassure her. Her eyes stung and she bit back the tears.

"Thank you," she managed. "It's been difficult."

Raina squeezed Autumn's hands. "I have lived long enough to see many of my comrades fall but I can tell you, despite the countless losses there have been many people we have managed to save."

Eric arched an eyebrow, intrigued. "Just how old are you Raina?"

Raina threw him a disapproving look over her shoulder.

"It is rude to ask a woman how old she is Mr. King. Haven't you any manners?"

As Raina left with Eric to begin their magic training, Stuart arrived and began setting up targets across the huge field. Ryan passed out handguns to everyone whilst reminding them to be responsible.

"They *aren't* toys and they *are* dangerous," he cautioned. "We will be instructing you on how to safely use them."

Autumn held the gun uncertainly, unable to rationalize the feeling of a loaded firearm in her hands.

Nathaniel, on the other hand, was thrilled.

"This is a sweet piece," he said, examining the gun with pride.

"All of our weapons are of the finest calibre," Vincent said matter-of-factly. "The king wouldn't have it any other way."

"The king?" Mandy repeated.

Vincent nodded and pointed to Ryan. He grinned mischievously.

"Why don't you show them Ryan?"

Ryan didn't look pleased by Vincent's suggestion, but he obliged him anyways.

"Cover your ears," he instructed.

Autumn and the others put on their protective headphones and Ryan took aim, pointing his gun at the target. He took a deep breath and pulled the trigger. A muffled bang escaped and a bullet soared, but didn't hit the bullseye.

Autumn pulled her headphones off and looked at Ryan, confused.

"I don't get it. You missed the target."

Ryan shrugged his broad shoulders, the ghost of a smile on his face. "Did I?".

Ryan strolled over and picked something up off the ground. He walked back over and opened his palm. Inside it was a large wind chime with each metal rod brandishing a bullet sized hole. The single bullet had ricocheted, puncturing each rod.

"That is awesome dude!" Nathaniel exclaimed, awestricken. "Way to go Geezerson!"

Autumn was suddenly aware that her mouth was agape. She closed it quickly and looked at Ryan.

"You did all that with one bullet?"

Ryan beamed, obviously proud of his accomplishment.

"I did."

"Dude you gotta teach me how to shoot like that," Nathaniel implored.

Ryan chuckled lightly. "You can't cultivate skills like that overnight Nathaniel. I have been training since I became a wolf. Being proficient with weapons gave me an edge when facing adversaries."

"Because turning into a massive freaking wolf isn't enough," Nathaniel deadpanned.

"Not if you are going head-to-head with another wolf," Ryan replied. "Or other supernatural beings. Being able to surprise your opponent during a fight is always to *your* benefit and *their* detriment. Remember that, all of you."

After Ryan's demonstration training began in earnest. It started with the basics of guns.

The mechanics, the dangers, the power of wielding a weapon that, with one single bullet, could save your life and end someone else's.

* * *

Autumn felt her hands shaking as she gripped the gun in both her hands. She knew this was something she had to do. Not only to save Rick from DSI but to survive. It seemed that the supernatural element was not going to disappear from her life anytime soon, especially with Rick possibly changing into a werewolf.

She took a deep steadying breath and forced her hands to stop trembling. Her face set with determination, she aimed at the target and pulled the trigger.

The bullet whizzed towards the target, narrowly missing the bullseye.

Autumn lowered the gun, and sighed, frustrated.

"You are doing amazing. Keep it up," Ryan said from behind her.

"I was close," she muttered, feeling embarrassed at her lack of skill. "I have been way off the mark with most of my other shots though."

"Autumn you will get it. You just need time."

"A luxury I don't *really* have."

Ryan smiled. "May I?"

Autumn nodded. She could use all the help she could get.

Ryan stepped behind her and wrapped his arms around hers. His hands gripped hers as she held the gun.

"Hold the gun firmly but you don't need a death grip," he instructed, guiding her with his hands.

"A trick I use when I am aiming? I remember what I am shooting and who I'm doing it for. Am I shooting a monster or a person? Whose life is on the line? Who am I saving? Is it my pack, an innocent bystander, myself?"

Autumn could feel Ryan's body, warm against hers. Her face flushed and guilt washed over her in a mighty wave. *If only Rick could see this,* she thought miserably. *He would hate us both.*

"In your case imagine Rick," he said gently. "You see him but the guards are rushing at you armed with their guns. You need to take them down. You can't let them shoot you because if you die, Rick dies. Game over."

Ryan let go. It was just Autumn and the gun. She raised her arms and pointed the barrel, focused on hitting her target, on saving Rick.

Ryan spoke. *"Now shoot."*

Autumn pulled the trigger and watched as the bullet blasted across the field, hitting smack-dab in the centre of the target.

"Right between the eyes," Ryan said, beaming with pride. "Congratulations."

A grin spread across Autumn's face.

Finally, she had hit the target.

It was then she made a silent vow: When the time came to rescue Rick, she would be a force to be reckoned with.

28

A week came and went in a blur of training. Garrett, using his "superior hacking skills" as he called it, managed to track down Rick. Raina had broken down the DSI warding, allowing Garret to locate their mainframe which created a digital trail to DSI.

Ryan wasn't exaggerating when he said as soon as they located Rick they would rescue him. After Garret informed Ryan he had found DSI's facility, Ryan began planning the rescue mission.

Everything moved quickly after that.

Saturday night, at midnight, they were going to storm the DSI hideout. They would free Rick and anyone else trapped within DSI's sinister grasp.

The week of training had been gruelling. Between that and having to make up excuses when her Aunt Katherine and Uncle James called looking for Rick, Autumn was at her wits end.

She had told them Rick had *lost* his cell phone, that he was in the shower, or out with Nathaniel.

All of it was lies, and it broke her heart to deceive the two people who had always treated her like family. Still, the truth would've been too much for them to bear, and she knew letting them into this bizarre world would only put them in danger. If and when Rick shifted, it would be his choice if he wanted to tell his parents who he was.

It was the day of the rescue and Autumn felt like a bomb quietly waiting to explode. The night before she had barely slept and the little sleep she got was haunted by the same nightmare she had been having since Rick disappeared.

Autumn was running through the DSI facility. Frantic, her mind raced as she searched for Rick. She could hear people screaming, cries of unadulterated terror. Some pleaded to be rescued, to be liberated from their cages.

Suddenly, DSI guards ran towards her brandishing weapons, but she wasn't alone.

Mandy, Nathaniel, Eric, Ryan and his pack trailed behind her.

Malaya began freeing people while the others fended off the guards.

"We've got this Autumn! Go get Rick!" Ryan instructed.

Autumn nodded and went on with her mission. Running so hard she felt like her lungs would explode, she heard the carnage behind her.

She didn't look back.

Her heart thudded in her chest, sweat trickled down her neck.

She called his name.

RICK!

She ran for what felt like forever, until her lungs burned and her legs felt like jelly.

At the end of a long and winding hall was the last cell.

RICK!

She repeated his name like a mantra.

She kept running until she reached the cell. She skidded to a halt.

She saw him between the iron bars.

Slumped against the concrete walls was Rick. His body was limp, his eyes stared up at her, lifeless, all the light snuffed out of them.

Terror washed over her like ocean waves and she screamed but no sound came out.

Except when she awoke, in Ryan's guestroom, she *was* actually screaming. So loud it took her a moment to realize the cries belonged to her.

Every time she awoke, panicked and terrified, Ryan rushed into the room. He knew of her nightmares, had even come to expect them. He held her trembling body in his strong arms and whispered soothing words.

Afterwards, she felt guilty and deceitful. He felt so safe and she couldn't deny how much she needed him.

Originally, Autumn had wanted to go home. To sleep in her own bed, to pretend Rick was there with her, safe and sound, but Ryan had insisted she stay in his guestroom.

He had warned her: "You are Rick's girlfriend and DSI knows that. Who's to say they won't come after you next? You just aren't safe at home by yourself."

She couldn't deny that out of everyone, Ryan was the best protector she could have. She would be undoubtedly safe with him. The last thing she needed was to get taken, attacked or worse. So she didn't fight it. She stayed with him.

* * *

Autumn watched the scenery going by outside her window. Everything was dark, lit only by passing streetlights and the pale moon.

Autumn, Mandy, Nathaniel and Eric were piled into the non-descript white van as Ryan, his pack, and Raina drove in another van ahead of them.

Autumn and the others were suited up in their bulletproof body suits and ready for action.

Autumn and Mandy were in the back of the van and Eric was in the front with Nathaniel. The radio played classic rock. Nathanial bobbed his head to the beat distractedly.

It felt strange not hearing Rick and him chatting like always.

Every so often Mandy would reach out and take Autumn's hand into her own and give it a reassuring squeeze. Autumn squeezed back but didn't say much. No one did.

The car was devoid of conversation, as everyone took in the levity of what they were undertaking.

Ryan had reiterated the plan before they left. They were going to take all prisoners tonight, not just Rick.

"We are going to liberate the people in the facility and take them back with us to the wolven territory," he had said. "They will be safe with us until we can determine if they are shifters or not."

Autumn wondered if the five missing students from Whitan High were at this DSI facility. Garret informed them that DSI had hideouts all over the country but it was likely because it was so close to Whitan.

They were parking a couple miles or so from the facility, which was in a relatively remote location. Ryan said it was an old abandoned warehouse, dilapidated and easy to miss, especially since it was far out in the country.

"Make no mistake," Ryan had said, sounding every bit the leader he was.

"There will be lives lost, there will be blood shed today but know these men are evil. They are not righteous, and they will continue to take people and use them for their own selfish whims. The people they no longer *need* don't return. They are disposed of. The only reason DSI lets anyone live is to experiment on them, and eventually break them. So do not fear doing what you must to stay alive. I do not relish dragging you all into this." He had looked at Autumn and her friends. "But I know you would never let us fight this battle without you. So tonight we are one unified pack. And together we fight."

Autumn thought about this speech. The words Ryan said were clearly meant to boost morale, but she didn't need his words. The rage in her heart had been burning the moment they took Rick and nothing, hell or high water, mountains, fire or brimstone would stop her from saving him.

Ryan's van pulled into a field bursting with wild and unkempt grass and weeds. Nathaniel followed. The van bumped along, jolting everyone inside until it came to a halt.

Autumn was the first to get out. She inhaled deeply, taking in the stifling heat, feeling her skin prickle against the humidity. She began stretching her limbs as the others exited the van. Beside them, Ryan and his people were readying the weaponry.

She was stretching out her stiff legs when Eric came over, his expression grave.

Grave Eric was never good.

Brooding and tortured Eric was rather sexy, but carefree and blissful Eric was too.

"Is everything okay?" she asked, moving into a lunging pose.

"I want you to promise me that no matter what the hell goes down in that building, that you will *not* do anything stupid," he said.

She chuckled lightly. "Please define *stupid*."

Eric didn't even crack a smile.

"No playing the hero. No taking bullets, no running in there half-cocked, no thinking with your heart instead of your head because I get it. You love Rick and you would do anything to save him. You of all people have the most riding on this rescue mission but you can't take foolish risks when people's lives, when *your* life, is on the line."

Autumn shot Eric a withering look. She was annoyed because he thought she would be that selfish to put Rick before everyone else, but another part of her knew what he was saying was true. When it came to Rick, she couldn't think straight. She was blinded by her love and desire to bring Rick home. That kind of sentiment could make her reckless.

She stopped stretching and jabbed him in his side playfully.

"Eric we have a plan remember? Ryan rehashed it for us for the zillionth time just before we left?"

Eric touched her face gently, stroking her cheek.

"I just worry about you. You mean so much to me Aut. Just be careful."

Autumn reached out and pulled Eric into a tight embrace. She buried her face into his neck and murmured, "You have my word Eric."

When they finally pulled apart Nathaniel and Mandy were coming towards them. Mandy handed Autumn her scythe.

"In case the gun gets boring." She grinned knowingly, holding up her nunchucks.

Ryan and his pack, Stuart, Vincent, Garret and Malaya, approached as Raina headed over to join Eric next to Autumn.

"Alright. Right to business," Ryan began in his authoritative voice. "If you hear the pack referring to each other with nicknames, we don't want you guys to get confused. So here goes. Garret is Tracer, Vincent is Reaper, Stuart is Night Owl, Malaya is Raven and I am Blaze."

"As in *Blaze of glory*," Vincent cracked. There was a teasing grin on his face.

Ryan rolled his eyes. "Yes and when we are werewolves we speak in a wolven tongue. In the event we actually shift of course."

"Man, if I could change into a wolf I would *always* fight like that," Nathaniel said wistfully.

"No you wouldn't," Ryan said then he went back to his speech.

"Lastly, as tempting as it may seem to be the big shot or the hero don't try it," he warned. "Dying young is *not* glamourous and I will *not* erect a monument in your name."

He smiled and reached into a large duffel bag. He pulled out the firearms and handed them out to everyone. After all the guns were dispersed, Ryan went over the mechanics of operating and loading the guns one last time. Then he handed out extra ammunition while explaining him and Vincent would take out the front guards. Once they got inside it was game on for everyone.

He looked at Autumn suddenly and said, "For many, this mission is extremely emotional but feelings *can't* cloud your judgment or lead you to make dangerous choices. We're going in together and leaving together. Is that understood?"

Autumn nodded her head with the others, fully aware that Ryan had been lecturing her.

"As we discussed before, we will have to split up eventually. Garrett managed to get the schematics of the warehouse. There are three floors, including the basement. We are guessing the majority of the hostages are down there. The other floors are most likely the labs and supply rooms."

Ryan adjusted his gun holster, his expression grave.

"Vincent and I will lead. Rookies in the middle and the rest of the pack will bring up the rear."

Vincent piped in. "Blaze and I will take out the guards around the perimeter of the warehouse. Once we're inside, the DSI staff and security will swarm us. A word of advice: they will *not* think twice before shooting. Neither should you. Now let's do this."

Walking along the dimly lit highway, not a single car passed by. Autumn looked out into the dense bush and acres of fields that surrounded them. Other than the critters and animals scurrying their way through the night, the area was completely deserted.

They were truly in the middle of nowhere.

They hadn't been walking long when Autumn spotted the warehouse up ahead. Shrouded by soaring oak trees with massive trunks, the DSI facility loomed, huge and menacing.

They snuck along the cover of trees, with Ryan and Vincent leading the way. Autumn could feel her pulse quickening and her heart racing.

Ryan held up his hand and everyone stopped moving. He gestured to the warehouse. Autumn looked over and saw two guards, dressed in crisp black uniforms, guns tucked neatly away in the holsters on their hips.

Ryan looked at Vincent and gave him the signal. They were going in. As planned, the others were waiting in the cover of massive trees until it was safe to proceed.

Autumn waited on baited breath as the two men armed themselves and rushed the building.

"Who the hell are you?" The guard blurted out as Ryan and Vincent charged towards them. "You are trespassing on private property assholes!"

Autumn watched as the other guard reached for his walkie-talkie, attempting to alert his comrades or request backup.

Ryan shot it out of his hand before he got the chance.

The deafening sound of shots being fired and bloodcurdling screams filled in the air. Autumn wanted to look away but she couldn't, fascinated by the scene unfolding before her. Another half dozen guards came rushing out from other sides of the building. Ryan was using two guns now, and his precision was impeccable. Every shot was fired with accuracy, his movements so swift and smooth. Watching him in battle was truly a sight to behold.

Vincent on the other hand, used brute force. He cackled and hollered his way through the guards, shooting some and cracking others in the head with his gun.

Once the guards were taken care of, Ryan and Vincent waited, armed and ready, in case any other stragglers appeared.

After a few minutes passed, Stuart spoke.

"It's safe to move ahead now. Follow me."

He led them carefully towards the warehouse, which up close looked more dilapidated then it had from afar. Moss and vines covered the exterior of the building, and the windows were filthy and cracked. To anyone that happened to pass, it would indeed look abandoned.

Autumn sucked in a breath as she stared at the lifeless bodies scattered haphazardly across the pavement. She tore her eyes away and looked ahead, where Ryan and Vincent stood in front of the steel warehouse door.

"Did they manage to call in the cavalry?" Stuart inquired as they approached.

"Nope," Vincent said, grinning. "But you can bet they have cameras somewhere and the gun shots weren't exactly quiet."

"That's exactly why we need to move fast," Ryan said impatiently. "Tracer, you are up."

Garrett nodded. "I'm on it Blaze."

Autumn wasn't sure exactly what Garret was about to do. She watched as he ambled toward the steel door, his lanky frame moving swiftly.

"Key pad lock. Exactly what I was expecting," he said and he began punching the keys, his fingers moving so rapidly they blurred.

A minute later, a loud clicking sound followed by a flashing green light indicated the door unlocking.

"And we are in!" Garret announced as he stepped aside to let Ryan and Vincent pass by.

"Good job Tracer," Ryan said, patting Garret's back with pride.

Vincent looked at Ryan, a wicked grin spreading across his face. "May I?"

Ryan smirked in return, aiming his gun at the entrance. "Of course."

Vincent lifted his leg, grunted and kicked, demonstrating his strength as the steel door flew open.

Everyone followed Vincent and Ryan into the building, weapons in hand, expecting to be greeted by an army of armed, pissed off DSI guards. Instead they were met by an empty corridor and eerie silence.

Ryan didn't lower his weapons, refusing to let his guard down.

"Stay vigilant. They *know* we are here. They are lulling us into a false sense of security," he warned.

"That's definitely not working," Autumn muttered as she scanned the area for suspicious activity.

"Just remember the plan. We clear the top floors then we hit the basement."

They were walking towards the staircase when the sound of many footsteps echoed through the room. Autumn watched as an army of thirty DSI guards came running towards them, their guns pointed and ready to shoot.

"Battle formation!" Ryan instructed. "Watch your back!"

Autumn, Mandy, Nathaniel and Eric fell into battle position just like they were taught. The wolves and Raina were no strangers to battle. They stayed on the outer circle, becoming a buffer between the DSI guards and their apprentices.

And everything after that was complete chaos.

29

The room was filled with expletives and gunshots. Autumn felt a bullet graze her arm. The guard that fired the shot moved closer to her, his eyes wild and menacing. Autumn felt her heart racing as she heard Vincent's words echoing in her head.

They will not think twice before shooting. Neither should you.

Autumn recognized it was one thing to *say* you could shoot someone.

It was another thing entirely to actually pull the trigger.

Rationally, she was doing this to protect her friends and save Rick. And she couldn't let this guard kill her and that didn't leave her many peaceful options.

The guard stood inches from her now and he was aiming his gun at her head. The eyes of a stone-cold killer fixated on her and before he could squeeze the trigger Autumn fired off a round.

She felt a mix of terror and relief when the bullet pierced him in the throat. The guard put his hand to his neck as the blood sprayed from the wound. She watched it running down his hand like a crimson river as his body began to jerk and he collapsed to the ground.

Autumn didn't lower her weapon as she began surveying the room. Mandy was fending off a guard who was swinging a club at her. Nathaniel was behind her shooting at two other guards. The wolves were holding their own without needing to shift. They fought off the bulk of guards along with Eric and Raina who zapped droves of guards with their lightning bolt spells.

Autumn spotted a cluster of vicious looking guards coming directly at her. This time she didn't hesitate and she began unloading rounds into them with fervor. Their bullets soared towards her and she moved to dodge them. She managed to avoid all but one and despite her armor absorbing the slug, it hit her with force in her shoulder.

Autumn felt the pain sear through her, burning along her shoulder and spreading along her collarbone and upper arm. It felt like someone had walloped her with a sledgehammer. Her eyes prickled with tears and her vision became blurred. She had never felt this kind of pain before, and though she was warned being shot while wearing armor still hurt, she could never anticipate this kind of pain.

Unwilling to fail at her mission, she managed to stay upright. She observed the guards she had managed to shoot. Some were on the ground, others were doubled over in pain but the one who managed to shoot her was moving in. He wasted no time and began firing at her, his eyes wide and crazed.

Autumn felt frozen as the bullets flew at her. She thought she was going to die when she felt arms seizing her. All of a sudden, she was out of harm's way as Ryan stood in front of her. He shot at the guard with his two guns, showing no mercy as he riddled his body with an array of bullets. When the guard was dead, Ryan approached her and that is when she noticed it.

All the guards had either been wounded or killed. Bodies lay strewn across the floor, blood and gore soaked the cement floors. Any person still twitching Vincent was finishing off with a bullet to the head. Like a dark executioner, his eyes showed no compassion or remorse.

Autumn understood Vincent's lack of sympathy. These men were not good people.

Maybe they had been once, but not anymore. They worked for DSI, who abducted and experimented on innocent people. DSI wrenched them from the safety of their lives and used them without remorse.

They took Rick from her and their blood was a minor sacrifice to get him back.

"Autumn, are you alright?" Ryan's voice interrupted her thoughts. He knelt down in front of her, his eyes taking her in with concern.

"He shot me." Was all she could manage.

Ryan nodded and put his hand where the bullet had struck her.

"You are going to be fine. I know the pain is excruciating but there will be nothing there but a huge ugly bruise. I don't feel anything broken."

"That is a relief," she said numbly.

He smiled. "Are you alright to continue?"

Autumn took a deep breath. She would not fail Rick. She would be an asset not a weakness. These were the things she promised herself before she began training with Ryan and the others.

She forced a smile. "Of course. Lead on."

* * *

The next stop was the labs upstairs. Ryan was certain all the upper level guards had already been taken care of. He asserted the majority would stay in the basement guarding DSI's most valuable asset: their prisoners. Still, they had to clear the whole building, leaving no stone unturned and Autumn informed Ryan beforehand that she wanted to retrieve Rick's labs results and personal records.

Though no one had any serious or life-threatening wounds mostly thanks to the high-tech armor suits, Raina doled out healing potions while Stuart went into the main office to snag keys.

Once the keys were obtained they walked along the second floor taking in the ghastly scenery. It was evident this was where the experimentation of the hostages took place. The rooms they went into were full of evidence. Stark white tables loaded with medical instruments, fridges jam-packed with blood samples, gurneys with straps and examination tables.

The whole floor smelt of blood, sweat and fear. The soundtrack was eerie humming and whirring of machines.

Finding all the rooms abandoned, they continued on, finally reaching the end of the corridor. The last room was by far the largest and required a key card to get inside.

"Allow me." Stuart grinned and he swiped the stolen key card. The door clicked loudly, opening before them.

When they stepped inside the vast room was packed floor to ceiling with filing cabinets. Autumn's heart sank. She wanted to get Rick's file but with this many cabinets it would take eons to find it.

"They are labeled *and* sorted. Alphabetical," Nathaniel said, practically reading her mind.

"Who knew villains were such sticklers for organization," Mandy said, chuckling lightly.

Ryan looked at Autumn, remembering their conversation and gestured towards the cabinets. She nodded and began looking for the cabinet labeled J. It didn't take long to find it. She saw his name JACOBS MARTIN RICK and grabbed the file, throwing it into her backpack.

When she was finished she noticed Garret grabbing some files as well. When he was done Ryan instructed everyone that when they hit the basement they would be splitting into groups. They had discussed this during the planning phase and though Autumn didn't like the idea of being separated from her friends she understood Ryan's logic. The basement was huge and there would be swarms of guards. Splitting up would be quicker and more efficient, making it easier to cover ground.

Also, they would be freeing hostages and traveling with a big a group wasn't the safest. Meaning if one group didn't make it, at least others would escape. Being one huge group made them one huge target. Splitting up meant the guards couldn't get them all at once. It made sense though most things Ryan said usually did.

* * *

The stairs to the basement were old and winding. Autumn looked down, seeing nothing but darkness spiraling below her. Raina touched Eric's shoulder encouragingly and he began reciting a spell. A floating orb appeared and filled the stairwell with light. With their path well-lit everyone started down the stairs, walking in pairs until they reached a large door. Stuart used another key card to open it. Anticipating guards on the other side, everyone was ready to attack. Instead all they found was a long empty hallway that branched out in three different directions at the end. The schematics had indicated as much and they had already planned which groups were going in what direction. They continued along the hallway in silence. A musty scent invaded Autumn's nostrils, above her florescent lights hummed without refrain.

When they reached the fork in the hall, everyone got into their designated groups. Mandy, Nathaniel, and Vincent were taking the hallway to the left. Malaya, Garret, Raina and Eric were taking the right. Autumn, Stuart and Ryan were going down the centre path.

"Everyone remember the plan. This is first and foremost a rescue mission. We want all the hostages out of here safe and sound," Ryan began, sounding again like the authoritarian. "And above all else, be safe. Being a hero is one thing, being a dead hero is quite a different story."

Vincent rolled his eyes, looking impatient. "The only people dying tonight are the people working for DSI Blaze."

"I love the positivity Reaper but can you tone down the arrogance?" Ryan smirked.

"Absolutely not," Vincent replied before turning to Mandy and Nathaniel.

"Let's get a move on rookies. I don't have time for tomfoolery."

Mandy gave Autumn's hand a reassuring squeeze as Nathaniel grumbled, "What the hell is tomfoolery?"

When everyone else had left, Ryan, Stuart and Autumn began their journey down the centre hall. Autumn had her weapons ready as they walked along slowly and cautiously. At first there was nothing. After traveling for a minute or so they saw something. Up ahead the hall widened into an opening and in the distance were rows upon rows of glass cells. In the opening stood two guards with guns in hand looking vigilant. Ryan placed a hand on Autumn's arm, indicating to stop. The three of them crouched behind a pile of crates to confer.

"There are definitely more than two guards in there," Ryan said, his voice barely a whisper.

Stuart nodded in agreement. "I'm not surprised. They are securing the hostages."

"I would imagine alarms have been raised and they are expecting us."

Autumn looked at him, confused. "Why didn't they come for us?"

Ryan met her gaze, his face grave. "Because they knew we would come to them."

Ryan explained the glass cells were most likely reinforced to avoid the hostages breaking out and escaping. It gave Autumn piece of mind to know she wouldn't accidently shoot anyone, Rick especially, while trying to eradicate the guards. The plan was simple: take out the guards, free the hostages. It was basic and straightforward. Still, Autumn's nerves were frayed. The night had taken its toll, but somehow she wasn't fraught. Her skin prickled, hairs standing on end. Her muscles throbbed and twitched, and her heart raced, thudding in her chest like the steady beat of a drum.

"Are you ready?" Ryan asked them. Both Stuart and Autumn nodded in unison.

He looked at Autumn and said, "Don't hesitate. You need to be faster than them and more ruthless if you want to survive."

A smile slowly spread across her face. She was ready. "Go in with guns blazing?"

Ryan returned her grin. "And leave in a blaze of glory."

30

The first two guards went down easily thanks to Ryan's double guns. After that the battle began in earnest, the chaos ensuing. Stuart was tired of fighting as a human and decided to shift, taking on his giant wolf man form. Something about seeing a werewolf biped was awe instilling, even though it wasn't Autumn's first time witnessing it. Guards with guns began shooting at Stuart, hitting his giant figure with ease. Stuart shook it off, literally squeezing the bullets from his hide and sending them tumbling to the ground.

"Normal bullets won't hurt him!" One guard bellowed above the din. "I got silver! Get out of the way!"

The guard aimed and began unloading the silver bullets but Stuart was too fast. He maneuvered out of the way, springing and dodging far too swiftly for a beast of his size.

"Try aiming the gun asshole!" Another guard called out.

Out of bullets, the guard began reloading the silver but it was too late. Stuart lunged at him with lightning speed. A few rapid swipes of his razor-sharp claws and the guard collapsed to the ground, his body sliced in half, eyes lifeless.

Autumn began unloading rounds into random guards who were coming at her as Stuart fought beside her, his claws an unstoppable weapon. Bullets soared through the air in every direction. Autumn stayed focused, moving swiftly, ducking, tumbling and flipping to avoid getting hit. She could feel the difference in her speed compared to when she fought in the caves months ago. Keeping up her training had paid off and she had Rick to thank for that. She was also more confident, her fear being replaced by strength and determination.

The battle was savage, and though weapons were aplenty it didn't stop the fists from flying. Autumn was facing off against a particularly brutish DSI guard. He towered over her, was built like a linebacker and when he swung his massive fist into her face she had to fight to stay conscious. She was literally seeing stars but she wasn't going down. She swayed side to side, forcing herself to stay upright.

The guard let out an obnoxious chortle. "I must admit my mother always warned me not to hit a lady but she never said anything about killing one!"

Autumn looked at the lanyard that dangled from his thick neck. His name was Buck.

"Well anyone that would name their son *Buck* probably wasn't expecting much from him later in life," Autumn spat.

She pulled out her scythe, a dark smile playing across her lips.

Buck narrowed his eyes and flashed a large hunting knife.

"It's a shame I have to kill you," he said, eyeing her from head to toe. "Such a beautiful girl. The things I would've loved to do to you." He licked his lips.

"I bet you say that to all the girls Buck," Autumn shot back. She was working hard to steady herself, her cheek throbbing with pain.

Buck simply grinned at her, his eyes so wild and crazed it sent chills down Autumn's spine. Then with a loud guttural cry he launched at her, the hunting knife glinting in the light.

Autumn mustered all her energy, swinging her scythe with everything she had. Before his knife made contact with her, her scythe landed against his torso. He let out a cry of agony as it stabbed into his gut, sending blood and innards spilling out across the cement floor.

Autumn let out a fierce growl of determination, pulling the scythe back to her. Buck's hunting knife clattered to the ground and she swung again, sinking the scythe into his leg for good measure.

Buck let out more cries of anguish before crumpling to the ground, his body lying still in the pile of blood and gore.

Breathing raggedly, Autumn looked around her. The only people still standing were Ryan and Stuart. She doubled over to catch her breath. Ryan had advised her to be ruthless but killing a human bring, no matter how sinister, was something she didn't relish. Still, she didn't want to die and it wasn't like Buck or any of the other DSI guards would show her mercy. These men were capturing and torturing innocent people. In her eyes that made them no more human than the demons in the caves.

"Are you alright?" Both Ryan and Stuart, back in his human form, were beside her now, faces filled with concern.

Autumn straightened and Ryan reached out, touching her cheek. She flinched at the pain his touch brought, her eyes prickling with tears.

"Wow he socked you good huh," Ryan murmured. Stuart, who was inspecting the disgusting remains of Buck looked impressed.

"That's nothing Blaze. You should see the other guy." He paused. "Well what's left of him."

Ryan looked at mess of blood and guts spread across the floor, and rubbed his temples slowly.

"This is why I use guns."

Autumn opened her mouth to respond but quickly shut it. The sound of clamouring echoed along the walls, something they were unable to hear over the din of battle. Autumn looked to Ryan and Stuart who exchanged perturbed glances.

Together they began moving further into the room, as the screams, screams of pure raw terror, rang through the air. Fear danced inside Autumn as she wondered which, if any, of these bloodcurdling cries were Rick's.

Stuart, who had stolen the key cards from the dead guards, handed a couple to Ryan and Autumn and they began freeing the innocent people locked inside the glass cells. Autumn was horrified at the state of the prisoners. They were filthy, dishevelled, emaciated and injured. Some practically raced out of their cells, seeing nothing else but freedom, others were too terrified to move a muscle. Some spoke, asking questions or thanking Autumn, Ryan and Stuart for rescuing them. Others were completely silent, almost catatonic; their fear so deeply embedded Autumn predicted it might never leave them.

Ryan, Stuart and Autumn led the charge, freeing prisoners from their pens as the liberated abductees trailed behind them.

Glass cell after glass cell went by until eventually Autumn felt panic rise inside her.

Only a handful of cells were left and they still hadn't found Rick. The negative thoughts she had been ignoring since Rick had gone missing began to take over.

What if Rick wasn't at this facility anymore? Would she ever see him again? Was he even alive?

The last thought sent shudders throughout her entire body. As they approached the last glass cell Ryan's hand fell upon her shoulder.

"The others might have found him already," he said gently.

Autumn couldn't wait any longer. With her heart thudding in her chest she walked towards the tiny cell, her legs feeling like rubber with every step she took. At first glance the cell looked empty but upon closer inspection she saw him. Crumpled in the corner, his eyes closed, still wearing the clothes he sported the night of his capture.

Her hands trembling, he didn't even look up as she swiped the key card into the slot. A beep sounded as the door clicked and opened. Ryan and Stuart stayed outside with the liberated prisoners as Autumn stepped into the cell, her eyes watching him steadily. When she was a few feet away his eyes jolted open and he sprung to life, standing up, his back pressed against the glass wall. He stared at her blankly, seeing her yet not really.

"Rick," she whispered, approaching him cautiously. "It's me. Autumn."

It took him a moment before he reacted and Autumn wasn't sure he would. Who knew what trauma he had endured and how it would affect him. But to her relief the confusion on his face finally gave way to realization, and his eyes locked onto hers. His expression softened, welcoming her and she launched at Rick without hesitation.

Autumn embraced Rick, his face nestled into the crook of her neck.

"It really is you," he said, his voice muffled by her hair. "You came."

That he even considered that she might have forgotten him made her heart wrench.

She could feel the sobs building inside her, the tears burning her eyes readying their escape.

"Of course I came. I would've been here sooner but it took us awhile to track this place down."

"Us?" Rick said and Autumn gestured to Ryan and Stuart who appeared to be explaining everything to the abducted teenagers.

Rick looked at Autumn, flummoxed. "Why are Stuart and Garrison here?"

"I can explain later. We need to meet up with the others and get out of this hell hole. Some of the prisoners need to be treated for injuries, including you."

Autumn traced the bruises and cuts on his face gently. Seeing evidence of his abuse was too much and the tears flowed from her eyes, spilling down her cheeks like salty streams.

Rick took her hand, squeezing it tightly in his. "I have spent enough time in this prison. Let's get the hell out of here."

Autumn squeezed Rick's hand in return as they exited the cell and headed towards Ryan and the others.

A sudden loud creaking noise drew Autumn's attention. Rick heard it too and they both began scanning the room for the source. Seeing nothing out of the ordinary, it took them by surprise when the rain of bullets began.

There was no time to react. Though it felt like time was moving in slow motion, everything was actually happening far too quickly. Ryan and Stuart were attempting to shield the cluster of teenagers and Rick jumped in front of Autumn, but he wasn't fast enough.

Autumn remembered Ryan warning her, if her armour was pierced too many times in the same spot, it would become vulnerable. She thought of this caveat as the barrage of bullets hit her body with brutal force. The wind was knocked out of her and her legs buckled, giving out beneath her.

Is everyone okay? She thought. *Please let everyone be okay.*

Autumn touched her abdomen and felt sticky wetness on her skin. She looked down at her hands. They were covered in blood. Logic told her, it was hers. She could smell it, almost taste the metal on her tongue.

She heard Rick, calling her name in distress. He was screeching, so close yet he sounded miles away. She closed her eyes, suddenly exhausted. She was so grateful when everything faded to black.

That was the thing about a sneak attack.

You don't see it coming.

Much like horror movies when the protagonist thinks they have prevailed, that they are safe. They let their guard down only to have the villain emerge from the shadows and stab them in the back.

Now Rick knew there was no such thing as safe. Since the day he realized the supernatural world actually existed, he knew this.

He could endure many things. Being captured, beaten, bruised and derided. Being pushed to his limits, pushed to the brink and back again, he could handle all of it.

But the sight of his beloved Autumn, limp and lifeless in his arms?

This was the one and only thing he couldn't bear.

He had never felt anything like this before. He had been *angry* of course. Much more frequently of late if he was being honest. But this tidal wave of pure, white-hot rage that was washing over him?

This feeling was foreign to him.

His body quivered and his skin burned so hot like it was on fire. Sweat dripped down his brow, trickling down his face as he looked around, taking in the scene before him.

Guards were shooting, aiming at everyone within range. Ryan was making his way over to him, as Stuart protected the horde of terrified teenagers. As Ryan maneuvered across the room, he shot his two guns at the guards who had emerged from the secret hatch.

Rick watched him, Autumn cradled in his arms.

Ryan didn't miss a shot.

Ryan arrived beside Rick. He said nothing, just looked at Autumn and that was when Rick saw it, when he knew for sure.

The grief in his eyes told a story Rick's former guidance counselor never would.

He loved her.

Ryan was in love with Autumn.

Rick's body was quaking now, making it difficult to control his limbs. Before he could worry about Autumn, he felt Ryan snatch her from his grip. He heard screams of terror ripping through the room. Was he the one causing this panic and mayhem? He couldn't think about that now. The pain was too intense. His muscles were enlarging, his bones breaking and reforming, the agony was overwhelming.

They would pay for killing her.

Pay with their blood and their lives. There would be no clemency, no one left standing.

31

The sound of insects chirping, the steady rhythm of cicadas singing invaded Autumn's ears. She was in the water, she was floating. Her bare body felt weightless and warm, like she was enfolded in a cocoon.

She opened her eyes and looked around, her confusion giving way to realization as she took in her surroundings. She was at the sacred werewolf grounds.

She was inside an enormous pond that was located in the middle of a massive field. The water was so perfect, so unblemished that she could actually see her body clearly underneath it.

Beyond the masses of towering evergreens that bordered the area, was the burgeoning sunrise. Daylight was on the cusp of snuffing out the night.

Autumn couldn't help but smile when she saw them.

Sleeping on the bank, curled up in blankets were Ryan, Mandy, Nathaniel and Eric. Her smile faded quickly when she didn't see Rick anywhere. Her stomach filled with knots as she tried to recall what had happened last night.

The last thing she remembered was the hatch opening, the guards ambushing them and the blood.

Her blood.

She had been shot. She moved her hand onto her abdomen. She felt nothing. No wound, no scarring just smooth healthy flesh.

Many questions raced through her mind.

If she was completely healed how long had she been out? Why was she sleeping in a pond? Where was Rick?

She needed answers. She stood up, trying her best not to wake anyone as she searched for clothes. She spotted a towel not far from her, so she stepped out of the water and headed for the shore.

She moved along cautiously, nearing the towel, when suddenly Ryan's eyes opened. He sat upright and yawned, his eyes focusing on Autumn who stood before him completely naked.

"I'm so sorry Autumn. I didn't realize you were awake," he said, turning away, his face flush with embarrassment.

Autumn couldn't help but take some pleasure in seeing the always composed Ryan Garrison flustered.

She snatched the towel, wrapping it around herself. "You can look now."

Hesitantly, he turned to look at her, as though he thought she might be playing a trick on him.

"I didn't see anything," he assured her.

Autumn chuckled at his fib. "Sure you did. But it wasn't your fault."

Ryan regarded her, a small smile on his handsome face. "How are you feeling?"

"I'm fine," she said. "Where is Rick?"

Ryan stood up, dusting himself off. He wore only jeans, his torso bare and glistening in the morning light. Autumn could see how in shape he really was, toned and lean without being too bulky. He ran both his hands through his messy brown hair.

"No questions about how *you* got here? What happened after *you* were *shot* in the gut?"

Autumn shrugged. She didn't care about that now. She needed to know where Rick was and that he was safe and sound.

Her eyes met Ryan's, unwavering. "Is he okay?"

"He is fine. I will send word to him that you've finally woken up."

"I can go tell himself myself Ryan," Autumn began, perplexed. "Can't I?"

"You can, with supervision." Ryan said. "Autumn, when you were shot you stopped breathing. He thought you were dead."

Autumn pulled her towel closer to her, her body suddenly ice cold.

"Well clearly I'm not. So what the hell are you getting at?"

Ryan sighed deeply, rubbing his temples in frustration.

"Rick shifted last night. The thought of losing you pushed him over the edge. Long story short, he went berserk. He tore the remaining guards' limb from limb and when he was finished, he came after the rest of us. The first change, you have zero control. Your only emotion is rage and your instinct is to kill. It takes immense training and loads of time to learn to control the werewolf inside you."

Autumn's face was ashen. The next logical question, she was terrified to ask.

"Did he kill anyone besides the guards?"

"No. Luckily, Garrett had arrived by then and he tranquilized him, but let me tell you, he didn't go down without a fight."

"So everyone is okay?"

"A few of the captives were injured, but nothing life threatening thanks to Stuart the human shield," Ryan said. "They are being treated in the medical ward. Eventually they will be sent home to their families."

"And those who actually shifted?"

"They are being welcomed into our werewolf trainee program," Ryan replied. "Once they are able to control their new abilities they are free to return home. Until then they are a danger to themselves and others."

Autumn felt her legs turning to jelly, unstable beneath her. She took a seat on a nearby log.

"So Rick isn't coming home?"

Ryan was silent, but his grave expression said it all.

"What about his mom and dad?" Autumn could feel the panic rising inside her. "What do I tell them?"

Ryan took a seat beside her, carefully placing his hand on her shoulder.

"I will figure something out. This isn't my first rodeo you know."

Autumn looked at her friends, Mandy, Nathaniel, and Eric. All things considered, she couldn't believe how soundly they were sleeping.

As though he read her mind Ryan said, "They were very worried about you and they couldn't sleep. Raina used some magics on them. They will be awake soon enough. After a fight like last nights they needed to rest."

Autumn and Ryan sat on the log together as Ryan explained everything in greater detail. Raina had used her magic to wipe the memories of the teenagers that hadn't shifted. Despite their potential to change, it wasn't something that always came to fruition. Not everyone with wolf blood shifted. Some would go their whole life never knowing what they were capable of. They couldn't be allowed to carry the knowledge of what they had seen last night, so Raina used her mind magics to erase their memories up until the day they were abducted.

As for Autumn's miraculous recovery, the pond was apparently the reason she healed so rapidly. After she was shot, she was on the verge of death. They rushed her back to what the wolves called The Healing Pond to let her recuperate.

"You have to be completely exposed for the water to penetrate your wounds," Ryan explained. "Hence why you were naked."

"And here I thought you just wanted a peek," Autumn teased.

Ryan smiled indulgently. "I can take you to see Rick but it has to be a quick visit. He has a lot to absorb on his first day as a lycanthrope. He needs to stay focused."

Autumn nodded, excited at the prospect of seeing Rick, if only briefly.

"Thank you Ryan. I appreciate it."

After walking for fifteen minutes, Autumn and Ryan arrived at their destination. In front of them was a massive stark white building with no windows and a huge reinforced steel door. The structure was bordered by trees, shrubs and wild flowers. Ryan led Autumn up the gravel walkway towards the entrance. Beside the door was an interactive console with an imprint in the shape of a hand.

Ryan noticed Autumn gaping and said, "This building is high security. We house an array of weapons, strategize and train here. You never know who might try and infiltrate."

He reached out and placed his hand into the imprint. An infrared light moved across his skin and a beeping resonated from the device as the locks clicked and the door opened.

Ryan led the way through the door, which took them into a sitting area. The room was sparsely decorated, with some plants, a few couches and a huge oblong dining table surrounded by chairs. In the corner there was a coffee station, a water cooler and a large stainless steel fridge.

"The break room," Ryan offered as they moved along into the hallway.

The first thing Autumn noticed was the beautiful artwork that adorned the hallway walls. The painting that caught her eye was that of a rust coloured wolf. It stood atop a rocky cliff face on all fours, its head held high in the air, as its fur blew in the wind. The painting beside it was of a regal looking snow white wolf. This wolf was much like the giant biped wolf Autumn was used to seeing now. It wore a robe ornamented with golden trim and tassels, and carried a long staff with different coloured stones encrusted along the length of it.

"The paintings are of our many courageous and noble ancestors," Ryan said, stopping to let Autumn get a better look. "Many of them have a lineage to the wolves here. These wolves were the bravest of our warriors. We celebrate our history on these walls."

Autumn and Ryan continued on, passing numerous doors. Each was labeled in gold embossed letters and Autumn read them as they went along. There was a sparring area, a gym, a library, and an arsenal.

When they reached the final door at the back of the building, the letters on it read: FLEDGLING QUARTERS. When Ryan opened it, him and Autumn were standing outdoors in an enormous field that had a dozen wooden cabins placed side by side.

"She finally woke up did she?" Vincent said, appearing from behind a cluster of trees.

"Rick's been waiting for her," he gestured to Autumn. "I swear Ryan. He can't be a true warrior if he spends him time swooning over her."

Ryan frowned disapprovingly. "*She* has a name Vincent. Try using it."

Vincent crossed his arms over his massive chest defiantly. "Is that an order *Sir?*"

Autumn and Ryan exchanged glances before he turned back to Vincent, his expression stern.

"I think you know the answer to that Vincent."

Vincent grumbled loudly before looking at Autumn, his lips forming an exaggerated smile.

"*Autumn.* I'm very sorry I was rude but listening to Rick prattle on about you is driving me insane," he said. "Please forgive me."

"Vincent, you are forgiven." Autumn said graciously. "Now can I see Rick?"

"Please do," Vincent said as he gestured to the cabin at the far right. "He's in there. Be careful."

"Thanks." Autumn started towards the cabin but Ryan grabbed her arm.

"You need to know seeing him right now is risky," Ryan said gravely. "If you upset him in any way he will shift. He lacks control and he will come at you. He doesn't know any better yet."

"He won't hurt me," Autumn protested but Ryan wasn't having it.

"Not intentionally Autumn, but you need to face the facts. Until he can control his wolf, Rick is dangerous."

"And you said I could see him," Autumn shot back.

After everything that had happened, she just wanted to be with Rick. There was no way Ryan was stopping her now, with Rick only steps away.

"And you can," Ryan said evenly. "Vincent and I will be right outside if you need anything. If you see Rick starting to change..."

"Run?" Autumn offered.

"Exactly." He stepped away from her. "Good luck."

Vincent and Ryan watched as Autumn traveled up the path that weaved throughout the subdivision of wooden cabins. When she reached the cabin door she knocked gently, her throat suddenly dry. The reality that she had no idea what to say to Rick hit her just as the door flew open.

Rick stood in the doorway, his face no longer battered, but looking exhausted. When he saw Autumn his blue eyes instantly lit up.

"Autumn!" He pulled her into his arms, his warm embrace soothing her frazzled nerves immediately.

"I was so worried about you," he murmured into her neck. "How are you feeling?"

"Quite good all things considered," Autumn replied, pulling away to examine Rick. "I'm much more concerned about you."

Rick pulled her close to him, his hands wrapped around her waist. He pressed his mouth against hers, kissing her hard and urgently. The kiss made Autumn weak in the knees, and her grip on Rick's shoulders tightened.

Rick broke the kiss and touched Autumn's cheek tenderly.

"I thought I'd lost you."

She ran her fingers through his curls. "But you didn't. Now you need to focus on your training. Until you learn how to control the shifting, you can't come home."

Rick sighed. "I see Ryan has filled you in on the monster I've become."

"You aren't a monster."

Rick let out a chuckle. "On shows they only change during the full moon. Apparently that's all bullshit."

"Can I come in? We haven't even made it past the front door."

Rick nodded, stepping aside to let her enter. "Of course! Come in."

Rick gave her the grand tour of his new lodgings. The cabin was small but cozy. There was a sitting room, kitchen and down the hall a bedroom and bathroom.

They had just sat down together on the couch when Rick looked at her, his expression grave. Autumn felt her stomach lurch. She knew Rick well enough to recognize when he was about to blindside her. Something was up. She could feel it in her gut.

"What's going on Rick?"

"Ryan neglected to mention something to you," he began, his hands folded on his lap. "Something important."

"Which is?"

"I am going to be leaving for a while. Vincent is taking us to a secluded area up north. All the newbies are going. When everyone has their wolf under control, we will return."

Autumn knew it was selfish, but she couldn't help herself. She didn't want Rick to leave. She didn't want him to be a werewolf. She didn't want *any* of this. The tears of frustration and fear that had been building suddenly broke free.

Rick reached out and grabbed her, pulling her into his familiar embrace. The feeling of his arms around her, the sound of his voice, and his scent only made her sob harder.

"Aut, please don't cry. The last thing I want is to leave you but if I can't control this, I might hurt you. I couldn't live with myself if I did that." He ran his fingers through her hair soothingly. "Besides, Vincent said if we work hard and focus, we will be home in no time. A month tops."

"A month?" Autumn balked. "How will I explain this to your parents?"

"Vincent will figure it out," Rick said softly. "He may act crass but the guy is actually pretty sly."

Suddenly the cabin door burst open, taking both Rick and Autumn by surprise. Vincent and Ryan stood in the doorway, looking rather displeased.

"Didn't I tell you Ryan?" Vincent said, sounding incredulous. "Hanky panky! Look at these two. If they got any closer they would be attached!"

Ryan acknowledged Vincent with a nod and clicked his tongue in disapproval.

"You both know better. If you had shifted with Autumn sitting so close to you Rick." He paused for effect. "You guys are playing a very dangerous game."

Autumn wiped the tears from her face discreetly as Rick stood up, his expression defiant.

"We haven't seen each other in more than a week!"

Vincent interceded gruffly, "We get it! You love each other but you can't be taking risks like this, for both your sakes. It only takes a second to lose control Rick."

Rick opened his mouth to reply but Vincent wasn't finished. He walked over to Rick, standing over him in a way one could only describe as menacing.

"Could you live with it?" He said, his tone even and calm.

Rick said nothing. He only hung his head, almost seeming to shrivel and cower under the weight of Vincent's glower.

"I said, *could you live with it?!*" Vincent spat. His rage sent a chill dancing down Autumn's spine.

"With what Reaper Sir?" Rick asked quietly, still staring at his feet.

"If you killed her, if you lost control for that split second it takes and you tore her inside out, could you live with that burden for the rest of your life?"

Rick winced at the thought. Autumn looked at Ryan. He was standing by idly, giving Vincent his reign as Beta. He was staying out of it.

"No," Rick said, defeated. "I couldn't."

Vincent smiled, looking smug and satisfied. "This is why you need to leave for training. To learn who you are with the wolf inside you."

Rick was leaving. The thought caused Autumn to weep again. As tears escaped her eyes, she wiped them away with the heel of her hand.

Vincent sighed, exasperated. "Wonderful. Now the girl is crying!"

Ryan started towards Autumn, but Rick got there first, pulling her close to him.

"Don't cry Aut. We have gone longer than a month without seeing each other."

Rick was right. They had spent years apart, only connecting via text or phone. Somehow that didn't make this separation any easier.

"I know you need to do this but I'm going to miss you."

"I will miss you too, but I will be back in no time." He took her face into his hands.

"Just promise me one thing," he whispered.

His face was inches from hers and even though Ryan and Vincent were in the room, it felt like it was just her and Rick alone.

"Anything Ricky," she murmured.

"No matter how hard it gets you hold on to us," he said, his eyes burning into hers. "No matter what it looks like, how it seems, how bleak, remember this." He reached for her hand and placed it on his chest. His heart was beating, a steady rhythm beneath her fingers.

"And remember how much I love you. It doesn't matter what kind of monster I become I will always love you."

"You could never be a monster Rick," Autumn said.

Vincent let out a snort. "Until she witnesses him morphing into a mangy slobbering beast."

Ryan shot Vincent a warning look. Autumn ignored him and continued on.

"When do you leave?" She asked, placing her hands on Rick's shoulders.

Rick touched her face, tracing her lips gingerly with his fingers. "Tonight."

Autumn closed her eyes, letting the tidings wash over her. If Rick had to go, she wanted him to depart on a positive note. She didn't want him to worry about her when he was gone. If he was worried he wouldn't focus and it would take him that much longer to return.

Autumn pressed her lips against Rick's and they kissed with desire and urgency. Vincent groaned in disgust but Autumn didn't care. He would have Rick for a while but she would be waiting for him when he finally came home.

32

Autumn watched the fire. She loved the smell of a burning campfire, but watching the flames was something else entirely. It was visceral. The way the flames danced, sending sparks flying into the ether of the night like auburn fireworks.

It had been a few days since Rick left, and Ryan had invited Autumn, Mandy, Nathaniel and Eric to a bonfire at the wolf territory. Initially Autumn had declined but Ryan insisted she be there for *the revelation* as he called it. Between him and Mandy pestering her, she eventually conceded.

Now she sat on a wooden log, encircled by her friends, Ryan and his pack and a crowd of random people that resided in the wolf sanctuary.

"So Rick's parents actually believe he's at skateboarding camp?" Mandy's voice cut through the hubbub. "I thought they were smart people?"

"They are," Autumn said, amused. "But Ryan can be quite charming. His tongue is more silver than cutlery."

"He sold the story like a pro did he?" Eric piped in.

Autumn nodded. "That he did. He was so convincing I started to believe Rick was at skateboarding camp."

Nathaniel let out a groan of disgust. "The guy can lie with impunity. It doesn't get shadier than that."

Mandy rolled her eyes. "That *guy* was covering for your best friend. Consider his ability to spin a believable tale a blessing Nate."

"If I could get everyone's attention please!" Ryan bellowed over the clamouring.

Immediately the crowd abided Ryan's request, going silent as he took a seat on a large hunk of wood situated in the middle of the campfire area. On his lap sat a massive tome with an aged cover that looked worse for wear.

"Good evening everyone," Ryan began. "Tonight we are celebrating. Our victory against the enemy known as DSI, the recruitment of new wolves and the truths that will be revealed to you all through this." He gently patted the book on his lap.

"Many of you have heard the prophecies. Our Perceiver Edmond has yet to mislead us yet still, much has been kept secret and for good reason. Tonight that will change. As our youngling wolves take the journey with Reaper to find themselves, we will take a journey of our own tonight."

Ryan held up the book. "This is the hallowed book of prophecies, written by generation after generation of Perceivers. In this book are tales of our history and ancestors. But the story I will be reading tonight, is one of our salvation."

Autumn felt goosebumps forming on her skin. Ryan went on.

"It has been foretold that war comes!" Ryan exclaimed. "It will come and we will lose. Or so we thought. Edmond saw something. Something that turned the tide and changed our fate."

Mandy leaned into Autumn whispering, "Not exactly a lighthearted campfire tale is it?"

Ryan opened the book, cleared his throat and began reading the story.

"The wolves were outnumbered on the field that day. The sinister creatures ravaged them, running rampant over corpses, their vileness spreading like a sickness. Blood had been shed and lives taken. It was a war made of nightmares, a war elder wolves spoke to their kin about. The war, they were going to succumb to it and it would happen again. To their kin and the kin of their children. The beasts' army would only grow in numbers and the war would rage on. The blood rain would fall once more and the river would overflow with bodies. History would repeat itself.

That was the belief until the day was prophesied. He would come, the boy with the hazel eyes, the boy with the spark of light inside him. He would fight beside them. The wolves would stand tall with him, their saviour and they would win the war. They would taste sweet victory.

So it was written. He would arrive, the salvation of all wolves, of all mankind. If he ceased to be born, so the world would perish. And they would be annihilated. All werewolves extinct.

The creatures would roam the earth, free to devour supernatural beings and humans alike, until none were left.

When his father is born, we shall rejoice. We Perceivers know when he comes, for the day he arrives the stars will align in the sky. He is the father of the saviour. He is The Starry Eyed Child."

Ryan stopped reading. He looked up at Autumn and when their eyes met, realization struck her.

Rick.

It was Rick.

Rick was The Starry Eyed Child the legends spoke of. All the attention Ryan had shown Rick and her, all the interest in their lives, suddenly it all made perfect sense.

Ryan read from the book once more.

"The mother of the liberator, the greatest love of The Starry Eyed Child, is a warrior herself. With hair akin to flowing black waves and eyes of piercing emerald, she will bear the child that will save the world."

Autumn remembered it then, the painting that was hanging above the fireplace in Ryan's study.

The woman was elegant and breathtaking, with alabaster skin and cascades of dark hair. The wolf rested its large head in the girl's lap, its eyes filled with a boundless love. The woman was cradling a baby, swaddled in blankets, in her arms.

Was she the woman in the painting?

Ryan closed the book and gestured to Autumn.

"Autumn, would you please join me?" He patted the hunk of wood he sat on.

"Sure," she said and though she felt like her legs might give out, she made her way over to Ryan. She could feel their eyes on her, everyone watching her. When she looked at her friends she saw it.

Eric, Mandy and Nathaniel were watching her like she was a stranger. What did she expect? Right now she felt like a stranger to herself.

Once Autumn was seated beside Ryan, he leaned towards her, whispering into her ear.

"You garnered the true meaning of the story I gather?"

She said nothing, just nodded at him slowly. He beamed at her, eyes filled with pride.

"Are you ready for this?"

"Yes." She lied. Her hands trembled and her heart pounded in her chest. Everything around her felt surreal.

Ryan turned to the crowd, addressing them once again.

"So it was written by The Perceivers, so it shall be! Autumn Kingston is the woman that will bear the greatest warrior the werewolves have ever known!"

Autumn didn't expect what happened next. When the cheering and hollering began, she nearly jumped out of her skin. She looked at her friends. Mandy, Nathaniel and Eric, looked astounded, but even they were cheering alongside the wolves.

"Rick Jacobs, the youngling is the man of myth and legend. He was born under the cover of fateful stars and he is indeed The Starry Eyed Child!"

* * *

Autumn stood alone, leaning against a tree, drink in hand.

She watched as everyone celebrated. The wolves, her friends. Under the glimmer of stars, they made merry. Nathaniel and Mandy bickered before kissing and making up. Eric and Raina were huddled together on a log conversing. They had approached her after the revelation, bombarding her with questions, asking if she was alright.

Just being the amazing friends they were. She told them the truth. She needed time alone to think. Autumn realized how ridiculous it sounded. A party wasn't a place to be solitary but she knew she wouldn't be much company tonight, at least not the fun kind.

"Autumn." Ryan was suddenly beside her, breaking through her reverie.

She looked at him, taking a long sip of her drink before speaking.

"The war that is coming...Is it demons again?"

Ryan was silent for a long time. For a moment Autumn thought he wasn't going to answer her.

"An army of supernatural creatures will join forces. Vampires, dark werewolves, demons, chimera, minotaurs, centaurs and succubae. So many different monsters Autumn, I can't name them all."

"What if something happens to prevent the prophecy from coming to fruition?"

Ryan's expression was grave. He knew exactly what Autumn was asking. If someone wanted to prevent the birth of the legendary liberator, and they found out who Rick was, who she was, they *would* try and kill them. They might even succeed.

"I have gone to great lengths to make sure your identities as the couple in the prophecy stay within these walls. You and Rick will be kept safe. I will make sure of that."

Autumn took another drink, praying it would quell her nerves. The next question she dreaded asking, but she had to know everything. She needed to know what was at stake.

She looked at Ryan, trying to remain poised, but the quiver in her voice betrayed her.

"And what happens if *they* win Ryan?"

Again, Ryan was silent. He stared up at the night sky, the millions of stars sparkling, his expression thoughtful. When their eyes met, she detected no fear in his. When he spoke, his voice was unwavering.

"It will be the end of the world, the end of everything."

EPILOGUE

Cairo, Egypt

Sweat dripped down his brow, pooling uncomfortably in his eyes, obstructing his vision. He wiped the sweat from his face with his sleeve, wishing he had opted to wear a hat like he'd originally planned on. The sun today, sizzling him at forty degrees or more, was ruthless and it wasn't like he could do his job indoors with air conditioning.

He had been digging for days at this excavation site, searching for the item that would help his nephew. He knew it was a longshot but based on his research, if any place in the world would have the artifact, it would be here.

When his nephew had informed him of the impending war, he wanted to be certain he'd have everything at his disposal to be a worthy adversary. Despite all he had learned, his nephew was still green when it came to the art of magics. He couldn't let him go into battle unarmed. Training with other sorcerers was advantageous, but it wasn't nearly enough. He was going to need a little something extra to unearth the power he had buried deep inside him.

He had no doubt this power existed within his nephew. His father and mother, his dearly departed sister, were the most powerful magic wielders he'd ever had the pleasure of knowing. He only wished they had lived, that they could be with their son to teach him their magics. To guide him through the journey he was undertaking and impart their wisdom upon him.

He continued on, digging under the cruel heat of the sun, well into the early evening.

"How's it going?" His assistant Wendy handed him a bottle of water. She had come with the wheelbarrow to clear away the spoil and bring it to the spoil heap.

"It goes," he said, taking the bottle from her absently.

"It is getting late Jeffrey-Allen," she said, as she gathered the dirt with a shovel, placing it into the wheelbarrow. "Maybe you should call it a day?"

Jeffrey-Allen shook his head in protest. "I can't. I just have this nagging feeling that I'm going to find it today Wend."

She continued shoveling the dirt, a small grin on her tan face. "You are so stubborn. At least drink some water. I don't need you passing out. I might be your sister, but I refuse to carry you."

Jeffrey-Allen opened the water bottle with flourish, taking a long exaggerated sip.

"See! I'm drinking!"

Wendy smiled approvingly. "Good! Now get back to it. It'll be dark before you know it."

Jeffrey-Allen continued digging, for what felt like days. He could hardly believe it when he hit something hard buried in the dirt. He felt his muscles tighten with anticipation, as the familiar feeling of hope flooded over him. *Was this it? Was he going to find what he was searching for?*

He used his trowel to continue digging, his hands aching. When there wasn't much dirt left to remove, he pulled out his lucky red toothbrush. He had used this toothbrush during many archeological digs and each time he used it, he had found something of great worth. Sometimes it was historically valuable, other times monetary, but the red toothbrush never let him down.

Delicately, he swept the toothbrush across the remaining dirt and debris. The light covering of dust was removed with ease, unearthing something that made Jeffrey-Allen gasp aloud. He looked around for Wendy, who came rushing towards him from the spoil heap.

She watched on as Jeffrey-Allen carefully used his gloved hands to remove the beautiful glimmering amber stone from its cocoon of dirt. Wendy's blue eyes were wide as she took in the stunning gemstone.

"Is that it?" she murmured.

Jeffrey-Allen nodded slowly, his heart pounding in his chest. "It is."

Wendy's expression was one of awe. "It's gorgeous. The pictures in the history books don't do it justice."

"I need to call him. Let him know right away!" Jeffrey-Allen said, pulling out his cell phone. He dialed the familiar number, trying his best to compose himself. This artifact was the biggest coup he might ever have, but it would remain a secret he would take to his grave. He knew his sister and nephew would do the same.

"Jeffrey-Allen?" He finally picked up after a few rings. "Please tell me you have good news."

Jeffrey-Allen took a deep breath before speaking. "I found it Eric. I'm holding the ancient relic in my hands."

Made in the USA
Middletown, DE
22 March 2019